The Vanished Child

**A Jayne Sinclair
Genealogical Mystery**

M. J. Lee

2

ABOUT M. J. LEE

Martin Lee is the author of two different series of historical crime novels; The *Jayne Sinclair Genealogical Mysteries* and the *Inspector Danilov* series set in 1930s Shanghai. *The Vanished Child* is the fourth book featuring genealogical investigator, Jayne Sinclair.

ALSO BY M. J. LEE

Jayne Sinclair Series
The Irish Inheritance
The Somme Legacy
The American Candidate

Inspector Danilov Series
Death in Shanghai
City of Shadows
The Murder Game

Historical Fiction
Samuel Pepys and the Stolen Diary
The Fall

This book is dedicated to the 130,000 Child Migrants who were taken from their homes all over the British Isles and transported to a foreign country.

'Every Childhood lasts a lifetime.'
David Hall. Child Migrant.

Contents

Chapter One 11

Chapter Two 16

Chapter Three... 25

Chapter Four.. 30

Chapter Five 33

Chapter Six 41

Chapter Seven... 46

Chapter Eight... 53

Chapter Nine.. 57

Chapter Ten 62

Chapter Eleven 69

Chapter Twelve.. 79

Chapter Thirteen 84

Chapter Fourteen 89

Chapter Fifteen... 94

Chapter Sixteen... 99

Chapter Seventeen 103

Chapter Eighteen 107

Chapter Nineteen 114

Chapter Twenty 117

Chapter Twenty-One.................................... 125

Chapter Twenty-Two.................................... 130

Chapter Twenty-Three 134

Chapter Twenty-Four 138

Chapter Twenty-Five..144

Chapter Twenty-Six...149

Chapter Twenty-Seven 154

Chapter Twenty-Eight 156

Chapter Twenty-Nine 163

Chapter Thirty..167

Chapter Thirty-One 174

Chapter Thirty-Two 182

Chapter Thirty-Three 187

Chapter Thirty-Four 191

Chapter Thirty-FIve 195

Chapter Thirty-Six 200

Chapter Thirty-Seven..204

Chapter Thirty-Eight 211

Chapter Thirty-Nine 215

Chapter Forty...218

Chapter Forty-One 223

Chapter Forty-Two 226

Chapter Forty-Three 236

Chapter Forty-Four 242

Chapter Forty-Five 248

Chapter Forty-Six..252

Chapter Forty-Seven...258

Chapter Forty-Eight 262

Chapter Forty-Nine 265

Chapter Fifty 272

Chapter Fifty-One...275

Chapter Fifty-Two...279

Chapter Fifty-Three 287

Chapter Fifty-Four..291

Chapter Fifty-Five..293

Chapter Fifty-Six 297

Chapter Fifty-Seven 300

Chapter Fifty-Eight...302

Chapter Fifty-Nine..306

Historical Note...309

10

Chapter One

June 22, 1952.

St Joseph's Farm and Trade School, Bindoon, Western Australia

The backs of his hands were raw and red, arms exhausted and all his strength gone. Harry lifted the stone anyway, resting it against the waistband of his shorts before heaving it up on to his chest.

Puffing like an ageing train, he shuffled over from the mound to the waiting wheelbarrow and dropped the rock into the wooden tray.

What time was it?

He glanced up, shielding his eyes. The sun was still high in the cornflower-blue sky, not a cloud in sight. He ran his tongue over his parched lips and raised his hand. 'Water, sir.'

A sleepy pair of eyes stared straight at him through thick lenses. The shiny leather boots shifted slightly in the sand and the tip of the man's stick raised itself from the dust, pointing to a wooden barrel next to a stone wall. 'Make it quick, ye lazy spalpeen.'

Harry loped over to the barrel before the man changed his mind, scooping up a ladle of warm water and pouring half of it into his open mouth, the rest over his head. The water dripped down his face, off his chin on to the dirty khaki shirt.

He rested his hands on the barrel and pushed, feeling the ache in his back muscles as he stretched his body. His face and arms were burnt by the sun, so different from a month ago when he had first arrived. His thin legs were bruised and battered, one toenail black where he had dropped a rock on his bare foot yesterday.

The sun blazed down, creating a haze that distorted the hills in the distance. It was as if the land itself were breathing hot fumes, like a sleeping dragon. A puff of wind arose from nowhere, swirling a cloud of red dust that coated the quarry and all those working there.

'Don't let Keaney see you. He's a bit nuts today,' whispered Slimo as he shuffled past, carrying a red-coated rock and dumping it into the wheelbarrow next to the stone wall.

Harry stretched upwards again and took a rag from his pocket to wipe the sweat off his brow. 'He's nuts every day.'

'Aye, he is, but today he's more crackers than usual.' Slimo picked up the wheelbarrow and slowly trundled it across the floor of the quarry to the spoil heap, making sure his bare feet gripped the wooden planks rather than risk the rocky floor.

'I don't care,' Harry whispered.

He took another ladle of warm water. Better enjoy the break while he could; the work would never stop.

'YOU!' Keaney pointed directly at him with his metal-tipped stick. 'Stop loafing and get on with it. I want this lot stacked and ready before nightfall.'

Harry hurried back to his wheelbarrow. The chiselled square of dressed stone lay at his feet. It had been cut from the rock face by another gang, chiselled into a perfect square under the watchful eyes of the

12

Italian mason, and left for him to move one hundred yards, ready to be lifted into place on the frontage of the main building.

He was tired and thirsty, his body ached and his skin was flaking off where the blisters from the sun had bubbled and burst.

'GET A MOVE ON.'

Keaney was walking slowly towards him, puffs of red dust rising into the air each time his leather boots hit the ground.

Harry bent over the stone and wrapped his thin arms around it, feeling the sharp edges dig into soft skin. He jammed his bare feet against the base of the stone, preparing to rock backwards and lift the front edge on to his thighs.

He took a deep breath and leant backwards.

The stone didn't budge.

'Put your back into it.'

He tried again, gripping the stone tighter, feeling it cut deeper into his skin. Breathe in, grit the teeth, lean back, pull up and... lift.

The stone stayed where it was.

He collapsed over it, panting.

A few of the others had stopped working for a moment, watching him, waiting for the punishment they were sure was about to come.

Harry heard the tread of Keaney's boots in the red dust of the quarry floor, getting closer now, louder.

A shadow loomed over him, blocking the heat of the sun. For a moment he basked in the coolness of the shadow, then he heard the words, a malevolent whisper through gritted teeth.

'You British are a bunch of lazy scum. What are you?'

Harry didn't answer.

Keaney's voice was slightly louder now so the others could hear. 'What are you?' he repeated.

Still Harry didn't answer, feeling his chest touch the hard stone as he panted.

The shadow leant closer. Harry felt the prod of the stick in the small of his back and heard the voice once more. 'Pick up the stone, ye lazy bastard, and take it over there.'

'Do it yourself,' Harry whispered. He didn't move, tensing his body for the blow he knew was going to come.

But Keaney was clever.

Harry waited and waited and waited. Finally, he relaxed – and then he heard the whistle of the stick through the air and the sharp pain on the back of his head. His small body was flung forward across the stone.

He tried not to cry out but a sharp screech erupted from his mouth.

Another strike, this time across the back of his legs. He sank to the floor on his knees, body draped over the stone, arms still gripping the edges.

'Pick it up and take it over there,' Keaney shouted now, an order.

Harry heard the swoosh of the stick being raised above Keaney's head, ready to strike down again. He pushed himself up, feeling the pain in his head as he moved. He gripped the stone with his arms once more.

As he did, a drop of blood flowed from the back of his head across his chin and splashed on to the rough surface of the stone. For a moment it sat there, red and viscous, seeping into the rock, leaving behind just a small stain where it had once been.

Another boy's arms joined him. 'We can do this, Harry. After three let's lift, okay?' It was Slimo.

Harry looked into Slimo's eggshell-blue eyes. He was twelve years old, or at least that's what he said. He'd been at Bindoon for a couple of years and already knew the ropes.

'Are you ready?'

Harry nodded.

'One, two, three. Lift.'

They both gritted their teeth and pulled. The stone rocked backwards and up, six inches off the floor. Slimo swivelled round, jerking upwards again and resting it on the edge of the wheelbarrow. They both pushed, sliding the stone to join the others sitting comfortably in the centre of the tray.

Keaney's stick came down across Harry's back. 'Next time, do it on your own. Nobody's going to help you here. Understand?'

He strode away, back to this place atop the rocky mound, his black cassock just touching the red dust of the quarry floor, giving the rough fabric a colourful hem.

Harry watched him go, imagining a knife stabbing again and again between those narrow black shoulders.

Chapter Two

June 17, 2017.
Buxton Residential Home, Derbyshire, England

Jayne switched off Elbow just as they began another mournful chorus of An Imagined Affair. The drive out to her father's nursing home from her house in Didsbury had been as difficult as ever.

The A6 had been designed by some evil planner to be the worst road on earth; a never-ending obstacle course of roadworks, traffic lights, speed cameras, more roadworks, bypasses, more bypasses, and traffic jams.

She had tried many times to find a different route to the residential home, but somehow she was always led unfailingly, as if by black magic, back on to the nightmare that was the A6.

The only rescuing grace was music. She could listen to the bands of her youth; the glory days of Stone Roses, the Mondays, and even Inspiral Carpets, when Manchester had earned the nickname 'Madchester'.

It was still a mad city but the emotion was more anger than excitement these days.

Her work as a genealogical investigator was quiet at the moment. One of those summer lulls, when everybody was thinking of their holidays rather than their family history. But she welcomed the break; a time to relax and spend time with her dad after a hectic couple of months.

Her last case had been particular trying and the trial was due to start soon. She had been shot at, chased and forced to go underground, while her father had been kidnapped and threatened with murder. Her police training had come in useful but it was not a time she had enjoyed. Her Jack Reacher days were long gone. There would be no more assignments from potential Presidential candidates. At least, she hoped that was the case.

For now, she just wanted to rest and spend time with her dad and his new wife, Vera. Being around them made her so happy.

She stepped out of the BMW and made her way up the steps. As ever, Jenny was sitting behind the reception desk.

'In their usual place?' Jayne asked.

The receptionist nodded. 'The happy couple are in the garden, doing a crossword. I don't know what they've got, but I'd like to bottle it and give a few drops to my old man.'

'Still lovey-dovey?'

'Lovier and dovier. Watching those two is like eating fudge, only twice as sweet.'

'What do you expect? They've just come back from honeymoon.' Jayne had picked them up three days earlier from Manchester Airport after their flight had arrived from Vancouver. Her father, Robert, and his new wife, Vera, had just spent two weeks aboard the Silver Shadow on a cruise to Alaska. In the car on their way back from the airport, her father couldn't conceal his excitement as he described the highlights of the cruise.

It was wonderful to see him so animated. It was as if he were a modern-day Rip Van Winkle, just emerged from a long sleep to see the world in all its beauty once again. His early-onset Alzheimer's was in abeyance. Or at least, that's what Jayne hoped. She would ask Vera later.

She touched the silver-mounted bone carving that hung around her neck. A gift from both of them. A symbol of love, they said. A love for each other and for her.

'I'll just go through.'

Jenny nodded. 'But you'd better be quiet. It's the repeats of the Great British Bake-Off. The residents get awfully upset if somebody disturbs their viewing. You might get a few custard tarts lobbed your way.'

'As long as it isn't rock cakes.'

She pushed through the fire doors and was confronted by the spacious day room. In front of the television, ten residents – mostly women – were gathered, eyes glued to the flickering eye in the corner. The curtains were drawn behind the television to help viewing, even though it was the middle of a beautiful summer's day.

'That's not how you make a Victoria sponge.'

'Look at her, creaming with a whisk. Should be beating the eggs in gently with a wooden spoon. My mother taught me as a little girl. Worked sixty years ago, still works today.'

'What's the bloody fool done? Can't have nowt like strawberry jam in't Victoria. Has to be raspberry, even if the seeds get under me dentures.'

Jayne crept past the armchair bakers. None of them noticed her, intent as they were on the rising of the sponges. She slipped through the patio doors and saw her father and Vera sitting close together on a wooden bench.

She tiptoed up behind them and whispered, 'No hanky-panky, you two.'

Vera started in surprise. Her father dropped his new wife's hand like a hot potato.

'You shouldn't do that. My heart is racing fit to burst.' Vera mimed panting.

Jayne bent over the bench and kissed her step mother on the cheek. 'Sorry, couldn't resist it, you two seemed so engrossed.'

'Just three clues left. Wish they wouldn't stick the difficult ones in the corners, it makes 'em hard to solve.' Her father laid down his crossword book.

Jayne kissed his cheek too. 'I'm sure you two will do it... eventually.'

'Aye, this one is like a dog with a bone, gnawing away at the clue till it surrenders.'

Vera bared her teeth. 'Had them sharpened last week when we were on the cruise.'

'A vamp or a vampire?' asked her husband.

Vera laughed. 'A bit of both, I suppose. What do you think?'

'Sorry to interrupt, but how's the jet lag?' Jayne sat down on the chair opposite them.

'Not bad. Finally fell asleep at three o'clock last night. Feeling tired now, though, not as sprightly as I used to be.'

Jayne's father was seventy-four and his new wife an energetic sixty-six, although she looked ten years younger. Good genes and lashings of moisturiser, she always claimed.

'He was wriggling all night, like those salmon we saw in Alaska.'

'Shush, love, don't tell Jayne everything.'

They nudged each other, obviously sharing a secret only the two of them knew.

'Now, what are you two planning for the next week? I have a new case starting at the end of June, and until then I'm free. I can drive you around, if you like.'

Jayne's father went silent. Then he looked across at Vera and nudged her. 'Go on, ask her. Now's as good a time as any.'

'Ask me what?'

Vera glanced down, suddenly bashful, not like her at all.

'Listen, love, if you don't ask then I will.'

Vera continued to look down, discovering a piece of lint on the hem of her dress.

Robert took a deep breath. 'It's like this, Jayne. When we were away, me and Vera, well – we got to talking one night...'

'We were sitting on the veranda of our state room, looking over the sea, and I'd had a glass or two too many,' she interrupted.

'Well, Vera finally told me...' His voice trailed off.

It was as if both wanted to tell the story but neither wanted to say exactly what it was. 'Well, what is it?' said Jayne. 'You've got me all ears now.'

Vera took a deep breath. 'You know my name is Thompson.'

'Your first husband's surname, isn't it?'

Vera nodded. 'My maiden name was Atkins and I was born in Saddleworth in 1951.'

'So you weren't born with a silver spoon in your mouth?'

Vera laughed again. 'Far from it. We weren't exactly poor, though. Dad worked at mill until it closed and then he found a job with the water board. Money was tight but we always had clothes on our backs and food on the table.'

Vera stared off into the distance. 'You'd have liked my mother, Jayne. A kind woman, but one who didn't say much. She was the real strength in our home – wore the trousers, she did. Not one for talking about her family or anything.'

Then it suddenly dawned on Jayne where all this was leading. 'You want me to research your family tree? Find out where you came from?'

Her father reached over and placed his hand on her arm. 'Let Vera finish, love.'

Jayne kept quiet.

Vera took another deep breath. Jayne could see her eyes glaze over with tears. 'It was on my mother's deathbed, she told me. We knew the end was coming, the doctor had been in to examine her. Old age, he said. He offered to take her into hospital but she wouldn't go. Hated them, she did, hospitals. Hated the smell of them. Me too, probably got it from my mother.'

Her father took Vera's hand in his own and smiled at her. She smiled back at him, moving a little closer on the bench.

'Anyway, she wasn't eating any more. Spent most of her time sleeping, coming in and out of consciousness, I suppose. My brother and I took turns to sit with her, reading the newspaper or a book aloud.' She stared off into the distance again. 'Always loved the news, did my mother. Almost as if she discovered the world through it.' Her voice dropped. 'Never went abroad, you know, not even to Spain. "A week in Blackpool is good enough for me," she used to say. I always wanted to take her to America, but we never went. And now we never will...'

Her voice broke and Robert put his arm around her. 'There, there, it's okay, lass,' he whispered in her ear.

Vera gathered herself together, sitting up straight. 'One night, a couple of days before she died, I was sitting in her bedroom reading to her when she suddenly spoke out loud. "I shouldn't have done it," she said. Well, Jayne, I didn't know what she meant so I asked her.'

"'Shouldn't have done what, Mum?'"

"'Shouldn't have given him away.'"

"'Given who away?'"

"'Your brother.'"

"'But you didn't. Charlie has just gone home. He'll be back tomorrow.'"

'By now I thought she was delirious or something. She was taking drugs they give old people and they were very strong. But then she sat up in bed and I could see her eyes were bright and it was like having my old mum back in the room with me. She said: "Not Charlie – your other brother, the one who vanished."

"'But, Mum, I don't have another brother. There's just me and Charlie."

'Then she let out a long sigh, her shoulders slumped and her head nodded forward. She turned to look at me, and I'll never forget the look on her face. It was as if all the regrets in the world were painted into every line, every wrinkle and every crease of her skin. She said in a low, quiet voice: "I never told you about him. Norman knew, of course. He was a good man, Norman. Wanted to be the boy's father but they had already given him away, vanished like he had never existed."

"'Mum, I don't understand. What are you saying?'"

"'I had another child during the war, in 1944. The father was a guard at the Glen Mill POW camp. He died at Sword Beach during the D-Day landings. I was already seven months pregnant. I never married him, and your grandmother, well, she was a tough old stick, upstanding member of the church and all that. I tried to look after the baby but after six months it was all too much. I had to give him up. Always wanted my baby boy back, though. After I married your dad and you were born, we tried to find him again. But they said he was already gone, already adopted. It was too late."

'Mum had stopped talking for a moment and stared at the picture of Jesus on the wall. I'll always remember that picture; this long-haired man with a bright red heart, his head surrounded by a golden light. She stared at the picture and said:

'"I remember him so well before he vanished from my life. He was a beautiful baby, always happy, with big black curls and rosy cheeks. I should never have given him away."'

Vera stopped speaking for a moment to wipe a tear from her eye.

Robert handed her his handkerchief. 'You'd better use this side, love, I've blown on the other.'

Vera smiled. 'He always makes me laugh, does your dad. That's why I love him so.' She leant over and gave Robert a big kiss on the cheek, leaving behind a scar of bright red lipstick.

'I love you too, Vera.' He pulled her closer to him.

She began speaking again. 'Anyway, after that last moment of clarity, Mum nestled back under the covers and went to sleep. She never regained full consciousness and died two days later. The death certificate said pneumonia but I don't think she died from an illness at all. It was regret that killed her.' She stared at Jayne. 'Do you think people can die from regret, Jayne? I do. I know my mother did.'

Jayne thought back over her past. Her time with the police and her time with her ex-husband, Paul. She had regrets, too many probably, but nothing that would kill her. 'I don't know, Vera,' was all she managed to offer in response.

'I can't have those same regrets, Jayne. I have to know if the things my mother said were true. Did she have another child, and if so, what happened to him? I know this is your job and everything, and I'd be happy to pay you...'

Jayne reached over and touched her step mother's arm. 'Shush, Vera. I'd be happy to look into the past for you. It's the one thing I know how to do.'

Chapter Three

June 17, 2017
Buxton Residential Home, Derbyshire, England

'I'm going to need a few details before I make a start.' Jayne pulled out an ancestor chart from her bag, which she had downloaded from the Lost Cousins website. 'This allows me to create a structure for the family members you know. Now what were your parents' names and dates of birth?'

Vera sat up straighter as Jayne's pen hovered over the form. 'My dad's name was Norman Atkins, and he was born in Oldham in 1921. He was older than my mum.' Her eyes looked up and left as she tried to remember the date of birth. 'I think his birthday was January twelfth. He served in the Army during the war, and stayed on afterwards, spending time in Palestine. They met after he was demobbed in 1950. Mum always used to joke he was in such a rush to get married, he proposed to her after two weeks.'

'That's quick, love. It took me two months.'

She reached over and kissed Robert on the lips. 'But we knew after two days. Must have been the same for them.'

'And your mother?' Jayne asked.

'Freda Atkins, nee Duckworth. She was born on June tenth, 1926. She passed away seven years ago. It's one of the reasons I came to live here. Dad died a couple of years after her, and with both parents gone, I didn't need to take care of them any more. My children had already moved away and made lives for themselves.' She glanced across at Robert. 'Best decision I ever made.'

'So, if she had a baby during the war, it will have been between 1939 and 1945. She must have only been a teenager when she gave birth.'

'She said it was in 1944. It was very young, even for those days...' Vera's voice trailed away, remembering her mother once more. 'I can't believe it. She was such a conservative woman. Went to church every Sunday without fail. Wore those two-piece suits with skirts below the knee.' She stopped for a moment and glanced down to the ground. 'I even remember an argument I had with her. I must have been fourteen. The Beatles had just released Rubber Soul and I was one of their biggest fans; beehive hairdo, skirt above the knee and all the rest. I thought Paul McCartney was the loveliest thing since sliced bread.

'I had a boyfriend then – David Endersby, a nice boy, looked just like Paul. One night my mother came back early from church, it must have been a Sunday. Myself and David were on the couch, just having a kiss and a cuddle, nothing serious. She walked in on us and exploded. And I mean went off like a hydrogen bomb, shouting at me and telling David to get out and never come back again. I wasn't allowed out for a month; just school, home, school, home. She kept watching me like a hawk all the time.' Vera looked up at Jayne. 'It makes sense now, doesn't it? She didn't want me to have a baby like her.' She began to play with the lint she had found on her dress. 'I wish she'd told me. I would have understood. Even then, I would have understood...'

'And when were you born, Vera?'

26

'April thirteenth, 1951,' Robert answered for her. 'She's my bit of young stuff.'

'Do you know anything about your grandparents?'

Vera shook her head and, still looking down, answered. 'I think the ones on my dad's side died in the bombing of Manchester. My mum had nothing to do with her parents. I only met my granddad once. I was already seventeen. One morning there was a knock at the door. I opened it and a small, thin man was standing there. He asked if a Mrs Atkins lived in the house. I called my mum and she came to the door. It was my granddad. Apparently, my grandma had died a couple of days before and he wanted my mum to go to the funeral. I remember them standing at the door arguing. I don't think my mum wanted to go. He said it was her mother who had passed away, she had to go.'

Vera reached for Robert's hand and took a few deep breaths before continuing.

'We went, of course. There weren't many people there. Apparently, my grandmother was an only child and had no living relatives apart from us. The only people at the Requiem Mass were parishioners she knew from church. My brother carried the coffin with the undertaker's assistants but I wasn't allowed.' She grimaced. 'A girl, you see. It all meant nothing to me then. All I cared about was music – I had moved on to the Rolling Stones by then – guys and my friends. Family didn't mean anything. I remember Mum was very quiet when she came back from the graveyard. Didn't say a word all night.'

'When was this?'

'I was seventeen, so it must have been some time in 1969.'

'What was your grandmother's name?'

Vera thought for a moment. 'Dora Duckworth, that was it. I remember thinking how old and uncool the name sounded.'

'And the church?'

'St Mary's on Union Street.'

'She was buried there?'

'No, at Royton Cemetery. Why do you ask, Jayne?'

'Because, as she died in 1969, her death certificate may give us her place and date of birth. They added those details in that year. The information could help build your family tree.'

'My mother hated her, you know. After the funeral, she never mentioned her again. Not once.'

'You never asked her why?'

Vera laughed. 'You didn't ask my mother such questions. And, if I'm honest, I wasn't interested. Young people don't think about such things, do they?'

Jayne snapped the lid back on her Montblanc pen. It was one of her eccentricities. When she was creating a family tree, she always wrote in the brightest vermilion ink. It was her way of commemorating the lives of the people she listed. On this form, they were going to be remembered once again. The dead brought back to life.

'I think I have enough to make a start, Vera. I should be able to find out more about your family.'

Vera reached over and touched Jayne's arm. 'Will you be able to discover if I have a brother?'

Jayne shrugged her shoulders. 'Honestly, I don't know. Adoption records are notoriously difficult to discover. Sometimes the baby was renamed completely and the date of birth changed. I can't promise anything, Vera. But I will try.'

Vera nodded. 'You know, the older we get, the more we want to know who we are and where we came from. And the more family means to us. My brother, if he exists and is still alive, will now be nearly seventy-three years old. Another life, another family. I would like to meet him before I die, Jayne.'

Jayne took hold of her step mother's hand. 'If he's out there, Vera, I'll find him. I promise.'

Chapter Four

September 27, 1951
23 Haggate Lane, Delph, Lancashire, England

He didn't know why the man took him away from Mr and Mrs Beggs. He sat on the floor playing with his soldier. He wasn't a real soldier, of course, but he looked like one. He was soft and cuddly, with a tall black hat – a busby, Mrs Beggs had told him – and a bright red coat with shiny golden buttons. His mother had given it to him for his birthday on her last visit. Ever since then it had never left his side, even sleeping with him at night.

The man talked with Mr and Mrs Beggs for a long time, and they drank tea from the best cups nobody was allowed to use unless it was Father Vincent when he came round for his cake on Thursday afternoons.

Harry knew Mr and Mrs Beggs weren't his real mummy and daddy. They had told him just before he went to school that they were his foster parents, whatever that meant. He didn't care what they said. He was a lucky boy – he had two mummies and one daddy. More than anybody else in school. His real mummy sometimes came to see him. She always brought him a present. On her last visit, she had given him the soldier, but it seemed such a long time since she had come to see him. He liked it when she came because she picked him up and gave him lots of kisses. He had to wipe his face afterwards, though. Her lipstick was very red and it made his cheeks sticky.

He always remembered her smell. Like all the plants in the garden had given up their flowers and crushed them together to spray on her neck. He liked the smell. A smell of the warmth of summer, the wind rustling through the trees and him on the warm grass, playing in the garden.

The man who came to see Mr and Mrs Beggs smelt of tobacco and sweat, with a hat that was too black for his head. Harry didn't like the man's smell. It was sour and burnt. He pretended he was playing, but he actually listened to what the adults were saying.

Mr and Mrs Beggs wanted him to stay with them. They said he would miss David and Geraldine and Grace and Flora, all the other children. But the man said he had to go back to the home, it was time for him to go.

When the man spoke he played with the hat that was too black for his head, his fingers stroking the dark lining inside the dark hat. Fingers stained brown at the ends, with nails that were a deeper shade of brown, like the man had just put them in his poo-poo.

When they had finished speaking and drinking their tea, Mr Beggs stood over Harry and lifted him in his arms, saying, 'You have to go with Mr Keaton now. They are taking you back to the home. You'll be happy there. There are lots of little children to run and play with.'

'But what about school?'

'You'll go to school there too. There's lots to learn and the fathers will tell you all about your catechism.'

Harry didn't understand that word, but at least in the home he would have a father, maybe he would have lots of fathers.

Mr Beggs handed him over to the man who smelt of smoke. The man put him down to stand on the floor and they walked out of the front parlour to the door. Mrs Beggs was waiting with his bag, which she gave to the man. She knelt down beside Harry and put his coat on him, fastening the buttons and tying the belt tightly around his waist. 'We'll miss you, Harry. Always remember we love you. We love you very much.'

Then she gave him a big hug and the man took his hand and they walked down to the gate.

At the gate, Harry pulled away and ran back to the house. Mr and Mrs Beggs were just closing the door. Harry rushed through it, hearing the footsteps of the man behind him and a shout: 'Stop him, he must come with me!'

Harry brushed past Mrs Beggs and turned left into the parlour. His red-coated soldier was still on the floor where he'd left it, arms stretched out on the old rug as if it were warming itself in front of the fire.

The man who smelt of tobacco ran into the room. Harry held up his soldier and made a charging noise with his mouth. The man snatched him up roughly, holding him tightly to his chest, the hard brim of his hat cutting into Harry's cheek.

Mr and Mrs Beggs were still standing at the open door. As they walked past, Mrs Beggs touched the man's arm. 'Does he have to go?'

The man said nothing and strode past her down the path, picked up the bag in his free hand, and marched out through the gate and into the waiting car that was as black as the man's hat.

It was the first time Harry had been in a car. It sounded just like a rocket, only louder.

Chapter Five

June 17, 2017
Didsbury, Manchester, England

Jayne pushed open the door of her house and was immediately greeted by her cat, Mr Smith, his long tail erect and his body rubbing against her legs.

'I know, I know, you're hungry and then you want to go out, right?'

The cat purred in agreement. Without taking off her coat, she went into the kitchen, booted up the computer and opened the fridge door. 'Lamb or chicken?'

The cat had followed her and was now standing beside his bowl expectantly.

'You had lamb yesterday, so it looks like it's going to be chicken.' She checked the title on the small pouch of food. '"Tender chunks of chicken breast with beef in a tasty, wholesome jelly." Hmm, sounds good, I almost fancy it myself.'

She tore open the pouch and squeezed the contents into the cat's bowl, adding a handful of dry food for a bit of crunch. Mr Smith tore into it as if he hadn't been fed for days. 'You just ate this morning, you greedy beggar.'

The cat ignored her, as he usually did.

'Now, what am I going to have?' She went back to the fridge. Nothing but a half-opened packet of cream crackers, four bottles of wine, a third of a box of French brie, a newly opened packet of custard creams and a tomato. 'That settles it. A bottle of Sauvignon Blanc and some cheese and biscuits. A gourmet meal for one coming right up.'

She suddenly realised she had been talking out loud again. Since Paul had left for Brussels, and their subsequent break-up, she had been spending most of her time alone. The sound of her voice in the emptiness of the kitchen was somehow comforting, as if she were still having a conversation with someone.

She placed a plate next to the computer, added a few stale crackers and twisted off the cap of the Sauvignon Blanc, pouring a large glass. She twirled the glass around, releasing the aroma of lemon, gooseberries and fresh grass. A classic New Zealand Sauvignon. The glass was already beginning to pearl with condensation as she drank the first crisp mouthful of wine. Immediately her body relaxed and the tension in her shoulders from driving drifted away on a cloud of New Zealand grapes. She checked the label. Villa Maria 2016, as fresh as the day it was poured from the steel vat.

The blinking cursor of the computer caught her eye. 'Time to begin. What secrets does Vera's family hold?' She took the Lost Cousins form out of her bag. 'Let's begin with Vera's mother.'

She logged on to the FreeBMD site to search the Births, Marriages and Deaths indexes and typed 'Freda Duckworth' into the fields, adding the date, 1926, and the district, Oldham.

Duckworth was a fairly common name in Lancashire, especially in the old mill towns, but Freda wasn't found so often. 'With a bit of luck, she'll be a loner.' Jayne pressed search and silently prayed to the gods of genealogy.

Just one result popped up on her screen almost immediately. 'Duckworth, Freda S. Mother's maiden name: Burns. Registration district: Oldham.' It was catalogued under January to March with a number of 8d, 1081.

Jayne punched the air and took another refreshing sip of the Sauvignon Blanc. A second Lost Cousins form, this one to create a family tree, was in her folder. She took it out, filling in Freda's maiden name and birth details into the boxes, the vermillion ink wet on the page.

She was on a roll; now to get the certificate itself. Unfortunately, the birth was after 1916, so even if the pilot scheme for online PDFs had still been in operation, she wouldn't have been able to get all the details.

Never mind. If Vera wanted her mother's birth certificate, she could order it later. At least she had the grandmother's maiden name to work with. Now she could go a little further back in time. It was tempting to jump straight in and check the FreeBMD for Vera's missing brother, but Jayne wanted context to the family. You never knew when the extra information might prove useful later on.

Vera had said her mother was an only child, but Jayne thought she better check it out. She broadened the search for Oldham Duckworths to ten years either side of 1926. Thirty-five results came back. Quickly, she scanned the hits looking for the same maiden name of the mother.

Nothing. Just the one hit in 1926.

Jayne relaxed. 'Great,' she said out loud. 'Looks like Vera's information is accurate so far.'

Hearing her voice, the cat sauntered over and rubbed himself once more against her leg. 'You want to go out, don't you, Mr Smith?'

A loud purr in response.

'Number nine on heat again? Or is it Mrs Brown's cat who is tempting you?'

No purr this time, just another pass across her leg, his body arching in pleasure.

'Okay, okay. I'll get no peace until I open the door.'

She stood up and stretched, striding over to the patio doors and opening them wide. The cat followed her and shot out through her legs, into the freedom of the garden.

'See you later.' She waved goodbye, but the cat was already gone. 'Men.' She shrugged.

It was a beautiful summer's night in Manchester. A blackbird was singing from the top of the chimney pot on the house opposite. A host of swallows were swooping across the contrailed sky, hoovering up insects. A car honked impatiently two streets away. There was a wonderful stillness to the evening, with not a breath of wind.

Jayne went back inside for her glass of wine, returning to the patio doors and sitting on the steps leading down to her small garden.

She closed her eyes. The sound of a woman's laughter, followed by the deeper guffaws of a man, came from the left. The faint screech of a violin note being played incorrectly on her right. Above her, the sharp squeaks of the swallows as they called to each other on the wing. Even though it was past eight o'clock, the light was perfect; a soft Manchester suburban summer's night, when the world was at ease after a long day at work.

She took another sip of wine. She liked being alone, not having to answer to anybody, nor worry what they wanted to do. She loved the peace of it, the stillness, never having to worry whether the other person was bored or restless. Now, there was just herself to consider. If she wanted to work, she worked. If she wanted to take five minutes off and smell the roses, she could do that too.

She thought about Vera and her discovery of another brother, a half-brother. What about Jayne's own family? Did her mother have secrets too? Robert was her stepfather, marrying her mother when Jayne was just three years old. Her biological father had vanished when she was a baby. She tried to remember him, his face, his eyes, his hair, but nothing came.

She laughed to herself. 'The big joke. You must be the only genealogical investigator who knows nothing about her own family,' she said out loud. One day, she would look for him and find out why he went away, but not today. Today, it was Vera she had to help.

She stood up and drained the glass. 'Break over, time to get back to the Atkinses, the Duckworths and the Burnses.'

She went back to the computer and pressed the 'New Search' button on the FreeBMD site. This time she clicked on the marriages section and entered the names of Vera's mother and father into the fields, expanding the time to seven years before Vera's birth.

Again, she whispered a prayer to the gods of genealogy as the little blue circle whirred, before it returned with a single result. Francis Duckworth married a Burns some time between January and March 1926.

Brilliant. Jayne would be able to give this information to Vera and order a certificate if she wanted. Then she stopped. The dates, they were too early. Vera said her mother's birthday was June 10, 1926, but her parents had only married six months earlier at the most. A shotgun wedding? Probably.

'Perhaps your mother wasn't the saint she made herself out to be.' As soon as the words came out of her mouth, Jayne regretted them. How could she so easily judge somebody and their actions of nearly one hundred years ago? What right did she have to be so high and mighty?

She got up and went to the fridge, pouring herself another glass of wine. Perhaps that's why Dora had been so tough on Vera's mother – not wanting her to be forced into an early, and perhaps unhappy, marriage, all because of a pregnancy.

Jayne sat down at her computer and checked the dates again, noting the index reference in her legal pad. Now for a bit of a long shot. There were no ages given in the entries but, with a bit of luck, both Francis and his wife had been older than seventeen when they married.

Jayne logged on to the Findmypast website and selected the 1911 census. People moved around a lot less in those days. Francis Duckworth had probably been born and raised in Oldham; time to check back a little further.

She entered his details, making sure the birth covered all ten years before 1911, and pressed search. One result came back. She was on a roll today. Vera's great-grandfather was Thomas Henry Duckworth, married to Annie Duckworth. They had four children, with Francis being the third. Thomas Henry earned his living as a coaster in a brewery. She wondered what a coaster did, but decided to check it later.

Now for the final search – the Burns family. She entered the surname and three results came back, all with the right age range. Her roll was over. Francis's wife could have been any of these women, and that was presuming she had been born in Oldham.

With a name like Burns, she could have been Scottish or Irish and migrated south or across the Irish Sea to find work.

38

No matter, she had gone back far enough. If Vera wanted to find out the surnames of her maternal grandparents, it would involve checking marriage certificates or the parish registers.

Jayne breathed out.

For some reason, she had been holding back from making the most important search of all. It wasn't like her to procrastinate when she was investigating somebody's family background, but Vera was her step mother. What if it was all just the imagination of an old lady who was dying? Did Vera really want to know if she had a mystery brother?

'That's not for you to decide, Jayne Sinclair. You're here to do the research, nothing more, nothing less.'

She logged back in to FreeBMD, clicking the 'New Query' button. In the search field she selected the year, 1944, and left the father's name blank but entered 'Duckworth' into the Mother section. Unfortunately, there was no way she could add the Christian name, Freda, into the search. The search only allowed the father's first name to be selected.

'More bloody sexism,' she muttered to herself. She then selected Oldham as the registration district and pressed 'Search'.

Nothing.

Even though it was not an unusual name for the area, there were no Duckworth mothers. She remembered Vera saying her family had links to Saddleworth. It was the next registration district along. She clicked Saddleworth district and said another prayer to the genealogy gods as she searched.

The result came back again.

Nothing.

Her lucky streak was definitely over. Now would come the hard graft of true genealogy. Perhaps Freda had moved to another area to have her baby? Jayne expanded the search to cover all districts. The site seemed to take an age to give her the result.

After almost a minute, 112 hits popped up for the year 1944, most of them situated in a swathe of old mill towns scattered around the north of England like warts. Only two of the hits showed the same surname, Duckworth, for both the mother and the baby, suggesting an illegitimate birth.

The small, dark print on the screen began to blur. Jayne rubbed her eyes; staring at the bright screen had made her tired. Or was it the wine? She glanced across – the glass was already empty.

She thought about phoning Vera with the news so far but decided against it. What did she really know? The names of Vera's grandparents and paternal great-grandparents. They were relatively easy to find from the census and existing information. But on the most important search, that of the vanished brother, she had hit a brick wall.

Vera's brother could be one of the 112 hits or he might be none of them. There were too many variables, too many unknowns at the moment.

Jayne rubbed her eyes again. She was also tired from all the driving. Switching off the computer, she decided she had done enough for that evening.

Tomorrow was another day. But without more information, this search wasn't going to be easy.

But they never were, that was the whole point.

Chapter Six

June 18, 2017
Didsbury, Manchester, England

Jayne was up with the larks at the break of dawn the following morning. It seemed wrong to waste such a beautiful day.

Outside, Mr Smith was sitting patiently beside the patio door, waiting to be let in. He was enjoying the freshness of a Manchester morning and desperate to find a warm windowsill to sleep off the adventures of last night.

She switched on the Nespresso machine and walked over to open the patio doors. The cat slinked past her, not bothering to acknowledge her presence, as if embarrassed by what he had been up to during the night. He stopped for a second beside his bowl, checking to see if there was any food there, before crouching down and cautiously lapping from his water bowl.

'Would his Lordship like breakfast?'

The cat miaowed in response.

'Kippers? Kedgeree? A poached egg on a freshly baked sourdough roll, covered in béarnaise?'

The cat ignored her.

Jayne opened the fridge, checking what was inside.

Not much. 'How about a pouch of "fresh lamb with carrot surprise"?' she read aloud off the label.

Mr Smith miaowed loudly, as if to say, 'Get a move on, woman.'

Jayne snipped off the corner of the pouch and squeezed the food into his bowl. She searched for the tell-tale orange flecks of carrot but saw none. 'I think the surprise is there's no carrot.'

The cat didn't care; he attacked the lamb with gusto.

Jayne selected a capsule of Nespresso – a 'jewel' in marketing speak – slotted it into the opening in the top and pressed the button. It wasn't the best coffee, but as an instant hit of espresso in the morning, it served its purpose of dragging her brain kicking and screaming into the day.

The cat ignored the whirr of the machine, wolfing down his lamb breakfast.

'My, we are hungry. Busy night at number nine, was it?'

The espresso cup was full. She took it, inhaled the aroma and took a fresh sip of hot liquid. Immediately, the caffeine surged from her tongue to her brain.

'Better,' she said aloud, booting up her computer. The cat slinked off to find a windowsill that had already been warmed by the rays of the sun, and to dream of nights gone and nights to come.

Jayne finished her coffee. 'Now, where was I?' She checked her notes and clicked on the saved hits in FreeBMD.

Last night's 112 results stared back at her. All she really knew was that she was looking for a boy, since Vera was sure her mother had given birth to a male child.

Jayne thought of having another coffee, but decided against it. Too much caffeine gave her a headache. Her search would have been far easier if the mother's Christian name had ever been included in the original files, but it never was. The mother was always just a surname.

'Get on with it, Jayne, stop faffing around.' She scrolled down the page. There were two hits where the mother's surname and the child's were the same, suggesting an illegitimate birth. She checked them first. Both children were girls. She crossed them off her list.

Now came the grunt work. She would have to individually check all 110 remaining Duckworth births in 1944, looking for clues. However, there was one thing she could do immediately to reduce the numbers. She cancelled out all the female births, which gave her forty-eight male births to look at.

'Makes life a little bit easier.' Next, she checked each name to see if there were subsequent births for the same father and mother. If the family had stayed together, it couldn't be Vera's mother.

Two hours later, Jayne had researched all forty-eight mothers with the surname Duckworth on the FreeBMD list of births for 1944. Forty-one had subsequent births, so they were eliminated. Three had births prior to 1944, so they were crossed off too, leaving just five women who could have been Vera's mother.

Year/Quarter	Name	Mother's Maiden Name	RegDist	Vol	Page
1944/March	Smith, John	Duckworth	Bradford	8e	456

Year/Quarter	Name	Mother's Maiden Name	Reg Dist	Vol	Page
1944/June	East, Alan	Duckworth	Haslingden	3b	235

Year/Quarter	Name	Mother's Maiden Name	Reg Dist	Vol	Page
1944/June	Bryan, George	Duckworth	Nelson	7a	127

Year/Quarter	Name	Mother's Maiden Name	Reg Dist	Vol	Page
1944/Sep	Brown, Fred	Duckworth	Chelmsford	4c	221

Year/Quarter	Name	Mother's Maiden Name	Reg Dist	Vol	Page
1944/Dec	Tyler, Walter	Duckworth	Preston	9d	189

Jayne discounted Chelmsford in Essex, as she doubted Vera's mother would have given birth so far away from home. Hadn't Vera said her mother had never travelled much in her life? So that left just four possibilities.

She checked the places and dates again, looking for clues. The four remaining towns were in the north of England, just a short drive or train journey from Oldham. Freda could have easily travelled to any of them to give birth.

In normal times, the father would have to attend the registration of the birth. But this was wartime. All Vera's mother had to say was her husband was serving overseas and register the child in his name. Generally, the registrar wouldn't ask for a marriage certificate, and particularly not back then, when so many men were serving in the Army.

Jayne quickly went online to check her facts.

The child of a married woman is, by law, always the child of her husband, and his name will appear on the certificate of any of her children – unless she, or her husband, tells the Registrar any different. It is, in fact, quite difficult for a wronged husband to get his name removed from a child's birth certificate – the Registrar will take some convincing, such as absence overseas for ten months or more!

The child of an unmarried woman – that is, a woman who admits to being unmarried – will have no father's name on the certificate, unless he attends registration with her, or swears an affidavit.

The words 'wronged husband' made Jayne snort. Why was the law so bloody male?

Had Freda convinced the Registrar her husband was overseas? Possibly. Only two of the births had no father's name, but both those children were girls.

'Sod it,' she said out loud. Before she did any more work she would need another shot of caffeine; this search was giving her a headache anyway. Selecting another espresso capsule, she slotted it into the machine and pressed the button. When it had finished whirring and clunking, she took the coffee back to her computer.

The child could be one of the four on her list, or it might not. She ordered the certificates anyway to make sure. At least the certificates would give the Christian name of the mother as well as her maiden name. There couldn't be many Freda Duckworths giving birth in 1944. She would now have to wait at least four days for the certificates to be delivered.

And then a new problem struck her with all the force of a double decker bus. What if Freda Duckworth hadn't used her real name when she registered the birth?

'Oh, shit,' Jayne said out loud.

Chapter Seven

September 27, 1951
St Michael's Home, Oldham, England

She wasn't a bad sort, Sister Morris – one of the better ones. Even when she used the strap hanging from her waist, it was more in disappointment than in anger.

Now Sister Tomasina, everybody knew you had to careful of that one. Her face could curdle cream and she went about the home with the permanent air of somebody looking for a bad smell yet unable to find it.

It hadn't taken Harry long to work out which sisters to avoid and which to stay close to. The others in his dormitory had whispered the rules to him on his first night.

'Don't be late for mass.'

'Don't be late for the porridge. It's shite but you have to eat it.'

'Don't run in the corridors. And especially don't be caught by Sister Tomasina. That one's a devil with the strap.'

'Don't talk when you're eating.'

'Don't eat when you're talking.'

'And definitely don't cross the Mother Superior,' said Tommy Larkin.

'Why not?'

There was a knowing laugh from Larkin's bed. 'You don't want to know.'

His other introduction to St Mike's, as it was known, had been brief. The man in the car had dropped him off at the entrance, saying, 'Go through those doors, a sister will be waiting.'

'A sister? But I don't have a sister.'

The man rolled his eyes up into his black hat. 'A Sister of Mercy.'

Harry stared at him.

'One of the nuns. They are going to look after you now.'

'I can't go back to Mr and Mrs Beggs?'

The man shook his head. 'Don't forget your bag.'

Harry climbed out of the car and stared up at the blue painted door and the black stone of the building towering over him. The rain had given a shiny gloss to the walls. Water was running down the front of the house where a gutter had broken. To Harry, it seemed like the building was crying.

He climbed the stairs slowly.

A woman dressed in black with just a hint of white peeping out from beneath a black hood appeared from nowhere. 'Hurry out of the rain, boy,' she said. She held a black umbrella over her head to stop her habit getting wet. 'This way.'

Harry ran up the steps as fast as he could. She pushed open the blue-painted door a little wider and Harry stepped through.

'Wipe your feet.'

Harry stood in a high hall with more steps leading upwards in front of him. There was a mirror and hatstand to the left, the floor was highly polished wood and the whole place stank of boiled cabbage. On the right, a black clock tolled 3 p.m.

The nun – Sister Tomasina, as he found out later (the one to avoid) – pushed him forward, shaking the drops of water from the closing umbrella over his head. 'Don't just stand there, boy. Come in here.'

She led the way into a small room that was hidden behind the mirror and the hat-stand. She sat behind the desk, picking up a sheet of paper.

'Is your name Harold?'

Harry nodded. 'Everybody calls me Harry.'

'We will call you Harold, it is your Christian name. Are those your things?'

He glanced down at the small green army bag he held in his right hand. He had forgotten it was still there. He nodded again.

'Cat got your tongue?'

He didn't recognise her accent. It was sharp, with edges like a rough stone. He shook his head.

'Well?'

'N-n-no, Miss,' he blurted out.

'It's Sister to you. Sister Tomasina.'

He followed her eyes to see the small puddle at his feet where the rain had run off his coat and dripped on to the floor.

Sister Tomasina sniffed. 'You're in number three, come this way. Welcome back.'

Welcome back? Had he been here before? He didn't remember living here or visiting with Mr and Mrs Beggs. Perhaps he had come to visit one day.

He followed the sister out of the door and up the stairs. He reached for her hand, as he had been taught by the Beggs. 'Always hold my hand climbing the stairs, Harry, you don't want to fall.'

The sister knocked it away and glared down at him.

He concentrated on climbing the stairs so he wouldn't fall, staring at the bottom of her hem as it glided upwards in front of his eyes. Occasionally the hem would lift to reveal the backs of her heels in her brown sandals: cracked heels with dry and flaking skin, looking like the old leather Mr Beggs used to clean the windows.

At the top, she glided down a long corridor. Two children were on their knees wiping the floor, dipping their cloths into steaming buckets of water.

For a moment, the children lifted their eyes to look at the new arrival, before dropping them again as Sister Tomasina strode past.

She stopped outside one of the rooms. 'This is your dormitory.'

The door opened. Harry saw a row of iron beds on either side of a narrow aisle. Each of the beds was neatly made, with a brown blanket folded at the bottom and white sheets turned down to the edge of a white pillow. Above each bed was a single wooden cross, alone and stark against the white wall. At the back of the room, facing the door, was a large picture window, revealing the grey day outside in all its glory.

'This is where you will sleep. Are you a bed-wetter?'

Harry knew about this. One of the other boys at Mr and Mrs Beggs did it sometimes in his sleep. He shook his head.

'Don't lie to me, boy. Are you a bed-wetter?'

He shook his head again, harder this time.

'We don't like bed-wetters.' She walked into the room. 'This is your bed. Number six.'

Harry looked around him, counting the beds. There were seven on each side. Seven times two equals fourteen. Where were the others?

As if she could hear his thoughts, Sister Tomasina answered him. 'The others will be along shortly when they've finished their work. They will explain our rules to you.' She touched the long piece of leather hanging from her belt next to the rosary. 'We have rules that must be followed. Am I clear?'

He nodded again.

'Am I clear?' she repeated.

'Y-y-yes, Sister.'

She nodded once, satisfied, and left the room.

Harry stood there at the end of his bed, not knowing what to do. For a moment, a small ball of pain rose from the middle of his chest into his throat. He knew he mustn't cry.

Not now. Not here.

He didn't know how long he stood there, not daring to move, a small puddle of water forming at his feet. The light through the windows had gone from a dull grey to a dark black before the others returned. Harry was still stood where Sister Tomasina had left him. They all crowded around him, friendly and curious.

'Are you the new boy?'

'What's your name?'

'Where you from?'

The questions kept coming until one boy took him aside. He was taller and older than the rest and seemed to be in charge.

'Hang your coat in the wardrobe over there and put your bag under the bed. The nuns will issue you with uniform tomorrow, they always do.'

For the first time, Harry realised they were all wearing the same clothes; a grey shirt, black shorts, a V-necked sleeveless green jumper and no shoes.

'She's given you this bed?'

Harry nodded.

'Vince used to sleep here, but he left yesterday. Jack Hopkins is the name.' He held out his hand like Mr Beggs used to do when people came to visit.

50

Harry shook it tentatively. 'Come on, it's time for supper. They won't let you eat if you're late.'

And that was his introduction to St Mike's. He soon got used to the place and its rules. The rest of the kids were great and the sisters were fine as long as you recognised which ones to avoid.

Most days, the children worked in the kitchen, cleaning the halls, sweeping the paths, or washing the floors. The thousand and one jobs that needed doing whilst the sisters watched and supervised.

Occasionally, they had classes when Sister Morris didn't have one of her headaches. But Harry wasn't very good at learning his letters, the shapes seemed all wrong to him. His hands smarted from the lash of the sister's tongue followed by the sharp edge of the metal ruler across his knuckles. But somehow, he didn't get much better at reading. Arithmetic was different, though. The numbers made sense to him, and even when he ran out of fingers it was easy to work out the answers.

He'd even made some friends. Jack, of course, and Denis, Ginger, Ernie, Fred, Georgie – all the rest of the gang in his dormitory. It was all boys there, no girls. The girls were in the dormitories at the end of the hall, guarded fiercely by Sister Grace. They saw them at mealtimes and stole a few words here and there. Jack's sister was one of them. But they vanished to the laundry every day except Sunday.

Sunday was Mass day. They were all assembled at 7.45 a.m. at the end of their beds, dressed in their cleanest clothes. They were told to put on their shoes and were then led down the stairs, out through the blue-painted door and around the corner to the church at the end of the road.

St Michael's was a vast church, towering above Harry's head as he sat in the pews. The priest led the congregation at the front, mumbling the words to the Mass. He was an old man who had to be helped by the altar boys as he moved in front of the altar or up the steps to the pulpit. The older boys, Jack included, sometimes went up for communion if they had been to confession. One day, Jack came back to the pew and sat next to Harry. He opened his mouth wide to show the host still sitting white and lonely in the centre of his red tongue and then rolled his eyes so only the whites could be seen. Harry laughed out loud and the whole church turned round to look at him.

He received six lashes across the back of his legs later that day. Sister Tomasina shouted at him after every lash of her strap, 'Jesus Christ died on the cross to save you! Jesus Christ died on the cross to save you, Jesus Christ died on the cross to save you.'

The backs of his legs were bruised and painful for the next week, changing colour from a livid red to a deep purple and finally ending in a lazy brown.

He would be more careful next time.

Jesus Christ had died on the cross to save him.

Chapter Eight

November 6, 1951.
St Michael's Home, Oldham, England

The acrid smell of gunpowder was still in the air. A pungent smell that seeped out from the brick walls and infested their hair, clothes and food.

But Harry didn't mind, last night had been fun. They all knew about the bonfire. Hadn't the local kids been building it for the last week on the waste ground between the church and the home? The day before, a guy had been hauled up to the top; the body of a shop mannequin dressed in old clothes with a football as a head, painted white with eyes, nose and mouth in bright vermillion red.

The nuns pretended to ignore it. 'Heathens,' Sister Tomasina whispered under her breath, making the sign of the cross.

November 5 had passed quickly. The next day, Harry was in the kitchens with Jack. Peeling the spuds, washing the cabbage, and helping the cook, Sister Iris, to roast the bacon for the nuns' table. Of course, the children wouldn't be having bacon – that was far too good for them, but if you were lucky, Sister Iris let you nibble on the ends the nuns wouldn't eat.

After they had washed their faces and brushed their teeth, Sister Tomasina had sent them to their beds in the dormitory at the usual time of 7.30 p.m., turning the lights out fifteen minutes later, after their prayers. Of course, she had closed the door with her evening goodnight: 'Dream of God, children, let him fill your head till morning.'

They all remained in their beds, the sheets and blankets pulled up under their chins to keep out the cold.

Sister Tomasina came back five minutes later, as she usually did, to check up on them. Ah, she was a clever one she was, but they knew she would return, so nobody had moved. She popped her head round the door, saw that nobody was 'awake' and went away.

Jack waited a minute before whispering, 'She's gone.'

Quietly, they crept out of bed. Jack went to the shutters in front of the windows, which the sisters closed every night to keep out the street lights. He folded back one side.

The bonfire was already alight. A crowd of children and adults were standing in front of it, watching the flames flicker through the gaps in the wood like dancing orange fingers. A few of the men were drinking out of bottles, their children eating something on sticks.

'Them's toffee apples, them is,' said Rocko.

'How do you know?'

'Me mam. She gave me one once. Lovely it was, too. The outside's toffee. It cracks in your mouth and then you bite into the soft apple inside.'

Harry's mouth was watering.

'You had one?'

'I did.'

'You did not.'

'I tell you I did too... Well, me and me brother shared it.'

54

The flames were reaching higher now, licking the feet of the guy. Some children had started dancing around the bonfire, forming a long conga line that weaved in and out of the adults, who were standing in groups, watching.

Snatches of a song drifted with the sparks to the home.

Won't it be fun on Bonfire Night?
Bonfire Night, Bonfire Night.
Won't it be fun on Bonfire Night,
On Bonfire Night in the garden.

We'll build a fire and it'll burn bright,
On Bonfire Night, on Bonfire Night.
We'll build a fire and it'll burn bright,
On Bonfire Night in the garden.

One man was fixing a pink circle to a pole. A match appeared in his hand and he touched it to the edge of the circle, stepping back sharply.

Nothing happened.

Then all of a sudden there was a loud whoosh and the pink circle begin to spin, giving off sparks of red and blue and yellow, spinning faster and faster until the colours blurred into one solid mass. The adults and children cheered.

Harry glanced across at Jack. 'It's beautiful.'

Jack didn't answer, his eyes shining bright, staring at the colours.

Then the spinning slowed down and the wheel shuddered to a halt. The man came forward once more, placing a bottle on the ground and inserting a long stick with a pointed end into the mouth.

'That's a rocket, that is. It can go to the moon,' Jack said.

They all waited as the man touched his match to the stick and stepped back again.

The rocket flared for a second before shooting up into the sky. All the boys leant forward to follow the rocket's progress, but they couldn't see it. For three seconds it vanished from view, and then above their heads in the dark night sky a flower of shimmering sparks exploded, dropping and sparkling till they vanished and the night sky returned.

The boys cheered loudly, only to be silenced by a loud 'Shush' from Jack. 'Don't make any noise, Sister Tomasina will hear.'

For the next hour, the boys watched the bonfire through the windows of the home. Rockets soared, sparklers sparkled, bangers banged, Catherine Wheels spun, little volcanoes spurted flame like Vesuvius and the citizens of the town ate their toffee apples and their parkin and drank their beer.

All this time the bonfire burnt fiercely, the flames illuminating the figures in a red, orange and yellow glow.

Jack and Harry. Rocko, with Little Tom. Denis the Menace and Georgie. James and John. Whitey and the Whatmough Brothers and Charlie all slept well.

Nobody wet the bed that night.

Chapter Nine

June 18, 2017
Buxton Residential Home, Derbyshire, England

It was time to tell Vera what she had found so far.

Jayne drove out to Buxton down the A6 with Oasis blaring out from the BMW's sound system, Liam Gallagher's Manchester whine a fitting accompaniment to her mood. What was she going to say? Everything depended on the birth certificates arriving from the Government Record Office in Southport, and if the name of the mother was not given as Freda Duckworth then they were stuffed, up the creek without a paddle?

The first and only job given to her by a relative and she had so far found nothing.

She had managed to discover a few grandparents, but that was easy – simply a matter of looking up the census. The important question – did Vera have a long-lost brother – was still unsettled.

Jayne switched off the engine and Liam Gallagher died too. Time to face the music. Luckily it wasn't Oasis.

She quickly said hello to Jenny sitting in reception and found Robert and Vera sitting out in the garden in their usual place under the shade of the old oak tree.

'Good afternoon, lass, it's great to see you.'

She leant forward to kiss her father on the forehead, noticing for the first time the bright liver spots at his hairline. 'How are you, Dad?'

He held his hand out horizontally and waved it in the air.

'He had one of his moments this morning.'

'Afternoon, Vera.' Jayne manoeuvred her way around the table to kiss her step mother on the cheek.

'One minute I was fine, the next I was stood there trying to remember my name. I couldn't remember my own bloody name.' Her father slammed his fist down on the table.

'There, there, Robert.' Vera patted his hand. 'You're getting older, these things happen.'

'But not to bloody me, they don't. Always proud of my memory, I was.'

'Vera's right, Dad, you shouldn't get annoyed with yourself, these things happen.'

'Wait till they happen to you, then see how you feel.'

There was a vehemence in her father's voice that Jayne hadn't heard before. Even when she was a teenager and had come home two hours late, he had always been gentle with her, reminding her this was not the correct behaviour.

Vera patted his arm again, but her voice had changed, the northern accent becoming far more pronounced. 'Now, Robert, that's no way to speak to Jayne. She's only trying to help.'

Her father appeared sheepish. 'Sorry, lass, I didn't mean... It's just...'

'I know, Dad. Don't worry, and don't be too hard on yourself.'

Vera smiled and sat up straight. 'Well, Jayne, have you discovered anything for us?' she said brightly, changing the subject.

'I'm afraid it's good news and bad news. First, the good stuff. I've found your paternal grandparents and I should be able to track down your maternal grandparents pretty easily.'

Jayne passed the LostCousins worksheet to her. 'Your great-grandfather, Thomas Henry Duckworth, worked as a coaster in a brewery in Oldham.

'What's a coaster?' Vera asked.

Jayne had tried to find out that morning. 'The nearest I can get is a man who pulled a sled around the brewery, probably with the ale barrels on it.'

'Sounds very physical.'

'It probably was. Thomas Henry had three other children as well as your grandfather.'

'So I probably still have other relatives somewhere?'

'I'm sure you do. Let's have a look, shall we?' Jayne booted up her laptop and logged on to the Lost Cousins website. She entered the details of Vera's grandparents from the 1911 census. 'Using the 1881 census would probably give us more hits. I'll take your ancestors back a bit further when I have time.'

'Isn't this exciting, Robert?'

Jayne pressed 'Search' and waited a few seconds. 'Well, here you are. Four hits. They all seem to be from the elder brother of your grandfather, Vera.'

'I've got relatives I didn't know I had.'

'They are your cousins, Vera.'

She glanced across at Robert. 'Wonderful! It's a lovely feeling to know there is family somewhere out there.'

Robert gave her a hug.

Jayne coughed, interrupting both of them. 'But to bring us down to earth, I've not been as successful finding your possible brother. The problem is, we don't know his name. I have checked the Duckworth births for 1944 and I've narrowed it down to four possibilities.'

'That's great, Jayne.'

'But it might not be one of these people. We'll only know when I check the birth certificates.'

A frown appeared on Vera's brow. 'I don't understand.'

'The Births, Marriages and Deaths indexes only give the surname of the mother, not the Christian name. I've ordered the original certificates. If Freda Duckworth's name is on one of them, then we've found your brother.'

'And if it isn't?'

'Then we're stuck. You see, when she went to the Registry Office in 1944, there are a few things she could have done.'

'Such as?' asked Vera.

'She may have registered the baby under her own name, Duckworth. This is what most women did when births were illegitimate. But I can't find any male births anywhere in England for 1944 with only the mother's name.'

Vera nodded, understanding the issue. 'What else?'

'She may have registered the birth under the father's name, giving her own maiden name as the mother. These are the four birth certificates I've ordered from the General Registry Office.'

'Are there more options?'

'If the baby was adopted, it may have been registered under the adopting family's name. But I've discounted this because you told me she looked after the baby for six months, which means she will have registered it herself.'

'I think I understand. It's getting complicated.'

'I'm afraid it gets even worse.'

Vera laughed. 'How can it get worse?'

'She may not have used her own name at all, and as we don't know the father's name…' Jayne's voice tailed off.

'Why wouldn't she use her own name?'

Jayne shrugged her shoulders. 'Guilt. Shame. Family pressures. The stigma of illegitimacy was still very strong then. And you did say your grandmother was a very religious woman.'

'How do we find out what she did?'

'Without more information, it's very hard. Can you remember anything else she said that might help us?'

Vera's eyes glanced up and left, dredging every conversation she had with her mother for clues. 'She wasn't the most talkative of women, my mother. Taciturn, I think you'd call her these days. She didn't tell us much and, as I said, I knew nothing about her baby until just before she died.'

'Would your brother know anything?'

'Charlie? I suppose he may do, but Mother talked to him less than she spoke to me.'

They both lapsed into a depressed silence before Robert spoke. 'It wouldn't hurt to go to see Charles. We promised we would visit at the wedding. Give him a call, Vera, tell him we're coming.'

'When?'

'Well, how about now? No time like the present, and if we're going to find this long-lost brother, Charles needs to know too.'

Chapter Ten

June 18, 2017
Eyam, Derbyshire, England

After a short thirty-minute drive from Buxton, they arrived in the Derbyshire village of Eyam, or 'Eem', as it was pronounced by the locals. Jayne had changed the music to Glenn Miller. She wasn't certain her father or Vera would be able to withstand the aural assault of Liam Gallagher at maximum Manchester whine.

'It's been ages since I visited him,' said Vera as Jayne parked the car opposite the museum. 'He lives in one of the old plague cottages.' She shivered dramatically. 'Couldn't do it myself. Too many ghosts, too many memories.'

'You shouldn't worry yourself about such things, my love.'

'Well, wouldn't you be a bit upset if you had sealed yourself in the village as the plague took hold, killing off your neighbours and finally yourself, one by one? I'd stick around and let people know how pissed off I was.'

Eyam was famous in England. During the plague year of 1665, the villagers had voluntarily quarantined themselves in order to prevent the plague spreading to the surrounding villages and district. Most of them had perished.

'Which cottage does he live in?'

'It's one of the little ones on the left, just before the church.'

They strolled down through the tourists and crowds of schoolchildren visiting the village, finally stopping outside a row of terraced cottages. 'This is it,' announced Vera.

In the garden stood a green metal plaque, with a sombre message printed in bright white letters painted on it.

Willow Cottage

Eight members of the Pilling Family lived here. They all died.
Thomas Pilling, died 26th September 1665
Mary (his daughter), died 30th September 1665
Elizabeth (his wife), died 1st October 1665
Thomas (his son), died 20th December 1665
Alice (his daughter), died 15th April 1666
William (his son), died 2nd May 1666
Henry and Anne Pilling, the parents of Thomas senior, died in 1666.

'I couldn't live here, but trust my brother to choose this place. Charlie was always fond of the macabre.'

They strolled up the tiny path leading to a small, terraced cottage. As they were about to knock, the door opened and a small round man, with the most florid face Jayne had ever seen, stood in the doorway.

'You're here, come in. Thought you said three thirty.'

Jayne checked her watch. It was 3.45. They were fifteen minutes late.

'Don't let the draught in. Put wood in't hole.'

Jayne stared quizzically at him. Vera came to her rescue. 'He means close the door.'

'Aye, that too.' He vanished through a doorway on the left. Jayne followed him, ducking beneath the solid oak lintel. The ceiling was so low, she felt she had to stoop to enter the room.

Even though it was the middle of summer, a fire was burning in the grate, filling the small room with the mellow aroma of burning wood. Every available surface was cluttered with stuff; magazines on a stool, books on a chair, old clothes on the sofa, a pile of vinyl records next to the fire. In the midst of it all, a small coffee table was set with cups and saucers, and a large teapot was hidden beneath a large tea cosy.

Vera moved the old clothes to join another pile on the floor, clearing a space on the sofa for herself and Robert. Jayne lifted up some old books from the chair and searched for a place to put them.

'Don't worry,' said Charlie, 'just put them on the floor. I'll tidy up later.'

She found a patch of empty space next to an old fireman's helmet beneath the coffee table, and sat down on the dusty chair.

'We'll let tea brew a little longer. I can't stand weak tea. Fancy a bit of Dundee?' A knife hovered over a fruit cake. 'Got from t'shop this morning. They do a lovely bit of Dundee, do Ramsdens.'

Both Vera and Jayne shook their heads, but Robert picked up a plate. 'I wouldn't say no. I like a bit of cake with me tea.'

'A man after my own heart. Jayne? Our Vera?'

They both shook their heads again.

Charlie cut a slice for Robert and for himself. 'Shall I be mother?' he said, pouring a thick, dark brew of tea into the floral-patterned china cups.

'Sugar?'

Vera and Jayne declined again. Robert held out his cup. 'Two, please.'

Charlie dropped two lumps into the cup and added three into his own. Without stirring it, he took a large slurp of tea, followed by a loud 'aaah'. 'Good tea, that. Puts hairs on your chest.'

Jayne glanced down at her cup. The tea was a dark, thick brown sludge that looked like it had been brewing for decades. She placed the cup back on the coffee table without drinking any, balancing it precariously on the edge.

Between mouthfuls of tea and Dundee cake, Vera's brother opened the conversation. 'What's this about our mother?'

Vera stopped as her cup was about to touch her lips and returned it to the saucer. 'It's like I said on the phone. I was thinking about Mother...'

'Not what she said just before she died?'

Vera nodded.

'Look, it's all claptrap, Vera. She was old, she was dying, she said stuff she didn't mean. Remember one night she sat up and talked about seeing her old friend from church, Myra, sitting in the chair?'

'Yes, but—'

'Our mother couldn't have had a child during the war. She wasn't the type.'

'And what type is that?' asked Jayne, an edge to her voice.

'Oh, you know, one of the good-time girls. There were lots of them during the war. Out with the men whilst their husbands were fighting in the desert or in Italy.' Charlie chuckled to himself, the red veins on his cheeks going redder. 'There were more than a few kids with American accents growing up in Saddleworth after the war, I can tell you.' He took a large bite of fruit cake, following it with an even larger slurp of tea.

'But what if it were true? What if she did have a child who was adopted? It would mean you and I had a brother somewhere.'

'A half-brother,' corrected Charlie, 'and it can't be true. Not our mother. You remember what a prude she was the day she caught you on the couch with that bloke having a bit of how's-your-father.'

Vera glanced across at Robert, who was suddenly obsessed with the currants in the fruit cake. 'It wasn't a bit of "how's-your father", as you put it. He was my boyfriend... then.'

'Aye, and I remember how she lost the plot. Went totally doolally.'

'Anyway, this isn't about me. Did you look for her old case?'

Charlie nodded and pulled out a small, battered suitcase, covered in stickers from Blackpool, Lytham St Annes and Southport. 'You mean this one?'

'That's it. Where she kept her stuff, wouldn't let anybody look inside it.'

'It was on top of the wardrobe upstairs. Didn't even know it was there. Haven't looked at it since the funeral. How did you know I had it?'

Vera glanced around the cluttered room, filled with knick-knacks, books and old newspapers. 'I knew you never chucked anything away.'

He chuckled again. 'Aye, true enough. Never have, never will.'

'I remember she used to sit by the fire sometimes on a Sunday night, after she had been to Evening Mass, and look in the case, picking through her old stuff. Wouldn't let any of us have a look in.'

'That was our mam. Kept herself to herself.'

'You never looked inside?'

'I had a quick rifle through, just in case there were old insurance policies or such like, but it was just a bunch of old pictures and letters. Nothing of value.'

'Memories are always of value,' said Robert.

'You know what I mean. Nothing valuable, just old papers. I chucked some stuff in from the funeral and closed it up.'

'Time to open it now.'

Charlie took a last slurp of tea and lifted the small case on to his knees. It had two locks on either side. He pressed the catch, expecting it to spring open.

Nothing happened.

He pressed again, harder this time.

Again, nothing.

'Looks like it's rusted shut.'

Robert held out his hands. 'Give it here. Have you got a hair grip, Vera, love?'

Vera pulled one from the side of her hair. 'Like this?'

'Perfect. Give me a second.' He unbent the hair grip, inserting one end of it into the lock and jiggling it around. As he did, he pressed the catch and it flew open.

'You never cease to amaze me, Robert Cartwright.'

Her father beamed. 'Just one of my many tricks, love. I'll show you a few more later.'

He inserted the hair grip into the second catch and a moment later it too sprung open. 'I think Vera should open it, don't you?' he said pointedly, looking at Charlie.

Robert's brother-in-law shrugged his shoulders.

Vera placed the case on her lap and touched the faded brown lid.

'Hold it.' Charlie put his hand on Vera's arm. 'Are you sure you want to do this?'

'I am. It's the only way we'll know for certain.'

'But... these are her things... her life.' A pleading tone had entered Charlie's voice. 'This was Mother's life.'

Vera stopped what she was doing and stared at him. 'You went through it, didn't you?'

Charlie nodded once and glanced away. 'Just before Dad died. He told me not to, but I did.'

'I have to do this, Charlie. I have to know.'

'You could never leave things alone. Even as a kid, you were always the one who went ahead, pushing everybody else out of the way.'

Vera stared at him and then down at the case. She had to know. If she didn't open it, she would forever wonder what was inside. 'Why didn't you tell me? Why did you pretend you hadn't looked inside?'

'Because you're like a dog with a bone. Once you get your teeth into something you never let go. Dad didn't want you digging up the past. He told me to throw it away.'

'The case?'

Charlie nodded. 'I couldn't do it. These were Mother's things. I should have listened to him.'

Vera scanned the small brown case sitting on her lap. The stickers from Blackpool and Southport and Lytham St Annes were faded now, just like the resorts they represented.

She lifted up the lid.

Chapter Eleven

November 10, 1951
St Michael's Home, Oldham, England

He crept up on him in the late afternoon, nearly scaring him half to death when he tapped his shoulder. Harry was scrubbing the corridor in front of Sister Tomasina's room, as he did every day.

'Hey.'

'Don't do that, I thought it was her.'

'Shoulda been working, not dreaming.'

'What are you doing here, Jack? I though you were takin' the slops to the pigs.' Every day the boys emptied out the slops into a large bin, which was collected by the farmer in his army jeep.

'Rocko and the Menace are doing it. Listen, Harry...'

Harry glanced over his shoulder. 'If they catch you here...'

'I know, I know.' Jack knelt down in front of Harry. 'Are you up for it?'

'What?'

'Tonight. The kitchen.'

Every Thursday, Mrs O'Kelly brought a large Victoria sponge to the home. It was supposed to be shared amongst the children, but somehow it always ended up on the nuns' table. 'A little treat for all their hard work,' Sister Mary used to say.

Harry sucked in his breath. 'I dunno...'

Jack stood up to go. 'If you're too chicken...'

Harry grabbed Jack's leg with his wet hand. 'It's just...'

'Just what?'

Perhaps it was seeing the townies eating the toffee apples. Or watching Sister Tomasina's fat finger wipe a blob of white cream from the side of her mouth. Or just the idea of something sweet and soft in his mouth instead of the usual fatty pork or half-cooked potatoes. But Harry wanted to do this with Jack more than anything else.

'I'm in,' he said defiantly.

'It's tonight.' Jack strode off down the corridor, stopping to check if any nuns were patrolling before hurrying down the stairs.

The rest of the day passed in a bit of a blur for Harry. He finished scrubbing the corridor, then cleaned the nuns' toilet. After pouring the contents of his bucket down the drain, he went into the dining hall with the others. They lined up in front of the long table and said Grace, led by Sister Tomasina.

'For what we are about to receive, may the Lord make us truly thankful.'

The metal plates were passed to the front where one of the older kids doled out the fatty pork stew with a ladle. The food was the colour of the sky in November, with just a touch of brown to suggest something edible.

Harry missed the food at the Beggs'. There always bread and butter for tea, with meat and vegetables, and trifle for dessert. 'You've got to eat properly if you young 'uns are to grow big and strong. Butcher's good to me, he is. Even with rationing I can still get my pork and a few sausages from under the table,' Mr Beggs always said.

Harry looked down at the food in front of him. It stared back at him. If he didn't eat now, there would be nothing more until breakfast tomorrow morning. He closed his eyes and dug in with his spoon, swallowed the first mouthful, feeling it crawl down his throat without touching his teeth.

The smell of roast meat stung his nostrils. Jack was carrying the plate of roast lamb up to the nuns' table, the sweet aroma of the meat lingering over the children's heads as it passed by.

'Shall I be mother?' Sister Tomasina began to carve.

The roast potatoes and carrots were passed around the top table, followed by a bowl of fresh green peas with a knob of rich yellow butter on top, just starting to melt.

'What are you looking at?' screamed Sister Mary at the congregation of children beneath her. 'Attend to your food, and be grateful for what you have.'

The children, thirty-seven in all, immediately returned their attention to the grey mass on their plates. The only sound was the scrape of metal against metal as the spoons mechanically shovelled food into small waiting mouths.

No conversation was allowed. Eating was to be silent and quick. A last supper before the final reading of a Bible and then bed.

Harry finished most of his food. Or, at least, as much as his excitement allowed him.

Just before they were ordered to take their plates to be emptied into the slops bucket, Jack walked in, carrying the large Victoria sponge up to the nuns' table with all the reverence of an altar boy holding the communion wafers.

Harry said a silent prayer to Saint Nicholas, hoping the nuns wouldn't eat too much of it. Sister Morris had told them the story yesterday. How, during a terrible famine, a malicious butcher had lured three little children into his house, where he killed them, placing their remains in a barrel to cure and planning to sell them off as ham. But the children were rescued by Saint Nicholas and the butcher was punished. Nicholas was a holy man who granted all the wishes of little boys.

The Mother Superior looked at the cake. 'I think we should save this for tomorrow, Sisters. I am so full after the lamb.'

The Saint had heard his prayers. Harry could see Sister Tomasina licking her lips, desperate to eat a slice. But she wouldn't contradict the Reverend Mother, not in front of the others, anyway.

'Take it back to the larder.' The old woman waved her hand and Jack turned to carry the cake back into the kitchen, winking at Harry as he passed.

After dinner, Harry washed and changed for bed. He wasn't one of the bed-wetters, so he didn't have to sleep near the window. Sister Tomasina came in at exactly 7.45 p.m. and turned out the light.

Harry was already falling asleep when he felt a nudge on his shoulder. 'You ready?'

Jack was standing beside his bed holding a box of matches.

'Where'd you get those?'

'The kitchen. Sister Mary wasn't looking. I also took this.' He held up a silver key.

Harry hesitated for a moment. Should he go? If they were caught, it would be a certain visit to the Mother Superior's room for punishment.

But the thought of the Victoria sponge, with its fresh cream and raspberry jam, chased away his fears. He threw back the covers and quickly pulled on his shirt and shorts.

'Where you going?' It was Little Tom, one of the new arrivals. He was quite a lot older than Harry but much smaller. Something, or somebody, had stunted his growth.

'Nowhere,' answered Jack.

'I wanna come too.'

'You can't.'

'I wanna come too,' he repeated, more forcefully this time.

'Shush, you'll wake the others.'

'You're going to the kitchen, aren't you, Harry?'

'Shhhhhh...' Harry felt a hand touch his arm.

'I'm coming...'

Jack was already at the door, his feet illuminated by the band of light seeping through the gap between the bottom of the wood and the floor.

'Are you two coming or not?' he whispered loudly.

Harry grabbed Little Tom's hand and they padded to the door. Jack opened it and stuck his head out.

They were all momentarily blinded by the harsh light of the corridor. From upstairs, they heard the sound of music coming from one of the nuns' rooms. A big band playing a swinging dance tune on the radio.

Jack crept out into the corridor and ran soundlessly to the top of the stairs. He waved the other two to join him.

Harry and Little Tom, still holding hands, slipped out of the room and crept along the wall to the stairs.

Jack was crouched down, gazing through the stair rods. 'They've already gone to bed, but there will still be one awake in reception.'

'How do you know?' asked Little Tom.

Jack smiled knowingly. 'You think this is the first time I've done this? Follow me, but don't make a sound.'

They crept down the stairs, past the reception room. The door was closed and they heard the sound of a loud snore coming from inside.

'Sounds like a pig,' said Little Tom.

'Shhhh....' Jack stared at him angrily.

For a second the snoring stopped, followed by the sounds of lips smacking together as if tasting food.

The boys stood still, frozen with fear. Then the snoring began again, softer now.

They crept across the hallway, pushing open the door of the dining hall. It was dark and strangely quiet, the only light a grey moonlit haze fighting its way through the window next to the nuns' table. Usually this place was full of children and the sound of metal plates being scraped clean of food. Now, the tables had been set for morning; a water glass, a spoon and a plate lined up evenly in front of each place. It was strangely lonely; a place that was missing people.

'The kitchen is on the left.' Jack pointed to a door.

They crept slowly towards it. In the dark, each boy kept as close as he could to the one in front. Jack taking the lead, Little Tom in the middle, Harry bringing up the rear.

They opened the kitchen door. Sister Iris had kept a single light burning above the stove, ready for one of the boys to start boiling the water for the porridge at five o'clock the next morning.

Jack ushered the other two in and closed the door. He produced the single silver key from his pocket. 'I have to put this back before breakfast. She won't miss it until then.'

He walked towards the larder door and inserted the key, turning it once. He pulled the door but it remained fastened. He pulled it again, but still it wouldn't budge.

Harry stepped forward. 'Let me.' He gave the key an extra turn, feeling a solid click between his fingers. 'This sort of key needs to be turned twice. Mr Beggs taught me.'

He grabbed hold of the handle and pulled. The old, wooden door swung open, revealing a small room with a single tiny window high up on the far wall.

On the other three walls, rows of shelves held tins of meat, bags of flour, bottles of milk, more tins, jars of jam, glass bottles full of red liquid, more flour, bags of sugar and, on the third shelf, a plate with an untouched Victoria sponge.

'How are we going to get it?' asked Little Tom.

Jack ran back to the kitchen, returning with the wooden step the boys used when they had to stir the porridge. He placed it under the shelf and reached up. For a moment Harry thought he wasn't tall enough, but Jack stretched up on his tiptoes and lifted the plate off the shelf.

'Close the door.'

'Why?' asked Little Tom.

'In case someone comes, stupid. The sisters don't sleep all the time.'

Harry pulled the door shut. The larder was instantly dark, the only light a vague glow through the thick glass of the small window. He could no longer see the Victoria sponge but he could smell its sweetness – the rich, buttery cream; the tangy jam; the seeds sitting in a jelly of liquid sugar; the light pillow of sponge encasing everything.

Harry heard the soft clink of a plate being placed on the floor, followed by the rasp of a match against sandpaper. The larder was suddenly illuminated by the flare of a match. Jack lit a candle that stood on the bottom shelf, next to some tins of Spam.

'I put this here yesterday, so we could see. "Be prepared." I learnt that in the Scouts at my last place.' He put the candle next to the sponge and sat down cross-legged at one side. 'For what we are about to receive, may the Lord make us truly thankful.' He plunged his bare hands into the centre of the sponge, grabbing a handful of cream and cake. 'Dig in, lads.'

Harry plunged his tiny hand into the soft, moist cake, grabbing a handful. He shoved the cake into his mouth, tasting the rich butteriness of the cream, the sharp sweetness of the jam and the soft crumb of the sponge.

'Ish good...' said Little Tom, spitting out mouthfuls of sponge as he spoke.

Neither Jack nor Harry answered him. They just carried on scooping up handfuls of cake like mechanical diggers clearing a drain, until the cake became a dishevelled mess on the floor between them.

Harry sat back first, unable to eat another mouthful. 'That... was... the... best...'

'Have some more,' said Little Tom, grabbing another handful.

Harry patted his stomach. 'Can't.'

Jack was the next to stop, but Little Tom kept scooping up handful after handful till it was nearly all gone.

'How do you do it?'

'Hungry... always hungry,' answered Little Tom, his mouth and teeth covered in cream and cake. 'Me mam used to make cakes. Not as good as this, though. No cream.'

'So you've got a mam?' asked Jack.

Little Tom reached for one of the last lumps of cake. 'She's going to come for me soon, when she's back on her feet. What about you?' Little Tom put another small chunk of cake in his mouth.

'No mam. No dad.' Jack seemed to think for a moment. 'Always been here. The sisters said they were killed in the war. I'm an orphan,' he said, a strange pride in his voice.

Little Tom scooped up the final morsel of cake on the plate, dropped it into his mouth and licked his fingers.

Harry felt the fullness of his stomach. He thought back to the last time his mum had visited him. She seemed fatter than usual and they had taken a long bus ride to watch a movie – Captain Horatio Hornblower with Gregory Peck – and then had afternoon tea in the Lyons Tea House.

'How are Mr and Mrs Beggs treating you?' she had asked.

'Good, they're nice.'

'And David?'

'He's my brother.'

'He's not your real brother.'

'I know, but he's as good as a real one.'

His mum had reached over and touched his hand. 'Would you like another brother or sister, Harry?'

He didn't know what to say, so he shrugged his shoulders.

His mum's lips were very red when she spoke. 'I've met a good man, Harry. We're going to get married, have a child and settle down. When we do, I want you to come back and live with us. Would you like that?'

Harry thought for a moment. 'Can David come too?'

'He can visit if he wants.'

Harry ate his salmon sandwich. 'Okay.'

His mum didn't say anything else after that, but took him back to Mr and Mrs Beggs that night.

'What about you, Harry?' asked Jack.

Harry was dragged back from the memory of his mother to a small larder, lit by a single candle and with the remnants of a Victoria sponge at his feet. 'What?'

'Do you have a mum and dad?'

'I think I do. I've never met me dad, he's new, but I know me mam. She said I was going to—'

As Harry spoke, the door to the larder suddenly flew open and a large black shape was silhouetted in the doorway.

'Big rats. We have big rats!' Sister Tomasina's eyes were blazing. 'Do you know what we do with rats?' She reached for the strap hanging next to the rosary at her waist.

Chapter Twelve

June 18, 2017
Eyam, Derbyshire, England

Inside, the suitcase was lined with brown silk, the colour still as vibrant and rich as the day it was bought. The photographs and papers were just stuffed inside, not neatly packed or sorted. On top of the pile were Mass cards, their black edges and messages of 'In Loving Memory' a stark contrast to the white card on which they were printed.

Vera opened the top one. On the left was an old picture of her father; flat cap on his head, smoking a pipe, a smile creasing his face as if to say, 'Don't take a picture now, I'm not ready.' Opposite the picture was a simple message:

'The Holy Sacrifice of the Mass will be said for the repose of the soul of' in bold type, followed by a handwritten message that said 'Norman Atkins by P.P. Edward O'Leary at St Hugh's.

She closed the card quickly. Memories of the funeral flooded back to her; her father's casket placed in front of the altar, the priest holding the host high in both hands, Charlie reading the prayer, and then standing in front of the grave just before the coffin was to be lowered into it, rain sleeting down, the priest beneath a black umbrella intoning some final words.

'There are a lot of Mass cards, for both Mum and Dad. Most are from other parishioners and Dad's mates in the water board. I put them all in the case after his funeral. Seemed like the right place.'

Vera gathered together all the different shapes and sizes, forming them into two neat piles; one for her dad and one for her mum. She didn't open her mother's cards. She couldn't bear to see the picture of her taken one day in Blackpool, her hair blowing in the breeze off the sea, her eyes squinting as Dad squeezed the shutter release. It was Vera's father's favourite picture of his wife and it was the one they had used at her funeral.

Beneath the Mass cards were a jumble of photographs, all with serrated edges and depicting faded black and white images. A line of women beside an old-fashioned bus. A young girl sitting on the grass, her legs tucked demurely beneath her. Two women staring into the camera with the stamp of a Southport studio in the corner. A soldier in British uniform, the flash of an armoured corps on his shoulder.

'I think that's Dad,' said Charlie.

Vera brought the picture closer to her face. 'It doesn't look like him.'

'He was younger then; it was probably taken as he joined up. I think the war aged him. You know, he never talked about it. I tried to ask him, "What did you do in the war, Dad?" The sort of question kids ask. But he wouldn't tell me. He never told me.'

'I can find out, if you like,' said Jayne. 'Some of the records are online now.'

Charlie shook his head. 'I don't want to know, thank you, not now. No point.'

Vera continued to search through the photographs. A group of women in a pub, a table of empty glasses in front of them, all smiling at the camera.

Another picture of the same child as before, carrying a soldier in a red coat and a busby. Older now, his hand covering his eyes as he shielded them from the sun.

She looked on the back, hoping to find a pencilled name or date, but it was empty apart from the stamp of the studio which had developed it: Marley and Sons, Oldham.

'Do you know who this is?' she asked.

Charlie shook his head. 'None of the pictures have captions written on them. I guess we'll never know who they were. Just friends or colleagues of Mum and Dad.'

When she had finished looking at the photographs, she sorted them neatly on the table in front of her. Pictures of her mum. Pictures of her dad. Pictures of relatives she knew. Pictures of places. And finally, the largest pile – unknown pictures. Memories that were buried forever with her mum and dad when they died.

At the bottom of the case was a pile of old corporation rent books from 1947 to 1958. The rent for each week paid, crossed out and signed by some long-dead council official. 'Why did she keep these?'

Charlie shrugged his shoulders. 'I don't know. Mum never threw anything away. Perhaps these were memories of a more difficult time. Or perhaps she kept them just in case the council ever asked again; as a record to show she had paid her way.'

'I remember it was always Mum who controlled the purse strings. Every Friday, Dad handed over his pay packet and Mum gave him back some money for his pipe tobacco and his fishing.'

'Nowt's changed, has it, Vera?' said Robert.

She nudged him with her elbow. 'I'm not that bad, am I?'

81

'You're not. I don't have a pay packet any more to give you, but I know I would if I were still working.' He smiled at her and gave her a peck on the cheek.

'When you two lovebirds have finished. They are in the pocket.' Charlie's voice was harsh, almost jealous.

Vera stared at the case. 'What's in the pocket?'

Charlie tapped the silk lining of the lid. For the first time, Vera noticed an elasticated flap. She pulled it open and inside was a thin bundle of letters tied with a purple ribbon.

'Mother kept them there, tied up.'

Vera closed the lid, putting the bundle of letters on top of the case. She undid the ribbon and held the first letter in her hand. On the cover, in faded blue ink, was the name Freda Duckworth and an address in Oldham. Vera tried to read the post-mark but the stamp was smudged, as if it had been rubbed out.

The letter was torn open roughly at the top. Inside was a single sheet of off-white lined paper with a bold typed message in black across the top. 'Save paper – there's a war on.'

Beneath it was an address in Delph – a village about six miles from Oldham – written in a neat, orderly hand, but undated.

Vera began to read:

'Dear Miss Duckworth, thank you for your letter enquiring after Harry. He came to us last month from the home and he's settled in very well. He's a happy, jolly boy who loves to play with our son, David. We have two other children from the home at the moment and they all get on very well together. Harry especially loves his food, he's got a tummy on him already.'

Vera paused for a moment, her voice beginning to break, and then she carried on:

'We'll be happy for you to visit Harry at any time but can you please write to us to let us know? We'd like to prepare him for when you come, but he does know he has a mother and that she loves him.'

Again, Vera stopped reading for a second, wiping her eyes before continuing once more. 'It says "yours sincerely" but I can't read the signature. Meggs or Beggs, or something like that.'

Jayne took a deep breath. It was her turn to talk.

Chapter Thirteen

November 11, 1951
St Michael's Home, Oldham, England

They were locked in a small storeroom filled with cleaning liquids and brushes until after breakfast.

They could hear the others through the locked door; their grunts as they carried the heavy troughs of porridge into the dining room, Sister Mary's shouts as she prepared the scrambled eggs for the nuns, and the clashing, cymbal-like sounds of the pots and pans as they were scrubbed clean by the boys.

'What are they going to do?'

'Cane us, probably,' said Jack nonchalantly.

'Will it hurt?'

'Of course it bloody hurts, that's the whole point. But don't worry, the pain stops after a couple of days. Georgie will get us some butter to rub into the wounds from the kitchen.'

'Doesn't sound good...'

'It was worth it though, hey?' Harry rubbed his tummy. 'I can still feel the cake inside me and taste the jam on my teeth.'

They heard the key turn slowly in the lock. The imposing black-clad frame of Sister Tomasina stood in the doorway.

'You, gutter rats,' she said, looking down her nose at them, 'you're going to Sister Mary's office.'

They followed her across the lobby, past the parlour and in through the open door of the Mother Superior's office.

The Victoria sponge plate was already sitting on her desk. A few crumbs of cake, a smear of jam and a careless blob of cream were all that remained.

'You have stolen from God.' The Mother Superior sat behind her desk, waving her finger at them. Little Tom was already whimpering. 'God doesn't love boys who steal. God is angry at boys who steal.'

Her hands wrestled with each other as she finished her sentence, the brown spots like dirt marks standing out against her wrinkled knuckles.

'But Sister—' Jack began to speak.

'BE QUIET,' shouted Sister Tomasina.

The Mother Superior carried on speaking, her voice menacing and quiet. 'What is the seventh commandment?'

Harry went through the commandments in his head: Thou shalt not have any strange gods before Me... Thou shalt not take the name of the Lord thy God in vain... Remember to keep holy the Sabbath day was the third. Honour thy father and mother was the fourth. Well, he hadn't met his dad yet, but he still honoured him. The fifth was Thou shalt not kill, and he was certain he'd never killed anybody. He racked his brain. The next one was Thou shalt not commit adultery, whatever that was. He had asked the nun what it meant but she had just ignored him. The seventh was Thou shalt not steal.

'Well, Hopkins?'

Jack shook his head.

'You?' She pointed at Harry.

'Thou shalt not steal.'

'Exactly. You three have broken the rules of God. Obey them and eternal happiness is yours. Disobey them and suffer the consequences.' She stood up. 'As the eldest, Hopkins, you will receive twelve strokes from the cane. You two will receive six each. Drop your shorts and bend over the desk.'

All three boys did as they were told. Little Tom was already whimpering.

Sister Tomasina handed the Mother Superior a cane. 'You're first, Hopkins,' she said.

The holy mother raised the cane above her head and waited, increasing the expectation. And then down it came with an audible whoosh across Jack's bare backside.

'One,' intoned Sister Tomasina.

Jack looked across at Harry leaning over the desk beside him and winked.

Another whoosh, slowed by a sharp thwack.

'Two.'

Jack winked again, but Harry saw his mouth tighten with pain.

Again and again the cane struck down on the boy's bare backside, the slap of the impact reverberating around the small room. Jack no longer winked at Harry. Instead he stared up at the cross of Jesus hanging above the Mother Superior's desk.

'Nine. Ten. Eleven. Twelve.'

Still Jack stared at the cross, his eyes fixed on the suffering Jesus. Throughout the punishment, he never cried out once.

'I think he isn't penitent, Mother Superior.' It was Sister Tomasina speaking, a sneer in her voice.

'Do you regret your theft, Hopkins? Are you penitent?'

Jack stayed silent.

Sister Tomasina had a strange smile on her face. 'I think another six would make him repent his actions,

Mother Superior. After all, the Bible does say "spare the rod and spoil the child".'

'Are you penitent, Hopkins?'

Again, Jack didn't answer.

The cane came down, swifter and harder now. Jack cried out in pain and then bit down on his tongue.

Harry heard Sister Tomasina's voice, gloating, mocking. 'One.'

After she reached the count of six again, the Mother Superior stopped.

'Are you penitent, Hopkins?' asked Sister Tomasina again.

Jack nodded slowly.

'I can't hear you.'

Jack mumbled something.

'I still can't hear you.'

The Mother Superior's cane rose once more above her head.

'I'm... sorry.'

Harry saw a smile of triumph cross Sister Tomasina's face.

'Your turn.' The Mother Superior pointed at Harry.

He bent over the desk, his head down, waiting for the sound of the cane through the air and the sharp pain of the wood across his backside.

Nothing.

He raised his head to look over his shoulder and down it came, the cane cutting through the air and striking the soft flesh of his buttocks.

For a few seconds there was nothing, and then a stab of pain shot down through his legs and up his spine into his head. Despite himself, he cried out.

The next one followed quickly afterwards.

The same swoosh of the cane cutting through the air.

The same stab of pain.

The same cry.

On the wall behind the desk, Jesus was on the cross, drops of blood dripping from a wound in his side and a tired, resigned look on his face.

He died for our sins.

'Three. Four.' Sister Tomasina called out the strikes.

The pain had vanished now for Harry. All that remained was Jesus on the cross, dying for his sins.

'Five. Six.'

The caning stopped.

'Are you penitent?'

Harry mumbled a yes.

'Your turn, Livesey.'

As Little Tom bent over the desk, Harry carefully pulled up his trousers. He glanced at Jack and received a large wink in return.

The same six strokes were followed by the same question. This time Little Tom answered before he was even asked. 'I'm sorry, I didn't mean to do it. I was hungry,' he screamed.

'That's no excuse,' shouted Sister Tomasina.

When all the punishments were finally completed, they received a long lecture on the importance of the seventh commandment from the Mother Superior.

For the next week, Harry couldn't sit down and had to lie on his side when he went to sleep.

Jack vanished from the home three days later. One moment he was there, the next he was gone.

Harry never had a chance to say goodbye.

Chapter Fourteen

June 18, 2017
Eyam, Derbyshire, England

Jayne pulled her laptop out of her bag. 'Finally, we're moving on the case.'

'This seems to confirm she had a son called Harry.'

'It does nothing of the sort, Vera,' exploded Charlie. 'All it does is tell us she was interested in this child. He could have been a neighbour's son. Or somebody else she knew.'

'Oh, come on, Charlie. She's a girl in her early twenties, visiting a young boy. Of course it has to be her son.'

Jayne held up her hands, trying to broker peace between the warring brother and sister. 'Let's read the other three letters before we come to conclusions, shall we?'

Vera nodded reluctantly. Charlie poured himself another cup of tea without checking if anybody else wanted one.

Vera picked up the second envelope. The paper was a different quality this time; light blue Basildon Bond notepaper and a matching envelope.

She peered at the stamp and the post-mark. 'It's dated June twentieth, 1950.'

'You'd better read it, love,' said Robert.

She pulled out the notepaper and cleared her throat.

'Dear Freda,

Harry loved your visit last month. He's been playing and sleeping with the soldier you gave him ever since, never letting it out of his sight. He loves the way it goes squeak when you press its tummy.

'He's also excited about having a new daddy. He's a lovely boy and, if you take him back, we will understand. We have been foster parents to a lot of children since we started before the War, but the best place for any child is with his mother. We look forward to meeting yourself and your new husband when you come next time.

'Until then, here's a kiss from Harry. He drew the X himself.'

Vera showed the notepaper to Jayne and Robert. A large red X, written in a shaky hand, was at the bottom of the page.

It was Jayne who spoke first after a long silence. 'The letter confirms it. She was Harry's mother.'

Vera suddenly began scrambling for the envelope, picking up and staring at the date. 'Why didn't I realise it before? The date is two weeks after my parents' wedding. They were married on June sixth, 1950, at St Luke's in Oldham. I've still got the pictures somewhere. She had a white wedding with all the trimmings. Looked lovely, she did.'

'Why can't you let stuff alone?' Charlie erupted again, harsher and louder this time. 'You're always shoving your nose into other people's business.'

Vera was calm and quiet as she answered him. 'This isn't "other people's business", Charlie, this was our mother.'

'Then read the next bloody letter. See what you find out now.' Once more, he petulantly turned away from them, attacking what was left of the Dundee cake with his fork.

Vera picked up the third envelope. 'This is from a year later. September twelfth, 1951.' She pulled out the note and began to read:

'Dear Freda,

We're sorry you couldn't make it for Harry's birthday at the end of August but it's a long way to come from Manchester. I know what it's like to deal with a young baby on the buses, particularly one only a couple of months old.'

Vera lifted her head and spoke to nobody in particular. 'They are talking about me. I was born on April thirteenth, 1951. I must be the baby. From the date on the letter, Dad was probably working in Manchester at this time.'

Robert reached over and patted her arm. 'Don't worry about it, love, just carry on reading the note.'

Vera wiped her eyes, swallowed and carried on reading:

'Harry is going to the school at the end of the road with our David now. He loves going there and playing with the other children. In all our years as foster parents, we can't ever remember having such a happy child in our care.'

91

Vera's voice broke then, but she continued to read on :

'Do let us know what you intend doing about Harry. My husband and I have decided, after much thought, that we will approach the home about adoption. But we won't do anything until we hear from you. We know how much you love him and will wait until we hear from you before taking this any further.'

'The signature is a lot clearer on this one,' said Vera. 'It's a Mrs Irene Beggs.'

Jayne began typing on her laptop, trying to get into Findmypast. 'Do you have Wi-Fi, Mr Atkins?'

Charlie stared at her, wide-eyed. 'I don't have truck with that sort of stuff. Haven't you noticed I don't even have a television?'

Jayne checked around the room. An old-fashioned radio sat in one corner, covered by an antimacassar, but there was no sign of any television. 'No matter, I'm getting a BT Wi-Fi signal.'

'It was my fault,' said Vera. 'She didn't visit him because of me.'

Robert patted her hand. 'Don't think like that, love, you weren't to know at all. Harry was obviously happy with the Beggses, they sound like lovely people.'

'Poor Mum, it must have been so difficult for her.'

'And they say in the letter that she loved him, too.'

'Here they are.' Jayne turned her computer around. 'I found them on the 1939 register. They were living at number twenty-three, Haggate Lane,

Delph.' She showed them the record, which ended in three blacked-out lines.

23 Haggate Lane, Delph Lancashire
Thomas Beggs M 07 Mar 94   M   Overseer
Irene Beggs   F   23 Jul 98   M   Housewife

XXXXXXXXXXXXXXXXXXXXXXXXXXXXX

XXXXXXXXXXXXXXXXXXXXXXXXXXXXX

XXXXXXXXXXXXXXXXXXXXXXXXXXXXX

'It's a small town, more a village really – a lovely place up in the moors.'

'I know it well,' said Vera. 'Used to go walking up there when I was young and the legs were still able to carry me for more than ten minutes.' She pointed to the laptop screen. 'Jayne, why are the entries beneath those of the Beggses blacked out?'

'The redacted people were probably born after 1917. They keep the records closed for a hundred years. To see them, you have to make a request and show a death certificate.'

'So they might still be alive?'

Jayne shrugged her shoulders. 'I suppose so.'

Vera returned to the letter. 'It says here they wanted to adopt Harry. Perhaps that's what happened to him. He was adopted by the Beggses and he still lives in Delph.'

Charlie had been silent until now, his body still turned away from them. 'Read the last letter,' he muttered under his breath, without looking at them.

Chapter Fifteen

January 22, 1952
St Michael's Home, Oldham, England

It was just after Christmas when the priest came to the home. The snow lay untouched on the ground surrounding St Michael's. In the streets of Oldham, it was already turning to an off-grey slush, churned up by pedestrians, bicycles, motor cars, buses and the occasional lorry.

Harry knew something special was to take place that day. In the morning, after breakfast but before they had begun their work for the day, Sister Tomasina had issued them with new shoes. Harry's were too big for him, but it didn't matter. The touch of the soft leather kept his feet warm against the cold wooden floor. He enjoyed sliding down the corridors outside the sisters' rooms with Little Tom, each one seeing how far they could go.

After a special lunch of cabbage and boiled bacon, the priest spoke to them in the dining hall. He was young, much younger than the priest at St Mike's, with a soft, mellow face and a voice like the hot chocolate Mrs Beggs made before bedtime.

'Good afternoon, children,' he began, clapping his hands together as if applauding their presence. 'Before we begin today, I'd like to say a quick Our Father. Please say it after me. Our Father…'

'Our Father…'

'Who art in heaven…'

'Who art in heaven…'

'Blessed be the womb of our Lord Jesus…'

Harry glanced up from his prayer to see the priest staring at Sister Tomasina as he said the words.

'Blessed be the womb of our Lord Jesus…'

Harry looked down quickly. If the sisters caught him not being respectful during prayers he would get a belt around the ear.

The prayer carried on, each word faithfully repeated by the children.

'That's very well done, that is; sure, the sisters have taught you well. Now, I'm just after looking out the window and it looks like it's beginning to snow again.'

Harry looked over the priest's shoulders to the sash window. Flecks of white cotton wool began to stick themselves to the glass before dissolving, only to be followed by more flecks of white.

'This country would freeze the arse off a saint.'

The children laughed. The priest had said the word 'arse'. Harry half-expected the Mother Superior to give him a clip around the ear.

'Does anybody know a place where it doesn't snow?'

Little Tom put his hand up. 'Heaven.'

'No, you're right enough. It doesn't snow in heaven. Or in hell, for that matter, if any of you are thinking of going there.'

The sisters laughed and so did the children, although none of them knew why what the priest said was funny.

'Anywhere else?'

'London,' answered Charlie.

'I think it snows there sometimes. Anywhere else? Anywhere you think of that could be hot?'

Harry remembered a newsreel he had seen with his mother on one of their outings. 'Australia?'

The priest smiled. 'That's the ticket. You're a clever fellow. What's your name?'

'Harry.'

'It's Harold,' said Sister Tomasina.

'Well, Harry, you're right. It's hot in Australia and it never snows. What else do you know about it?'

Harry tried to remember the newsreel. It was about a family who had just gone there after the war. The boy rode a bike and the girl was feeding a kangaroo. 'Well, it's hot, and there are lots of trees and kangaroos and fruit...'

'You do know a lot, don't you? Well, children, Harry is right. It's always sunny and you can pick fruit right off the trees. One of the Fathers told me he used to go to the tree in his garden when he needed a lemon. No need to go to the shop, he just picked them from his own tree. Now isn't that amazing?'

All the children nodded.

Daisy Moore put up her hand. 'Is it true the kangaroos keep their babies in their tummies?'

The priest laughed. 'I think it is. The young kangaroos are called Joeys, so I've been told, and they stay in a pouch on their mother's stomach. Wouldn't you all like to see them?'

All the children nodded.

Little Tom raised his hand. 'Can we play with them?'

The priest thought for a moment. 'I'm sure you can, but you'll have to ask the mother politely.' He waved his finger. 'Not the Reverend Mother, the kangaroo's mother, of course.'

The children laughed again. Even the Reverend Mother's face broke into something approaching a smile.

'Now, I've an important question for youse.' The children watched as the priest paused and scratched his nose. 'How many of you would like to go to Australia?'

The children looked at each other, not understanding.

It was Little Tom who spoke first. 'And leave England?'

The priest smiled. 'Let me put this a different way. How many of you would like to play with the kangaroos in Australia?'

Little Tom's hand shot up, followed by the others. Not wanting to be left out, Harry slowly raised his own hand.

The priest and the Mother Superior smiled broadly, nodding to each other. 'That's very good, very good. The lucky ones might just get the chance to play with them. I'll have a chat with Sister Mary and choose just a few of you to come with me when I leave in a couple of months' time. Now, just to check again. Who would like to play with the kangaroos in Australia?'

This time all the hands, including Harry's, shot up.

'All of you? Grand. I'm afraid we only have places for a few, but we'll let you know just as soon as we can who'll be going.'

The Mother Superior told Harry he would be going to Australia two weeks later.

'But what about me mum?'

'I thought you wanted to play with the kangaroos?'

'I do, but...'

'Your mother is happy for you to go. See, she's signed the form.' The Reverend Mother held up a piece of paper with a scrawled signature on the bottom.

Harry's soul shrivelled up inside him. His mum wasn't coming for him after all. He wasn't going to meet his new dad or his younger brother or sister.

'Me mum wants me to go?' he finally said.

The Reverend Mother smiled. 'She thinks it's for the best. You'll have a much better life in Australia. Besides, she has a new family now and she doesn't want anything to do with you any more.'

'I have a new brother?'

'You have a new sister, actually. That's why it's best you go to Australia.'

'Can I see my mum before I go?'

The Mother Superior smiled again. 'She doesn't want to see you any more, Harold. You only have us now. We're your family.'

Chapter Sixteen

June 18, 2017.
Eyam, Derbyshire, England

Vera picked up the last envelope. 'The post-mark is clear; September 28, 1951, only two weeks since the last one. Two letters from them in a month is a lot.'

'We don't know, love, perhaps she didn't save all the letters, just the most important ones.'

'I hope you save all my letters, Robert, even the unimportant ones.'

'Hurry up and read the letter, Vera. All this lovey-dovey stuff is a bit sickening.'

'You know, you've become the tired cliché, Charlie; a grumpy old man. They should draw a cartoon of you.'

Her brother picked at what remained of the cake. 'At least I don't go sticking my nose in where it's not wanted,' he sniffed.

'Read the letter, love.'

Vera coughed twice, clearing her throat.

'Dear Freda,

I'm afraid we have some news. Mr Keaton from the home came yesterday. They have decided to take Harry back. Apparently, he has reached an age where he needs the support of a

proper Christian education. Just taking him to church on Sunday was not enough. The sisters will make sure he receives a good education.

He's lucky there is a place for him at the home. These days there are more children than beds, that's why we took him in the first place. Thomas and I will miss Harry immensely. His broad smile was a ray of sunshine even on the greyest day. And our son, David, is already missing his playmate. He keeps asking when Harry is coming back. Unfortunately, we can't give him an answer.

Has the home written to tell you? Sometimes they can be a bit slow at keeping parents informed. So we thought we'd tell you as soon as possible.

If you have time, I would go to visit him to make sure he's settling in properly. I'm afraid we're not allowed to go, just being foster parents.

Have you given more thought to what we talked about last time you were here? We are serious about adopting Harry permanently if you feel you can no longer look after him. We would love to have him stay with us forever. Please let us know as soon as you can. The church can be very slow when it comes to adoption and we have to set the wheels in motion.

Please consider it. I know you've always planned to take him back one day, but now he's in the home again, we should make a decision.

Yours sincerely,
Irene Beggs

'What does it all mean, Jayne?' asked Vera.

'It means he went back to the home and Mum never saw him again!' shouted Charlie, standing up from his chair. 'Are you happy now you've brought Mum's dirty linen to light?' He leaned over Vera. 'Didn't it occur to you, when you were off traipsing after your men friends, that she was so sad? All those years, missing him every day, wanting to see him again.'

Robert stood up, facing Charlie. 'Back off. Don't speak to my wife like that,' he said through gritted teeth.

Charlie stomped over to the far side of the room, staring out of the small window.

Vera was still sitting on the sofa, her hands clasped in front of her, tears streaming down her face. 'I never knew... I never knew.'

Charlie ran his fingers through his hair. His voice was softer now, quieter. 'She told me one Christmas. We'd been to Mass that afternoon, Dad had already gone to bed. We were sitting together in front of the fire, drinking a small whisky. You remember how a wee dram helped her sleep. Well, this time she must have had more than one. She blurted it out as we were both sitting there quietly. "You have a brother, you know."

'I'll never forget those words as long as I live. She then told me the whole story. The soldier she thought loved her, who was already married. The baby, how happy he was. But her mother wouldn't hear of her keeping him. So she had him placed in a home, visiting every couple of months when she could take time off work. Her new marriage...' He lifted his head. His face was in shadow, the small round body silhouetted against the late evening light streaming in through the window. His voice low, almost a murmur. 'Dad wasn't too keen on him coming back. He thought Harry was happy with the Beggses...'

Vera stared at him. 'Why didn't you tell me?'

'She swore me to secrecy. I promised I would tell nobody, least of all you.' He stopped speaking for a moment, swallowing a lump in his throat. 'She loved you, you know. She wasn't very good at showing it, but she did.'

'But we argued and fought so much, that's why I left when I did.'

'Perhaps it was her way of showing she cared.'

The room fell silent. In the corner, an old clock ticked away the hours. Outside, a blackbird sang his independence from the top of his perch in the approaching dusk. In the distance, a church bell began to ring, calling the faithful to prayer.

Jayne coughed, clearing her throat. Her voice, when she spoke, was strangely muted. 'Do you want to pursue this, Vera? Searching for Harry, I mean?'

Vera thought for a moment and then stared at her brother. 'We have to. Harry might still be out there somewhere. I'd like to meet him before I die.'

Chapter Seventeen

June 18, 2017
Buxton Residential Home, Derbyshire, England

Jayne, her father and Vera sat in the common room of the home, drinking a cup of coffee. Most of the other residents had already turned in for the night. Just one old man was sat in front of the television in his wheelchair, watching Strictly Come Dancing.

'He used to be a professional, you know,' said her father.

'A professional what?' asked Jayne.

'Dancer. Went all over the world with it. Brazil. Argentina. Hong Kong, Blackpool. Then the arthritis got the better of him, so here he is. Never misses a programme, though.'

'Can we get back to the job at hand?' said Vera sharply.

They had driven back from Vera's brother's with the case. It now lay open beside them, the letters at the side and the solitary picture of a child with a toy soldier on top.

'This is what we know,' pronounced Jayne. 'Your mother, Freda, did have a baby in 1944. She called him Harry or Harold. He was fostered out to faster parents, the Beggses, by a charity, probably in 1946, staying with them until September 1951 when he returned to the home.'

103

'Can we call him Harry? "He" is so impersonal.'

'Sorry, Vera, you're right. We'll call him Harry.' Jayne picked up the picture of the young boy. 'This is probably a picture of him, as it mentions in the letters that your mother gave him a toy soldier. We can't be certain, though.'

The boy in the picture was looking directly into the camera, his hair styled in a cute quiff and a confident smile on his face. A happy boy. A cheeky boy. The eyes had a little mischief, a little devilment in them.

Jayne took a deep breath. 'Now, here are the two major problems. We still don't know Harry's surname, the name he was registered under at birth. I'm certain it wasn't Duckworth, though.'

'How can you be sure?' asked her father.

'I've checked all the Duckworth births for 1944 and there are no Harolds or Harrys.'

Vera took the photo from Jayne. 'So he must have been registered under a different name?'

'Correct. It could have been the father's name or something else entirely. Without a surname, he's going to be difficult to find. And if he was adopted, we can't ask for any information unless we know his birth surname.'

'But you've requested the birth certificates of the four Duckworth mothers in 1944, haven't you?'

'I did, and I'm hoping Freda is one of them, but...'

'But what, Jayne?'

'But it all depends what name she used when she actually registered the birth. If she didn't use her real name...'

The people sitting around the table were all silent for a moment trying to understand the implications of Jayne's words.

Her father ran his hand through his thinning hair. 'You said there were two problems, Jayne. What's the other one?'

Jayne logged on to the childrenshomes.org site. 'We don't know the name of the home he was sent to. According to this site, there were over seven hundred and fifty residential care homes in Lancashire at this time.'

Her father whistled. 'So many?'

'War, poverty, hunger, fear; they all take their toll on the most vulnerable in society.'

'But the Beggses and my mother were Catholic,' said Vera. 'The letter said he was going to be taken care of by nuns.'

Jayne pressed a few keys on the computer. 'If we search for just the Catholic homes, it still gives us over a hundred in Lancashire, and more than thirty-five in an area ten miles around Oldham.'

Her father tapped the computer screen. 'Why that area, Jayne?'

She noticed the liver spots on the back of her father's hand had become much more numerous. 'Reading between the lines of the letters, I feel the Beggses had a relationship with some of the Catholic homes, to foster children. I could be wrong, but I don't think they would take them more than a short drive, otherwise it would be too much of a nuisance to visit and check up on them.'

Her father nodded. 'It makes sense, but it doesn't help us very much. It still leaves thirty-five possible homes where Harry could have been sent.'

Another silence enveloped the table. Off to the left, tinny Argentinian tango music came from the television's tiny speakers.

'There's only one thing we can do.'

'What's that, Jayne?'

'Visit here. Go to Delph.' She tapped the top of one of the letters with the address of the Beggses.

'But the letter was sent over sixty years ago, Jayne. The Beggses must be dead by now.'

'I know it's a long shot, but perhaps a neighbour remembers them. And they had a son called David, perhaps he's still alive.'

'The chances are not great, Jayne.'

'Well, Dad, unless you have a better idea, that's where we're going.'

'When?' asked Vera.

'Tomorrow morning. We'll leave early, put a full day in. How does nine a.m. sound?'

He father scratched his nose. 'It sounds like I'm going to be setting the alarm.'

Chapter Eighteen

June 19, 2017
Delph, Lancashire, England

It was nearly eleven o'clock before they finally arrived in Delph. They had come from Buxton on the A624, the looming hills of the Peak District National Park on their right and the industrial wasteland of Greater Manchester on their left.

Jayne was tired of driving. The evening before, she had considered staying in one of Buxton's B&Bs for the evening, or even treating herself to a night at the Palace Hotel, bathing in the spa and maybe having a massage to ease her tired limbs.

But then she remembered the cat hadn't been fed and he would by then be bellowing for his dinner with all the ferocity of caged lion. So she had driven all the way back to Manchester.

At home, she had treated herself to a nice glass of Aussie Shiraz and an even nicer block of Valrhona chocolate.

With Mr Smith fed, watered and released out into the neighbourhood to prowl, she settled down in front of the computer to see if she could make any more progress on finding the vanished child.

She stared at the screen for a long time before it occurred to her. Could she come at this problem from a different angle?

They now knew the child's Christian name was Harry or Harold. How many children were born with that name and a Duckworth mother in 1944?

She typed 'Harold' into the FreeBMD search area, leaving the surname blank, but keeping 1944 as the year.

The computer seemed to take an age to respond.

In the whole of England, there was just one baby with the Christian name Harold born to a Duckworth mother. It was one of the four names she had already found.

For a second, Jayne's hopes soared, only for them to plummet back to earth when she realised the woman lived in Nelson and had four other children by the same man before the arrival of Harold.

A quick slurp of wine and a square of chocolate gave her the energy to continue.

Could Freda have used a different surname when she registered the birth? But how? Surely the Registrar would have asked her for proof of identity? During the war, everybody had to carry Identity Cards. As Freda was under 21 at the time, hers would have been brown, with a code indicating the year and quarter in which she had been born. But there were no Duckworth mothers in Oldham – she had checked the FreeBMD site twice. How had Freda avoided telling the Registrar her real name? Had she used a fake Identity Card? In those days, there were no pictures inside and no description, so it would certainly have been possible.

Jayne shook her head. Sometimes the past was a different country with no map to guide you. She took another chunk of chocolate, letting it melt slowly on her tongue.

Come at it a different way.

She now knew Harry wasn't adopted, which meant Freda registered him herself. She went back on the website and isolated all the Harrys and Harolds born in Oldham in 1944, writing down the names of fourteen individuals.

Births Mar 1944

Child's Name	Mother's Name	Birthplace	Vol	Page
Butler, Harold	Quinlan	Oldham	8d	985
Cook, Harold	Thomas	Oldham	8d	1030
McNally, Harold	McInnes	Oldham	8d	1045
Mungo, Harold	Hampson	Oldham	8d	960
Stone, Harold	Arnold	Oldham	8d	991

Births Jun 1944

Child's Name	Mother's Name	Birthplace	Vol	Page
Daly, Harold	Davenport	Oldham	8d	1088
Richards, Harold	Hinton	Oldham	8d	938

Births Sep 1944

Child's Name	Mother's Name	Birthplace	Vol	Page
Stout, Harold	Mooney	Oldham	8d	1040
Britton, Harold	Burns	Oldham	8d	978
Davids, Harold	Hulley	Oldham	8d	957
Press, Harold	Roberts	Oldham	8d	1035

Births Dec 1944

Child's name	Mother's Name	Birthplace	Vol	Page
Brain, Harold	Lockett	Oldham	8d	1007
Court, Harold	Haughton	Oldham	8d	1011
Massey, Harold	Andrew	Oldham	8d	956

She stared at the list, not really taking it all in. The Harry they were looking for could be any one of these children. Then it occurred to her that Freda may have had the baby in another area. She added the filter of the county, Lancashire, and the results came back for 156 Harolds born that year.

This wasn't helping. Unless she could find out more information, it was going to be a long, lonely slog through the records trying to find the right Harold, presuming he was born in Lancashire. She was dreading going through the records of all the surrounding counties.

She switched off the computer and went to bed — maybe tomorrow would be a better day.

But the next morning started badly. They left the nursing home later than intended; Robert couldn't find his glasses and Vera forgot her knitting.

'I always knit in the car, Jayne, it takes my mind off the rocking, otherwise I get motion sickness.'

Eventually they reached the outskirts of Delph, avoiding Manchester and Oldham completely.

'Nothing to see there any more, dear, they ripped the heart out of my home town when they "developed" it in the seventies. I wouldn't say it's ugly, but it makes a slag heap look elegant.'

Jayne keyed in the address on the BMW's satnav. 'Let's find Twenty-three Haggate Lane, shall we?' She drove up Delph New Road. Despite it being close to the town, the road still had the feel of a tree-lined rural lane.

'Delph's a pretty place, but difficult to get to,' said Vera, looking up from her knitting.

They passed an old blackened mill on a hill to the left, its soot-stained walls, tall smoke stack and broken windows a reminder of Delph's once-busy industrial past.

'I suppose the mill would have been buzzing with workers making textiles the last time Freda visited here. Now it's just a decrepit empty shell. Makes me angry, what's happened to our industrial past. I blame Thatcher and her lot. Bloody vultures, all of them.'

'Shush, Robert, Jayne wants to listen to her voice.'

'Turn right and then immediately left,' said the impersonal female voice from the dashboard.

'It's amazing how it knows the right way to go.'

They drove up a hill, past the high stone walls of the old factory buildings.

'That one's still making cloth. Mallalieus, I remember it from when I was a girl.'

'One of the few, that is,' grumbled Robert.

'You've been here before, Vera?' asked Jayne.

'I came with my mother a couple of times when I was little. I never knew why. Ooh, Jayne, I've just thought, do you think Mum came here looking for Harry?'

'Perhaps, Vera, we'll never know.'

As they climbed up Millgate, the road narrowed considerably, hemmed in on both sides by tall three-storied buildings. On the left an old Cooperative Hall with the words 'Unity is Strength' carved into the stone facade had been turned into an Arts Centre.

The satnav spoke again. 'At the next junction, make a sharp left on to Haggate Lane.'

Jayne swung the car round and they headed steeply uphill on an extremely narrow road. On the left, modern bungalows squatted close to the ground.

'This doesn't look good. These houses were all built in the sixties.'

Then the satnav spoke again. 'Your destination is on the right.'

From nowhere, a row of old three-storied weaver's cottages appeared, built from local stone and still with the mullioned windows created so the weavers could use every bit of ambient light.

Jayne stopped the car. 'At least these buildings were around in 1944,' she said. 'Number Twenty-three is on the right, the last of the four.'

'What are we going to do?' asked Vera.

'I'll show you. This is fieldwork. Not the easiest way to find links to the past, but sometimes the only thing we have.'

Jayne marched up the stone-flagged path. On the left a small garden was in full flower, with hanging baskets decorating each side of the door. She knocked and stood back. Vera and Robert watched from the gate.

A young woman opened the door cautiously. 'Yes, how can I help you?'

'Hello, my name is Jayne Sinclair. I'm—'

The woman moved to close the door. 'I'm not interested in buying anything, thank you.'

'Please, I'm not selling anything. I'm a genealogical investigator and I'm researching somebody who used to live here.'

The woman stopped and seemed to be thinking.

'It would help me immensely if I could ask you a few questions.'

The young woman nodded and opened the door wider. 'Can you be quick? I've got my hands full at the moment.'

Jayne saw she had a young baby in her arms and another one with tousled blonde hair clinging to her legs. 'Of course, I just want to know if you knew the people who lived here in 1952?'

The woman laughed. 'I wasn't even born then. We only moved in two years ago. Before then it had been empty for a couple of years, that's why we picked it up cheap.'

'It looks wonderful.'

'My husband is a bit of a handyman. Sometimes I think he's married to his Black and Decker, not me. He certainly treats it better.'

'Okay, sorry to have bothered you.'

The woman went to close the door then opened it again. 'You might want to ask David. He's the man who sold us the house.'

'David?' Jayne took a stab in the dark. 'David Beggs?'

'That's him. It was all getting too much for him, what with the stairs and all. He's in one of the bungalows down the hill. I guess he didn't want to move far.'

'Do you know the number?' Jayne asked tentatively.

'It's over there. The one with the red door, number eight.'

Chapter Nineteen

June 19, 2017
Delph, Lancashire, England

'I remember Harry well. My parents were very fond of him.'

They were sitting in the spotless lounge of David Beggs's bungalow, drinking the ubiquitous cup of tea. At least this cup was vaguely drinkable, unlike the one served by Vera's brother.

Jayne scanned the room. It had the obsessively tidy look of a person who spent too much time alone; the cushions were in exactly the right place, the carpet had been freshly hoovered, the pictures were all aligned perfectly.

'You must have played together as children.' Jayne encouraged the old man to keep talking.

David Beggs was as tidy as his lounge, wearing a green tie, poplin shirt and freshly pressed trousers. A man who takes pride in himself, thought Jayne. The only thing out of place were his eyebrows; they were bushy, like a hairy caterpillar gone to seed.

'Aye, we did. Even went to school together for a short time, before Harry was sent back.'

Jayne knew she would have to lead this man carefully. One wrong move and he would clam up. It had taken a long time to convince him they were simply genealogical researchers and not potential intruders. It

114

was only the mention of Harry's name and the reminder of his parents living at number 23 which gained them access and the requisite cup of tea.

'What was the name of the school?' she probed.

'St Alphonsus, at the bottom of t'hill. Me mam and dad were staunch Catholics, wouldn't let me go to any of them Protestant schools.' He was silent for a moment, obviously back in the past. 'I remember one day, Harry and I climbed the wall of Haggate House. It used to stand where these bungalows are now. They had a lovely orchard at the back, all chopped down now, of course. Well, us two, we ate those apples like they weren't making them any more. Sick as dogs, we were. Both of us got a tanning from me dad. Nothing too bad, though, it were the telling off that was worse.'

'When did that happen?'

'Must have been 1950. No, I tell a lie, 1951. We were already in school.'

'And then Harry was taken back by the home. When was that?'

'Later in 1951. I don't remember exactly when. We weren't at school, so it must have been a weekend. A man in a big black car came for him. I remember being so jealous when Harry went in the car. I wanted to sit up front in those big leather seats too.' He paused for a moment, taking a drink of his tea. 'He had this toy soldier – a guardsman, really – and he slept with it, took it everywhere with him. As he was leaving, he pressed the soldier up to the window of the car. It was like the soldier was saying goodbye, not Harry.'

'Who took him away?'

'Like I said, a man in a big black car. I didn't know his name.'

'I meant which home did he go to?'

'The one where all the other children came from. St Michael's.'

Vera was about to speak. Jayne glanced across at her, signalling with her eyes to let the man continue talking.

'Mum and Dad loved kids. I think they wanted them so much but nothing happened for a long while, so they decided to foster instead. And then I came along. God's grace it was, said Mum, for looking after the children from the home. So she carried on caring for them, just so God would look after me.'

'St Michael's, you say?' Jayne repeated.

'Aye, the one on Harris Road, next to the church. Harry came to us from there when I were a nipper. He was slightly younger than me, so I were always his big brother. Mum and Dad missed Harry so much when he left. We always thought he would come back but he never did. They even tried to adopt him but the home said he had gone away. I never saw him again. I always wondered what happened to Harry when he went away.'

'Went away? What do you mean?'

The old man looked up from his tea. 'You don't know? He went to Australia with all the other migrant children.'

Chapter Twenty

April 12, 1952
St Michael's Home, Oldham, England

Harry knew it was today.

For some reason the sisters had been nice to him and the others for the last few days. A week ago, a doctor had come to the home and examined the eight of them who were going to Australia. Himself, Little Tom, Georgie, Ginger Jones, Fred Whatmough and Ernie Laurie from the boys, and the Astley sisters – June and Doris – from the girls. His hands had been cold and his voice gruff. He barely looked at the boys as they stood in front of him in their vests and underpants.

'Wish he'd get a move on,' whispered Georgie.

'It's freezing. And we missed out on breakfast this morning.'

'You never finish the porridge, Ginger, so why you complainin'?'

'Not the point, is it?' Ginger said. 'I—'

'Be quiet, boy,' shouted Sister Tomasina.

They waited for the inevitable swoosh through the air as the strap swung down to catch one of them on the back of the legs, but it never came.

Instead, she spoke in a strangely affected voice: 'How long are you going to be, Doctor? The surgeon is waiting for our boys.'

117

'Not long, not long. This one has something on his lungs.' He pointed to Charlie, who was always coughing, especially when he first woke up. 'Might be a spot of TB. Have to check him out, but he can't go – not till he's had an X-ray.'

'Not to worry, Doctor. I'll fetch another boy to take his place.'

She went to get Ernie. He hadn't put his hand up to go when the priest came round, but it must have been his turn anyway. The doctor passed him as fit, barely glancing at him. Ernie was only eleven but looked older and was built like a strongman at a circus.

After the doctor had finished, a nurse had given each of them an injection in the left arm. 'Won't hurt,' she said.

But it did. Harry's arm was still aching when he finally left the home a week later.

After the injection they had been led next door, still wearing their vests and underpants, and told to lie on a trolley.

'What's happenin', Matron?' asked Fred Whatmough.

'Well, if you're very good, each of you will get one of these.' She held up a bag of gum drops.

'I like the orange ones,' said Ginger.

'No you don't. You never had them before.'

'Shut your mouth, Georgie. I have too, me Da bought me some.'

'Liar. You don't have a Da...'

'I do, he's gone away, that's all, but he's coming back for me.'

'He's never coming back for you, Jones.' Sister Tomasina pulled the boys apart. 'He's in prison. And if you don't want to end up locked away like him, you'd better mend your ways.'

The boys fell silent. The nurse offered the bag of gum drops to Ginger. 'You can have the orange one. They're my favourite too.'

'You shouldn't spoil these boys, Nurse. Sets a bad example,' sniffed Sister Tomasina.

They all took a gum drop. Harry's was blackcurrant, whilst Little Tom chose strawberry.

'In a few moments, the doctor is going to cut your tonsils out. It won't hurt at all. I'm going to put you to sleep with this.' The nurse held up what resembled a rubber mask.

Little Tom nudged Harry. 'It's like what a pilot wears in the RAF.'

'Why are you cutting out our tonsils, Matron?' asked Ginger.

'Well, sometimes they get infected, especially in young boys. And you don't need them anyway.'

'But Sister Mary said we are made by God. Why did he give us something we don't need?'

'It's not your place to question God, Jones,' Sister Tomasina stepped in. 'Who are you to say want God does or doesn't do? You're nothing to him.'

'But Sister Mary said—'

'I don't care, Jones.' She stepped forward and grabbed him by the arm, forcing him to lie down on the trolley. 'Is the doctor ready, Nurse?'

'I think so.'

'This boy can go first as he seems to be the most talkative.'

The nurse moved to the side of the trolley. 'If you could hold his shoulders, Sister.'

Sister Tomasina pressed Ginger down into the trolley, digging her fingers into the soft flesh beneath his collarbone.

'Now, Ginger – that's your name, isn't it?'

Ginger nodded, wide-eyed with fear.

'The boy's name is Jones, Nurse,' barked Sister Tomasina.

The nurse stared at the sister before continuing. 'I'm going to place the mask over your mouth and pour a few drops of this liquid into it. Then I want you to count backwards from ten for me. Can you do it?'

Ginger nodded without saying a word.

Harry could see his bare foot, the dirty sole trembling against the white sheet covering the trolley.

'Are you ready?' She placed the mask over his mouth and poured a little of the liquid on it.

Ginger tried to get up, but Sister Tomasina pressed down on his shoulders, stopping him.

The foot trembled faster.

'Don't forget to count, Ginger,' the Nurse said gently.

'Ten, nine, eight, seven, six…'

Ginger stopped counting.

'What's happened to him?' asked Harry.

'He's just gone to sleep. He'll wake up in ten minutes.'

Another nurse came from the next room and rolled the still body of Ginger away on the trolley.

'He'll be okay?'

'Of course he will. His mouth will be a little dry, that's all, and he won't have any tonsils. So, who's next?' she said cheerily.

Within less than an hour, they were all done and de-tonsilled, the doctor working with all the speed of a miner on piece rate.

The next week passed slowly for Harry. He was sure his mother would come to see him before he was sent to Australia. He had played with the globe in Sister Tomasina's room; the country seemed far away. It would take at least a week for him to go there, see the kangaroos and come back. What would happen if his mother came for him whilst he was away?

A couple of days before they were due to leave, all eight of them were taken in a bus to Afflecks, the department store in Manchester. It was the first time Harry had been out of the home, other than to walk to Mass on a Sunday, since he had been taken back there. They drove down Oldham Road, past row upon row of terraced houses. It was a beautiful spring day; the sun shone down and the trees were just breaking into leaf. Harry stared out of the window, not talking to Little Tom by his side.

There was a buzz of excitement as they were led by Sister Morris into the store. First, the boys were taken to the third floor and told to sit down.

An assistant came out and measured them. 'And how old are you?' she asked Harry.

'Seven, but I'll be eight in August.'

'You are tall for your age. We'd better give him the size for a nine-year-old. What do you think, sister?'

The nun shrugged her shoulders. 'Whatever you think is right.'

The assistant came back with a raincoat, khaki and corduroy shorts, two khaki shirts, a white shirt, tie, belt, three pairs of socks, three vests, three pyjamas, a pair each of sandals and pumps, a dark cap, a sun hat, three pairs of white underpants, a toilet bag with all the necessaries, two toothbrushes and a face flannel, complete with a small brown patent-leather case to put it all in.

'Aren't you a lucky boy? You're going to look very smart in your new clothes.'

Harry said thank you very much.

'And so polite. You have trained them well, sister.'

Sister Morris smiled proudly. 'We try our best. With God's grace, we'll succeed.'

After the rest of the children had been outfitted with all their needs, they trooped back on to the bus.

On the way back from Afflecks, Harry plucked up the courage to sit next to Sister Morris at the front of the bus, just behind the driver. 'Will you tell my mother to wait until I come back, Sister?'

The sister had peered at him quizzically. 'Why, whatever do you mean, Harold? Ask your mother to wait for what?'

'In case she comes while I'm away in Australia seeing the kangaroos.'

'Oh, get away with you and your silly questions. Sure, haven't you got enough to do, packing your things for Australia? And don't forget your new underwear, you'll need it on the voyage.'

But his mum hadn't come. And now a young woman was standing in front of the eight of them, with the Mother Superior introducing her.

'Now, this is Miss Anstey, she's going to accompany you on your trip to Australia.'

The Mother Superior held up her index finger and waved it in front of their faces.

Harry noticed it had a brownish stain at the end covering the nail, the same as the man who had brought him to St Michael's. He wondered if they were brother and sister.

'You must obey her in everything, children. Remember, God is watching you all the time. He will punish those who behave badly.'

'So He has a strap too...' said Ernie under his breath. Harry started to laugh.

Mother Superior stared at him. 'Why are you laughing, boy? Do you find God funny?'

'No, Mother Superior...' mumbled Harry.

The old nun turned to the young woman. 'Would you like to say a few words, Miss Anstey?'

She stepped forward and slapped her hands in front of her as if in prayer. Harry noticed that she wore the whitest of white gloves and a matching hat covering her short dark hair. When she spoke, her accent was strange; high and drawling, not like anything else he'd ever heard.

'Hello, children, my name is Claire Anstey. I'm Australian and I'm going to escort you to my home country. We're going to have a good time together on the ship, but you must remember to listen to me and do everything I tell you.'

Harry looked at her. She smiled back at him, and winked. He was going to like this woman.

Ginger put his hand up. 'Please, miss, are we really going to see kangaroos?'

'Of course you are. There a lots near Perth, where we're going.'

'And when are we coming back? I don't want to miss my dad when he comes to get me.'

Miss Anstey glanced across at the Mother Superior, whose voice when it came had an edge of threat. 'I've told you before, Jones. Your father is in jail, he will not be coming for you, ever.' Then the voice modulated to that of a gentle old woman. 'Now, when Sister Tomasina calls your name, you are to walk over to the table, collect your name tag and number, and put on your hat and coat.'

'Ernest Laurie,' Sister Tomasina shouted.

Ernie stood up, adjusted his shorts that were already too small, and walked over to the table. Sister Tomasina ticked a sheet of paper in front of her, handing a tag to Ernie to wear round his neck. 'You are number 417, Laurie. Do not forget the number and do not lose your tag. Put on your hat and coat and wait over there.' She turned over the second sheet of paper. 'Dora Astley.'

The procedure was followed until she shouted, 'Keith Jones.'

Nobody responded.

Louder now. 'Keith Jones...'

Harry nudged Ginger in the ribs. 'That's you.'

He stumbled up and ran over to the table, collecting his tag.

'Harold—'

Before she had said his surname, Harry was already at the table. He had a question to ask. 'Sister...'

'Here's your tag. You are number 423.'

'Sister, I wonder...'

'What?' answered Sister Tomasina, without looking up from her papers.

'What if my mum comes for me while I'm away?'

'She won't.'

'But she might, Sister, she sometimes comes to see me.'

Sister Tomasina glared up to the heavens. 'See this here?' She thrust a sheet of paper in front of his face. 'It's your mother's signature. She knows you are going to Australia, so why would she come here for you?'

Harry stared at the scrawl just above Sister Tomasina's finger.

'But she wouldn't want me to go away without saying goodbye. I know she wouldn't. She always says goodbye.'

'Well, this time she didn't. Now go and get your hat and coat. You're keeping Miss Anstey waiting.'

Harry put the tag with its block letters, 423, around his neck.

Why hadn't his mum come to say goodbye?

Chapter Twenty-One

June 19, 2017
Delph, Lancashire, England

'Are you sure, David?'

David Beggs's eyes went up to the ceiling as he recalled the past. 'I remember my mum and dad telling me. You see, I missed Harry so much and wanted to know when he was coming back. They said he had gone to Australia. I guess the home must have told them.'

'What does it mean, Jayne? Why was he sent to Australia?' asked Vera.

Jayne tapped her laptop. 'I've only dealt with one of these cases before. He was one of the child migrants and I helped him trace his relatives in England.'

Vera frowned. 'Child migrants? I don't understand. How can children be migrants? And I'm pretty sure my mother didn't sign any papers for him to go to Australia. I mean, she wanted him back, didn't she?'

Jayne scratched her nose. 'It's a difficult story, Vera, not one many people know about. From about 1870 to the 1960s, Britain exported nearly 130,000 children to the colonies – mainly Canada, Australia and New Zealand.'

'"Exported"? You're talking about children, Jayne, not bits of machinery. They weren't cargo.'

Jayne sighed and spoke softly. 'Not cargo, no, but workers. Farm hands and domestics, mainly.'

'But you said they were children, Jayne.' Her dad spoke for the first time.

'They were, some as young as four years old.'

'I don't understand.' Vera leant forward and touched Jayne's hand. 'Please explain it to me clearly.'

Jayne took a deep breath. 'As I said, about 130,000 children left the United Kingdom for the colonies. From 1870 to 1928, they were sent to Canada to work on farms and to be servants. After the First and Second World Wars they were also sent to Australia.'

'You said they were children – how old were they?' Robert asked.

'Most were aged between four and twelve years old. A few were in their teens, but not many.'

'Four to twelve… How could they send children so young? Were they orphans?'

Jayne shrugged her shoulders. 'Some were orphans, but most weren't. Perhaps they were from broken homes, or a parent had died, or their family had simply fallen on hard times…'

'Or they were illegitimate, like Harry.'

Jayne nodded. 'Or they were illegitimate. Anyway, they ended up in a variety of children's homes run by charitable organisations.'

'It was the charities that sent them?'

'All the famous ones were involved: Barnardo's, the Salvation Army, the Catholic Church, the Fairbridge Society, the Anglican Church. Even the Methodists.'

'But why, Jayne?'

'It was a different time. I think the charities believed they were doing the right thing; taking these children from broken homes or a difficult upbringing and giving them a new life in the colonies.'

'But Harry wasn't from a broken home. He was illegitimate but my mother wanted him back.'

'And my mam and dad loved him, they wanted to adopt him,' David said quietly.

Jayne shrugged her shoulders. 'What I don't understand is that these child migrants were supposed to have nobody left in England, that's why they were sent abroad.'

There was silence in the room, save for the clock ticking on the mantlepiece and the gentle music of an ice-cream van off in the distance.

'Would you like an ice cream?' David asked. 'He always comes around at this time. It's my little treat for myself.'

They all shook their heads.

'You don't mind if I go? Only it wouldn't feel right without a ninety-nine for my lunch.'

David was up from his chair with all the energy of a teenager going out on his first date, and through the front door before the ice-cream van had a chance to escape.

When he had gone, Vera spoke quietly. 'Well, I never expected that. Australia... Harry went to Australia.'

'We don't know if he did, Vera.'

'But David just told us he went there in 1952.'

'We need to check the files properly. It wouldn't be the first time a children's home had written one thing but done another.'

'And how are we going to do that? If he wasn't adopted, there won't be any records, will there?'

'True. But we now know which home he was in — St Michael's.'

Vera frowned again. 'I remember the church when I was growing up. St Michael's on Harris Road. There was a home attached to it. We used to go for

Mass there sometimes, when Mum wanted a change of priest. She didn't get on well with Father O'Malley. Said he was too modern for her taste. She liked a more traditional service. The priest at St Michael's was very old school.'

'Good, I can pay it a visit. See if they have any records of their children in 1952.'

David bustled through the door, carrying his ice cream with a chocolate flake sticking out of the top. 'Have I missed anything?'

'We were just talking about St Michael's.'

'The church is still there but the home is gone, knocked down years ago. One of those bloody road-widening schemes the local councils were so fond of back then. Knocked every bloody thing down so people could drive to wherever they were going five minutes quicker. Bloody choughs.'

Jayne thought for a moment. 'Never mind, the records were probably sent to a central location. One of the Catholic migrant organisations will have them.'

'Is there anything else we can do, Jayne?' asked Vera.

'Well, we can check the passenger registers for Australia. Do you know when Harry left, David?'

He shook his head. 'I'm pretty certain it was 1952, not long after he went back to the home, but I can't be certain.'

'It's easy to check other years too. And there's always the Child Migrants Trust.'

'There's an organisation for these people?'

'Set up in the late 1980s by a woman called Margaret Humphreys in Nottingham. For the last thirty years they've been very successful at reuniting these children with their parents. In all that time they've been the one group who have been consistent with support and help.'

Robert leant forward. 'But they can't be children any more. If they went to Australia after the war they will be the same age as Vera.'

'Shhh… Robert, going on about my age.'

He smiled at her. 'You'll always be twenty-one to me, Vera.'

'Get away with you.'

Vera slapped his hand playfully but Jayne could see she was pleased at the flattery. 'Some are older than twenty-one. Most are into their seventies now.'

'That means their parents would be in their nineties. Can't be many still living.'

'I don't think there are many, Vera. But the children still want to know if they have relatives. Can you imagine never knowing if you had a family or not?'

Again, there was silence in the room before Vera spoke. 'It must be awful. So many years separated from the ones you love. No wonder it drove Mum to distraction.' She gripped the edge of the chair. 'We have to find Harry, Jayne. Whatever it takes, we must find him.'

Chapter Twenty-Two

April 13, 1952
Tilbury Docks, London, England

There weren't any bands or cheering crowds of people as the ship pulled away from the docks in Tilbury. The rain was sleeting down and a grey-brown mist hung over the derricks and wharves like a shroud. Harry was standing next to Little Tom and one of the Astley sisters, with Miss Anstey behind them.

They had come down on a train yesterday from Manchester. It was the first time any of them had ever been on a railway. They crammed into a single second-class compartment with Miss Anstey, all fighting for a place next to the window. Of course, Ernie won, being the biggest and the eldest, and he invited Harry to join him.

They spent the rest of the trip looking out of the window as the green and pleasant English countryside whistled past in front of their eyes.

'It's like something from the movies, isn't it? said Harry.

'What is?'

'Looking through the window. It's like there's a whole world out there. Like a movie rolling past in front of you.'

'Dunno, never been to the movies. Have you?'

130

'Went with me mum on me birthday. We saw Horatio Hornblower, and some newsreels. It was terrific.'

After a couple of hours, a man with a trolley came round offering them tea, but only Miss Anstey took a cup.

'With sugar?'

'Two, please.'

'You've got a lot of kids with you.'

'They're orphans. Taking them to London.'

'Poor kids. Bombed out, were they?'

'I don't really know the stories, I'm just their minder.'

The man with the trolley gave them all a Cadbury's Fudge. 'Now, you tuck in to those, kids. If I've got any sarnies left over after I've done the train, I'll come back and see you right.'

As they were nearing London he came back with another man, who was wearing a large hat like an officer. 'This is the lot I was telling you about, Bill.'

The man with the hat stared at them and they stared back, silent.

'Give 'em whatever we've got, George. I'll fiddle it somehow.'

George came back five minutes late with cheese and tomato sandwiches, ham rolls, shortbread biscuits and two boxes of Mars bars. 'Don't eat it all at once, kids, you'll be sick as parrots.'

That night, they ate everything they have been given in the dormitory of one of the Catholic homes in London. Miss Anstey had tucked Harry into his bed with his soldier, and then kissed him on the forehead.

'My mum and Mrs Beggs always kissed me goodnight.'

'Do you like it?'

Harry nodded.

'Okay. Every night, I'll tuck you in and kiss you goodnight. That's a lovely soldier. A guardsman, isn't it? What's his name?'

'Trevor.'

She laughed. 'A funny name for a soldier. Who gave him to you?'

'Me mum.'

A frown creased Miss Anstey's forehead. 'But I thought you were an orphan?'

'No... I've got a mum. She'll be waiting for me when I get back from Australia.'

Another frown. 'Hmmm. Goodnight, Harry. Sleep tight and don't let the bed bugs bite.'

'I won't, miss.'

The ship gave three long toots from its whistle, waking Harry from his dream of Miss Anstey kissing his forehead. One of the sailors unhitched a rope from the bow of the ship, throwing it on to the dock to be caught by another man. Harry felt the throb of the engines beneath his feet becoming stronger. The bow swung away from the dock and the breeze ruffled Harry's hair.

Little Tom turned to Miss Anstey, tugged her skirt and asked, 'What time do we arrive in Australia?'

'What time?'

'Will it be after bedtime?'

She laughed. 'Yes, Tom. In fact, we're going to be on this boat for quite a while. At least six weeks.'

'So we won't be back in England for me tea?'

She laughed again. 'No, Tom, we won't.'

'What are we going to eat then?'

'Don't worry. See those men in white coats?'

Little Tom nodded.

'They're called stewards and they will give you a cup of tea any time you want it.'

132

Harry stared out at the mist rising from the river, a grey-brown haze which enveloped the wharves and clung to the brick walls. In the distance, the lights of London were just being switched on, fighting their way through the smog, a dim glow warming the dusky sky as the boat pulled away from the dock and headed slowly, inexorably downstream towards the open sea.

He wasn't going to think of his mum.

He wasn't going to think of Mrs Beggs.

He wasn't going to cry.

A gob of sick rose from Harry's stomach into his throat as he watched the river widen and the shore vanish into the mist.

Chapter Twenty-Three

June 19, 2017
Oldham, Lancashire, England

Even with the satnav, they became lost three times before Jayne finally found the area they were looking for. There were patches of the old Oldham Vera recognised, and she gave a running commentary to her life and a city that had changed.

'I had my first kiss over there. I was fourteen and it was with Neville Harrison. He was the school dreamboat – looked just like Mick Jagger, only thinner. Tried to put his hand up my skirt but I put an end to that.

'Used to be a corner shop there,' she said, pointing to a piece of waste-ground strewn with litter, plastic Coke bottles and discarded McDonald's wrappers. 'Gave you six gobstoppers for threepence and an extra one if you gave him a smile. Lovely man, he was, Mr Turner. Had a heart attack one day and keeled over. The place wasn't the same without him.'

'And that's where I used to work on a Saturday, wrapping up the fish and chips whilst Mr Harkins stood over the hot fryer. When he closed at seven, I used to get as much scraps as I wanted plus two haddock and chips and two plaice and chips. Mum used to love it – the one night she didn't have to cook. On the way home, I'd stop in at Turner's and buy a block of Wall's Neapolitan ice cream for everybody. Three different colours it was – pink, yellow and brown – but they all tasted the same to me.'

Jayne parked outside the church, stopping the running commentary. Vera got out with her, but Robert stayed in the car.

'Are you feeling okay, Dad?'

'Fine, lass, just a bit tired. I'll rest here, you go ahead.'

'We won't be long, Robert. You wrap up well.'

'Aye, I will, love. Might have a little nap, it's been a long day.'

They strode across the road to St Michael's. It was a squat little church, built from the local stone, blackened with age and pollution. There were no large spires or elegant stained-glass windows to adorn it. Just a single small tower standing next to a simple nave, like one of the guardsmen at Buckingham Palace.

A notice on the door stated bluntly:

Due to a shortage of priests, Mass will only be said in this church on the last Sunday of every month. We apologise for the inconvenience.

The notice was signed by the Diocese of Salford. Beneath it was the same message in Polish.

Jayne stared up at the single blackened tower, its stone finger pointing directly up to heaven.

'It wasn't a rich area. Poor Irish, mainly,' said Vera. 'Many came during the famine and stayed. There used to be riots around here during Holy Week. The local Protestants didn't like the parades and suchlike. Just an excuse for a barney, if you ask me.'

Jayne looked around. 'Still not the richest area.'

'The Irish have moved away now and new waves of migrants followed in their footsteps. Bengalis and Pakistanis in the eighties and nineties, Poles and East-

135

ern Europeans after that. Like all migrants, they will eventually assimilate. When I was growing up, it was still the Irish who were the most plentiful. They kept Catholicism and churches like this going.'

'The church looks lonely and solitary. Nobody to keep it warm.'

'I think the home was over there,' Vera said, pointing. 'I remember there was a piece of wasteland, something must have been knocked down in the war. But why the Germans would want to bomb round here is anybody's guess. Perhaps they were after the train station at the Mumps, or they just weren't very accurate. Anyway, there was a piece of waste-ground here and the home overlooked it. I remember they used to have marvellous fireworks on bonfire night; rockets, Catherine wheels, bangers. People used to bring all their spare rubbish and dump it on the bonfire.'

'It's over here?'

Vera nodded, pointing again back over her shoulder.

Jayne walked towards where the home used to stand. A three-storey block of flats stood there now, modern in the ugliest sense of the word; grey concrete, rusty iron railings, flaking paintwork. A dull, depressing place to live for anybody.

And then she saw them.

Walking along the road in twos, a nun leading the way, her habit billowing in the wind and her rosary flapping at her waist. She was followed by the girls, dressed in their Sunday best, and the boys bringing up the rear, smart in their clean shirts, shorts and newly polished faces. They walked past her and up the steps into the church, the nun turning to guide them through the large oak door, admonishing any who were talking with a vicious stare and a loud shush.

And then, just as quickly as they had appeared, the column of children and nuns vanished. Jayne shook her head, staring at the modern building.

It had happened again.

The past coming alive. She didn't know how it happened. Maybe it was her imagination or maybe something more. Like an image embedded in the walls of the old church Jayne could somehow access, like playing an old tape machine. She had no problem believing in her scenes, as she called them — for her they were as real as any documentary on television.

'Are you okay, Jayne? You've come over all pale.'

'Fine, just a little tired, that's all.'

'You and your dad. Two peas from the same pod. Well, we've seen all we're going to see here. Shall we head back to sunny Buxton? I'm dying for my tea.'

'Let's go, Vera.' Jayne put her arm round her step mother and guided her back to the car, glancing over her shoulder at the place where the home used to stand.

What was it like to live here?

And then a shiver went up her back.

Had somebody just walked over her grave?

Chapter Twenty-Four

April 20, 1952
On-board the SS Otranto, somewhere in the Mediterranean Sea

In many ways, the time he spent on the Otranto was the happiest of Harry's life.

He was never scared on the ship, except one time just before they put into Gibraltar, when the wind and the waves made the ship rock from side to side. When he went to the toilet, he had to hold on to both rails in the corridor to prevent himself falling over. Ginger and Little Tom were both sick as dogs, but Harry wasn't. He had a 'Mariner's Tummy', one of the crew had told him, whatever one of those was.

He shared a large cabin with Little Tom, Ginger and Ernie. They soon settled down into the rhythm of ship life. In the morning, one of the stewards from Goa – his name was Arthur – brought them tea and orange juice in bed. Then they had breakfast in the lounge. At first, Harry didn't believe his luck as he sat down at the table covered in a linen tablecloth, where a white-jacketed waiter served them cocoa, fried eggs, bacon, bread and butter, and toast with jam, golden syrup and marmalade.

The rest of the morning they played on the boat and the promenade decks, running up and down the gangways and getting in the way of all the passengers.

The ship was big, with two large metal funnels through which smoke poured at all times of the day and night. Harry had once counted all the steps from the front to the back of the ship: 623. It was the biggest thing he had ever seen.

At the front and back were two masts, like on the sailing ships he had seen in the pictures, but the crew never hauled up the sails. He asked one of them when they were going to start sailing.

'Never, matey. This ain't no sailin' ship.'

'But why do you have masts?'

'Those are for haulin' up your food when we get to port. Wivout 'em, you wouldn't have nothing to eat.'

There were other kids on-board; some Catholic children from other homes and a small group of Protestant kids from the Fairbridge Society. At first there had been a stand-off, with Ernie out in front flexing his muscles and showing them who was boss. But that soon ended and they all became friends, playing together and getting to know each other.

At noon exactly, the bell would ring and they would all troop back to the lounge for lunch. At first, Harry had been confused. He asked Miss Anstey, 'Why do we have lunch at dinnertime?'

She stopped talking with the man, Alfred Grey, who was escorting the Fairbridge kids. 'I don't understand, Harry.'

'Well, miss, in Oldham we have our dinner at one o'clock and our tea at six o'clock and that's it for the day. But on the ship there's lunch, then tea at four, but dinner doesn't come till seven thirty. Why don't they eat dinner at the proper time?'

'They do, Harry. It's just the different words. On the ship they call dinner "lunch".'

'But that's not right, is it, miss? Dinner is dinner and we have it at one o'clock.'

She put her arm around his shoulders, leading him away. 'Well, think of it this way. When you have lunch at noon, just call it your dinner.'

'And what about the evening meal? We call it tea where I come from.'

She glanced back at Mr Grey. 'Call it what you want, Harry. You like having another meal, don't you?'

Harry nodded.

'Well, there you are. Just call it supper instead.'

Harry thought for a moment. 'Okay.'

With it all sorted out, Harry could go back to playing with the gang until teatime, which wasn't a proper tea, just some biscuits, scones and clotted cream and more orange juice. Sometimes the crew organised games in the afternoon. Harry was best at deck quoits, which involved tossing a ring on to a number on the deck. He even beat one of the Fairbridge boys, Tommy Hardy, who was nearly twelve.

After tea, he always went to the Reading Room to draw in his diary. Miss Anstey had suggested this to all of them on their second day out of England.

'It's going to be quite a long voyage, children, and we're going to visit many interesting places. Perhaps you would like to keep a record so that when you're older, you can remember these times.'

'You mean something to show me mam when I get back to England?'

'Something like that, Tom. Here's some paper I took from the Reading Room earlier. There's plenty more on the ship. Now, fold it in half, like so, then turn it on its side and what do you have?'

One of the Astley sisters put her hand up. 'It looks like a small book.'

'What are you going to put on yours, Harry?'

Harry chewed the end of his blue pencil. 'I'm going to call mine "My Trip to Australia", because that's what it is.'

'Very good, Harry, and what are you going to put on the cover?'

He thought again. 'Well, I could cut a picture of the ship from one of the menus and stick it on.'

'Brilliant idea, Harry.'

Ever since then, before supper, Harry dutifully filled in his diary in the wood-panelled Reading Room, surrounded by shelves and shelves of books. In his own small way, he thought he was writing a book like all those other people; a book of his adventures at sea. It used to take him a long time, as he was slow with his writing and often got the words jumbled up. Miss Anstey used to sit with him sometimes, patiently showing him how to write. She even helped him when he wrote letters home to his mum. These used to take him longer than the diary, but every week he wrote back to her, posting the letters when they reached a port.

He never received a reply, though. He guessed she didn't know where to write, and if the ship were moving all the time, how would the postman ever catch up with it?

In the letters, he told her all the things he did. Like running three times around the boat deck without stopping. Or eating four bowls of ice cream for lunch. Or throwing sugar cubes at the rats on the wharf at Naples, watching as they raced each other to be first to grab the lump of sweetness. Or standing at the front of the boat and seeing a group of big fish – dolphins, Miss Anstey told him – jumping and gliding at the point of the bow as it cut through the blue water.

He also wrote about the things he'd seen.

The seagulls stealing food from the waiter. And the monkeys in Gibraltar who thought they were Kings of the Rock. And the men who had tried to sell them real Egyptian antiques when they had docked in Suez, which nobody bought because they were cursed.

All the things his mother would love to read, even though she had never left England. And when he met her again, he would give her the diary, telling the stories of his travels through the words and the pictures. When she read it, his mum would know he had been all over the world like a proper traveller.

After he finished his writing, it was time for a shower and then dinner – or as he preferred to call it, supper. It wasn't like the food in the home at all. Despite being on a ship far from anywhere, they still managed to eat like lords.

He copied the menu from one night in a red pencil, so his mum could see what he was eating.

Veloute Benin
Fillets of Sea Bream, Mornay Sauce
Braised Haunch of Mutton, soubise
Roast Ribs of Beef, paysanne
Baked and Boiled Potatoes
Cabbage
Golden Pudding
Cream Ices
Dessert

He copied it as neatly as he could. When he finished, he thought the shape resembled a strawberry. Some of the words he didn't understand, but he liked the food. Especially when you could go back and have as much ice cream as you wanted.

Miss Anstey tucked them all up in bed at 9 o'clock on the dot. It was the one thing she was very strict about. They must be in bed and in their pyjamas by then or she would be very angry.

Harry never saw her angry at any time during the voyage. But he always made sure he was in bed waiting for her to come round and tuck him in, giving him a kiss on the forehead and Trevor, his soldier, a kiss on the top of his busby.

Despite everything he did during the day, it was still the time he enjoyed most.

It reminded him of his mum and Mrs Beggs.

Chapter Twenty-Five

June 19, 2017
Didsbury, Manchester, England

Jayne was exhausted when she arrived home. She opened the front door and was about to shout, 'Paul, I'm home,' when she realised he wasn't there. In fact, her husband hadn't been back to the house for two months. He now lived and worked in Brussels.

The emptiness of the house, the silence as her voice reverberated on the walls, hit her like a punch in the chest. She swallowed, trying to fill the emptiness inside her with something, anything.

As she closed the door, the cat meandered out of the kitchen and rubbed his body against her legs. She picked him up, feeling him resist her embrace and then finally give in to welcome it, licking the side of her neck. 'You've missed me, have you?'

A voice in her head, a nasty wheedling voice, answered her. He's the only one who does.

She put Mr Smith down and he flounced off to check his bowl. She followed him into the kitchen. Why was she feeling this way? She hadn't missed Paul before, so why was she suddenly aware of his absence?

She opened a pouch of cat food without looking at the label. What's the matter with you today? Are you just tired or is there something else? She poured the contents of the pouch into the bowl as the cat waited expectantly.

This sense of loneliness was new to her. All her life she had been surrounded by people. At school she had been a popular girl, involved in so many clubs and outings it had driven her mother crazy. In the police, she was always with other coppers, either on a case or for the inevitable socialising after the shift had finished. Then Paul had come along, and even through her breakdown after Dave Gilmour's shooting, he had been by her side, constantly tending to her every need.

She wondered if he preferred her as she was then; totally dependent on him rather than the independent woman she had become.

She had always had people in her life. 'About time you learned to enjoy your own company, Jayne Sinclair,' she said out loud.

As she did so, the reason for her unhappiness struck her. It was her father and Vera. She had just spent the day with them, only leaving them an hour ago when she dropped them back at the residential home in Buxton. They were so loving, so conscious of each other, so aware of the other's moods and feelings. A stroke on the arm. A touch of the hand. A glance to each other when they thought she wasn't looking.

And what did she have?

Nothing.

An empty house. A cat. And a few investigations to keep her occupied.

'God, you are feeling sorry for yourself today,' she said out loud, thinking, I'm even talking to myself now.

There was only one balm for moods like this.

Chocolate.

A block of the very best she had. Chocolat Bonnat Chuao. She took it out of the fridge, letting it come to room temperature before she would eat it. For a moment she was tempted by a bottle of Tempranillo softly calling her name, but she wouldn't drink, not tonight. A nice cup of tea would be much better.

She put the kettle on, happy with her decision. You should never be jealous of somebody else's happiness – that route only led to bitterness and envy, and there was enough of that in the world already.

She booted up her computer. On the way back from Buxton, an idea had struck her just as Liam was in mid-yowl, singing the words, 'Don't look back in anger'. There was something she had missed. Perhaps that's what had started this mood. The knowledge she had missed a clue she should have picked up.

What was it?

She poured the hot water on to the tea bags and put the lid back on the pot.

Vera's file was on her computer desktop. She clicked on it and began to read through her notes on the case. The paternal side of Vera's family was pretty easy to find in the 1911 census. They had even found some relatives on the Lost Cousins website. Should she look for the maternal side? And what about going back a little further, checking out the 1901, 1891 and 1881 censuses? Or was the plural censi?

She could do that later. It wouldn't help with problem at hand; finding Vera's long-lost brother. 'Stay focused, Jayne.'

She snapped off one of the squares of chocolate and popped it in her mouth, letting the sweet and bitter richness dissolve slowly across her tongue. Finally, she swallowed, enjoying all the tastes of its Venezuelan home; honey, flowers and powerful tropical fruits, clove and allspice as the chocolate slipped down her throat.

She remembered a survey in the papers. Given the choice between sex and chocolate, 57% of women would choose the latter. Now she understood why.

She turned the page to the names she had saved for all the Harolds born in Oldham in 1944, and scanned down it as she snapped off another piece of chocolate.

Births Mar 1944

Child's Name	Mother's Name	Birthplace	Vol	Page
Butler, Harold	Quinlan	Oldham	8d	985
Cook, Harold	Thomas	Oldham	8d	1030
McNally, Harold	McInnes	Oldham	8d	1045
Mungo, Harold	Hampson	Oldham	8d	960
Stone, Harold	Arnold	Oldham	8d	991

Births Jun 1944

Child's Name	Mother's Name	Birthplace	Vol	Page
Daly, Harold	Davenport	Oldham	8d	1088
Richards, Harold	Hinton	Oldham	8d	938

Births Sep 1944

Child's Name	Mother's Name	Birthplace	Vol	Page
Stout, Harold	Mooney	Oldham	8d	1040
Britton, Harold	Burns	Oldham	8d	978
Davids, Harold	Hulley	Oldham	8d	957
Press, Harold	Roberts	Oldham	8d	1035

Births Dec 1944

Child's name	Mother's Name	Birthplace	Vol	Page
Brain, Harold	Lockett	Oldham	8d	1007
Court, Harold	Haughton	Oldham	8d	1011
Massey, Harold	Andrew	Oldham	8d	956

'Now, we know Harold was born in Oldham in 1944, so he must be one of these Harolds, unless he was given another name at birth. But probably not, because the letters from Mrs Beggs only referred to him by the name "Harry"...' Jayne mumbled to herself. She was certain this was the Christian name Freda had given him.

And then it her like a runaway bus.

'You've been stupid, Jayne, very stupid,' she said out loud.

Chapter Twenty-Six

May 12, 1952
On-board the SS Otranto, somewhere in the Indian Ocean

It was during one of these times, before they sailed too far south and the weather became too hot, that Harry had his first real adventure. They were playing Hide and Seek and Ginger was It. At first, Harry had thought to hide in one of the lifeboats hanging from davits along the upper boat deck, but he couldn't reach up far enough and the boats were covered with tightly fastened ropes.

Instead, he went down into the bowels of the ship, going further than he had ever gone before. Down past the cabins, down the steps next to the galley, filled with raucous voices shouting in a strange language, and down past the cordoned-off stewards' area.

One time, he heard footsteps and slipped behind one of the metal stanchions. Three dark, hairy men walked slowly past without seeing him. Behind his hiding place was a large metal door with a red notice saying: DO NOT ENTER.

In for a penny, in for a pound, thought Harry. He lifted the metal lever locking the door and slipped through it. Nobody had ever been here before, Ginger would never find him.

He was in a darkened corridor with a high ceiling. Blinking red and white lights shone from the top of large metal boxes. He took a few steps, hearing his feet clang on the metal of the floor. There was another door at the end, fastened with a metal lever.

He lifted it up and opened the door. Instantly, a wall of sound attacked his ears. A metal thump beat beneath him, accompanied by the hiss of steam and the roar of a furnace.

He stood there, letting the sound wash over him. And then he felt the heat, rising through the metal floor wash over him. His forehead broke out in a sweat, the drops drenching the roots of his hair and running into his eyes.

'What the bloody hell are you doing?' said an accented voice, and someone grabbed his shoulder.

He tried to wriggle out of the grip, but the fingers were too strong.

'I said, what are you doing down here? Can't you read ze sign?'

The hand let him go and he backed against the wall.

'Are you one of ze orphans?'

Harry felt himself touch a metal pipe. The man stepped forward. He was tall, with a dark beard and a dirty white cap.

'I'm not an orphan. I've got a mum.'

'Zohhhh, you 'ave a mother, do you?' The man pronounced some words like they began with 'zed'. 'Zen why are you going to Australia?'

Harry didn't know. He kept quiet, looking for a way to escape.

The man noticed his darting eyes. 'No escape. Engine room is my world. Didn't you see sign saying DO NOT ENTER?'

Harry nodded.

'But you came in anyway?'

Harry nodded again.

The man's voice softened. 'You like breaking rules. A man after my own heart. Now you here, would you like to zee engines?'

Harry thought for a moment and nodded again.

'Do you ever speak?'

Harry shook his head.

'Is a no or a yes?'

'It's a maybe.'

'Good, I like maybes. Come and I will show you engines.' The man turned left down some metal stairs. Harry followed him. The sound grew louder all the time as they descended.

'What is your name, little Englishman?'

'Harry.'

'A good name, 'Arry.'

'Suits me.'

'I'm sure it does.'

They reached the bottom and stepped into a large room. In the middle, four large metal shafts were going up and down and round and round, glinting in the light hanging from the ceiling. Two men stood checking out a panel of flickering gauges.

'Lads, zis is 'Arry. Come to see engines. Well, what do you zee, 'Arry?'

Harry gazed at the shafts and the gauges, the boilers and the turbines. His mouth and his eyes opened wide.

'She was built 1925, in Barrow in north England. Do you know how big is she?'

Harry remembered the figures he had read. 'Twenty thousand tons, eighty feet in width and six hundred feet long.'

'Very good, pretty close. Come over here.' He beckoned him over to a guard rail.

Harry looked down to see a row of sweating men shovelling coal into the open mouths of fires. Each

151

time one of the furnaces was opened, a blast of warm air rose to brush past Harry's nose.

'Men shovel coal into fifty-six furnaces to keep six turbines filled wiz steam.'

'Do they drive the prop… prop… proplars?'

'Exactly. And propellers drive ship. It's zimple, 'Arry. Zat's how we get to Australia. Remember, when you in the world above, looking over stern and seeing white wake, it's my men's sweat zat drives ship forwards.'

Harry touched his heart like he had been taught to do by Mr Beggs. 'I'll remember.'

'Good, now you must go back up to the top. If Captain catches you down here, he'll string you up from yardarm. And we wouldn't want zat, would we?'

Harry didn't know where the yardarm was, but it didn't sound a nice place to be strung up from.

'Would you like to be ship's engineer when you grow up, Harry?'

'Do you mean me? Running a place like this with the engines and the boilers and the men shovelling coal into the fires?'

'Of course, who else would I mean?'

Harry eyed the gleaming metal and the shiny, flickering gauges. 'But I…'

'If I – a German from Hamburg with no parents – can do it, you can too.'

Harry smiled and nodded.

'Good. Ralph will show you how to get back topside. Look after yourself, 'Arry.'

As Harry walked up the stairs of the Engine Room, he glanced back at the man with the dirty cap. The man waved and then turned to stare into his gauges.

Harry never told anybody about the trip down to the Engine Room, not even Little Tom. Before they reached Australia, he went twice more through the forbidden door. Each time, he chatted to Friedrich, the Chief Engineer, and his men.

It was on the last trip, when he had spent five minutes shovelling coal into the fire, that he said to Friedrich, 'I want to be an engineer like you when I grow up.'

'You won't see much of world, 'Arry, not in dark and dirt of an engine room.'

At that moment, it didn't matter to Harry.

He knew what he wanted to do when he grew up and that was far more important to him.

Chapter Twenty-Seven

June 19, 2017
Didsbury, Manchester, England

Jayne Sinclair rechecked her saved results for all the Harolds born in Oldham in 1944. She went back to one of the original FreeBMD hits. There it was, staring her in the face and banging her about the head like a police truncheon.

'How could you have missed it?'

She clicked on the result.

Births Sep 1944

Name of Child	Name of Mother	Birthplace	Vol	Page
Britton, Harold	Burns	Oldham	8d	978

The date range was correct. In the letters from the Beggses, they had written about a birthday in late August and here it was in the right quarter. But the giveaway was the surname of the mother: Burns. Freda must have used her grandmother's Identity Card to register the birth. It wouldn't have been a problem, there were no pictures on the wartime cards and nor were there any birth dates.

But why?

Perhaps her mother or father had asked her to. Or perhaps she felt shame at using her own surname, Duckworth, on the form. Or perhaps her grandmother had promised to look after the child and thought it would be easy if they had the same name.

Or simply because they wanted to keep the real mother's name secret.

Jayne snapped off another chunk of chocolate and poured out her tea.

As with many things that happened in the past, she would never know. She could find the records if they existed. She could even track down people who were difficult to find and discover links where none had existed before. But human motivations, the secrets hidden in the human heart – well, they stayed buried in the past, locked in the memories of those who would never be able to reveal them.

At least she could now order the correct birth certificate and show it to Vera.

She completed the form on the GRO website for Harry, adding in Freda and Dora's birth certificate, as well as Freda's marriage certificate, just in case she needed them. All in all, the fees for the priority service came to £93.60. A pretty penny to add to the government's coffers.

Within the next couple of days she would have all the certificates, including Harry's, and would be able to show them to Vera. Her step mother's long-vanished brother was slowly, inexorably, revealing himself.

Jayne added a splash of milk to her tea and brought the cup up to her lips. 'Here's to you, Harry, I hope we find you soon.'

Chapter Twenty-Eight

June 20, 2017
Didsbury, Manchester, England

The next morning Jayne woke bright and early, feeling strangely refreshed. It was always like this when she was making headway on a case. It was when she was blocked or couldn't find a link that tiredness crept in like a thief in the night.

But this morning the sun was shining through the curtains, the birds were singing in the garden and, more importantly, she had two leads she needed to follow up.

'I wish all mornings were like this,' she said out loud as she bounded down the stairs.

Mr Smith was waiting for her outside the patio door. She opened it and he sauntered straight in, tail erect.

'You're back early this morning. Mrs Roberts' cat at number nine not in the mood? Or has she gone off with the Tom in number twenty-three? Have you been jilted for a younger model?'

From his corner next to the bowl, the cat let out a plaintive miaow.

'Poor thing. I guess it means you're hungry.' She took out a pouch of cat food and poured it into his bowl. Have to buy some more, she thought, he's eating me out of house and home.

156

The cat attacked his food, purring quietly as he did so.

She chose a Roma capsule from the Nespresso rack and put it in the machine. The kitchen filled with the delightful aroma of coffee.

'Time to get to work, Jayne, make an early start.'

She booted up her laptop and sat down with the espresso. Two leads to follow up; the Catholic Migrants Centre and the passenger lists for Australia. She checked the time on the wall: 7.14 a.m. Nobody would be at the Centre yet, so she'd call later.

'Let's attack the passenger lists first.'

She logged on to Findmypast, selected the A-Z of record sets and then typed in 'Passenger Lists Leaving UK 1890-1960'.

There were over 24 million records. She hoped he would be easy to find, but with a surname like Britton, the name under which he'd been registered, it shouldn't be too difficult.

She laughed to herself. 'Thank God it isn't Harry Smith.'

She typed his name in the search field, added a departure date of 1952, plus or minus two years, and finally chose Australia as the destination country to narrow the field even further.

She pressed 'Search' and crossed her fingers.

Just one hit.

She was back on her roll.

She clicked on the result. Two rotating arrows stared back at her for a few moments before a page began to form on her screen. A long passenger list appeared for the SS Otranto, a liner leaving Tilbury Docks on April 13, 1952.

Printed at the top, in big, bold official letters, were the words:

NAMES AND DESCRIPTIONS OF BRITISH PASSENGERS EMBARKED AT THE PORT OF LONDON

Interesting.

The word 'British' was in much bigger type, as if this was a badge of honour to distinguish these passengers from everybody else.

She scanned down the list of names, looking for a Harry. There he was.

| Britton. Master H. | " | " | " | " | " | " | " | 8 | 1 |

The compiler of the passenger list had saved himself the trouble of repeating information by adding a long line of ditto marks. She went back up to the top of the list, adding in the missing information.

Name	Last Address	Class	Port	Profession	Age	Country
Britton. H.	St Michael's Oldham, Lancs.	A	Fremantle	Student	8	England

Jayne punched the air. She was sure it was him; the age and dates were correct, but the final confirmation was the address. It was the same home David Beggs had said was linked to his parents.

The cat joined her in the excitement by rubbing his body against her chair on his way to find a place to sleep.

Finally, she had some good news for Vera. They were catching up with her long-lost brother.

Jayne returned to the shipping register. On either side of Harry's name were eight others, all listed as being from the same home:

Anstey. C.M	St Michael's	A	Fremantle	Nurse	24	Australia
Jones. K.	St Michael's	A	Fremantle	Student	10	England
Laurie. E.	St Michael's	A	Fremantle	Student	12	England
Livesey, T.	St Michael's	A	Fremantle	Student	10	England
Britton. H.	St Michael's	A	Fremantle	Student	8	England
Astley. J.	St Michael's	A	Fremantle	Student	8	England
Astley. D.	St Michael's	A	Fremantle	Student	11	England
Whatmough. F.	St Michael's	A	Fremantle	Student	8	England
Rice. G.	St Michael's	A	Fremantle	Student	9	England

So these were the other children from the same home who had accompanied Harry to Australia. He didn't travel alone, other children went with him. Were they all orphans? Or were they more like Harry, the illegitimate child of an unmarried mother? She didn't know the answer, but she would try to find out.

There was one person who wasn't a child. Miss Anstey, a nurse whose birthplace was given as Australia.

Was she the guardian of the children during the voyage?

Probably. She had the same address as the children. The home obviously employed her to look after them.

Out of curiosity, Jayne checked the page before on the passenger list.

There were five more children here, this time from a different children's home – St Joseph's in Birmingham.

Lillis. J.	St Joseph's	A	Fremantle	Student	11	England
Rafferty J.	St Joseph's	A	Fremantle	Student	7	England
McGahey H.	St Joseph's	A	Fremantle	Student	5	England
McNulty. J.	St Joseph's	A	Fremantle	Student	6	England
Bunney. W.	St Joseph's	A	Fremantle	Student	8	England

And above the listing, another four children and their guardian from the Fairbridge Society:

Grey. A.	Fairbridge Society	A	Sydney	Teacher	29	Australia
Bone. O.	Fairbridge Society	A	Sydney	Student	8	England
Camps. C.	Fairbridge Society	A	Sydney	Student	8	England
Hender. I.	Fairbridge Society	A	Sydney	Student	8	England
Done. M.	Fairbridge Society	A	Sydney	Student	8	England

Seventeen children on just two pages – what the hell was going on?

She spent the next couple of hours going through all the passengers on the SS Otranto for the voyage to Australia. It seemed most were migrant families heading out from England to Australia after the war in the assisted passage scheme. 'Ten Quid Poms', she remembered they were called. All looking for an escape from dreary post-war Britain and a new life in the sunshine and beaches of Australia.

But she counted twenty-seven children, some as young as four years old, travelling on the ship too. All sent by a variety of charities: Catholic orphanages, Fairbridge Schools, Barnado's, and the Church of England.

From the back of her mind came a vague memory of something Gordon Brown had said in 2009, or was it 2010? She hadn't paid much attention. At that time, her squad was in the middle of a homicide investigation in Moss Side; two rival drug gangs were fighting over turf, with one poor innocent bystander shot dead just because he happened to be in the wrong place at the wrong time. She had been working horrendous 20-hour days, dragging herself home to sleep for a few hours before going back to the nick once again. They got the bastards in the end, though. Put the shooter away for twenty years. Should have thrown away the key.

Quickly, she Googled Gordon Brown and child migrants. Within a second there appeared an article from BBC News on February 24, 2010:

The headline was very blunt: Gordon Brown Apologises to Child Migrants Sent Abroad.

...'To all those former child migrants and their families... we are truly sorry. They were let down. We are sorry they were allowed to be sent away at the time when they were most vulnerable. We are sorry that instead of caring for them, this country turned its back.

'And we are sorry that the voices of these children were not always heard, their cries for help not always heeded. And we are sorry that it has taken so long for this important day to come and for the full and unconditional apology that is justly deserved.'

Gordon Brown also said they were cruelly lied to and their childhoods 'robbed', and described the scheme as 'shameful' and 'a deportation of the innocents'.

More than 130,000 children, aged between three and 14, were sent to Commonwealth countries...

Jayne stared at the screen in shock. 'How come more people don't know about this?' She checked the figures again – 130,000 children sent to Commonwealth countries? She whistled audibly and the cat came running, thinking it was his lucky day; feeding time twice in one morning.

As she sat, staring at the screen, the phone rang beside her.

'Hi Jayne, it's Vera.'

'Hi there. There's some shocking news I've just discovered about Harry.'

'Me too, Jayne. He didn't go to Australia. My brother's found some other letters. He was adopted after all.'

Chapter Twenty-Nine

May 28, 1952

On-board the SS Otranto, Fremantle harbour, Western Australia

The land crept up on them slowly.

Harry first noticed a change in the crew. They were more active, rushing here and there as if hurrying for a party. Then he leaned over the gang rail and noticed the sea had changed colour from a deep ocean blue to a darker, greyer green. The birds arrived soon afterwards, squawking and crowing as they danced in the slipstream of the funnels.

It was Ginger who first spotted land not long after breakfast. A light smudge, like the smear of ash across the forehead during Easter. Gradually edging closer and revealing layers of colour, hill tops and the beginnings of miniature trees.

They hadn't seen land since they had left Ceylon almost two weeks ago. The boats had come out to greet them when they arrived in the port of Colombo, and the fare to go onshore had been one shilling and sixpence, or two rupees in local currency. Of course, none of them had any money, so at first they thought they couldn't go. Then Miss Anstey and her new friend, Mr Grey from the Fairbridge Society, decided to treat them all, Protestants and Catholics both. They had wandered round the markets and visited the temples, shrugged off the sellers of the carved wooden statues (even though Harry had wanted to buy one for his mum), and avoided the coloured ices because Miss Anstey said they were bad for your stomach.

But what Harry would always remember were the elephants. Now, he had seen pictures of them before, but nothing showed how big they were. When he stood next to one of them, he only came up to the top of its leg, the big, flapping ears wafting gently over his head.

Miss Anstey had given him a banana to feed to it. He started to peel the banana, but before he could even get it open, the trunk swung across and ripped it out of his hand, stuffing the banana into its gaping mouth, skin and all. Ginger and Ernie thought this was hilarious; an elephant who was bananas.

They walked around the town a little, seeing the local children playing in the street and even swimming in the dock. They didn't have much, those children – not even clothes, as they were often wearing nothing but a pair of shorts – but they seemed happy with big, beaming smiles.

Ernie tried to talk to them, but they all ran away. He was so big now, he even scared adults.

'Look, there's the town,' Ginger shouted now, as they leaned eagerly at the balustrade. 'It must be Fremantle.'

Miss Anstey joined them at the gang rail with Mr Grey. Harry noticed they were holding hands. He supposed that's what adults did when they liked each other. He hadn't seen much of either of them since leaving Colombo. Miss Anstey still came to tuck him in every night, but she did it quickly, not spending long in his cabin. Sometimes, she and Mr Grey even missed lunch and dinner – they must have been very hungry, Harry thought.

'Look, there's the harbour. I can see the derricks.' It was Ginger again. He had the best eyes of any of them. At night, they sometimes sat on the promenade deck and stared at the stars. It was always Ginger who pointed out the brightest ones shining down on them.

'Have you all packed your cases?' This was Miss Anstey.

They all nodded.

'Good. When we dock, we'll be met on the quay and one of the brothers will take you to your new home.'

'How long will we stay here, miss? I want to go home for my tea.'

Miss Anstey put her arm round Little Tom. 'This is your new home, Tom. Australia. It's my home too.'

'But what about England?'

'England's a long way away. You're stayin' here. Don't you get it? You're never going back.' This was Ernie at his most brutal.

Little Tom took one look at his face and shut up. There was no point arguing with Ernie.

The ship moved quickly up the channel and edged closer to the docks.

Miss Anstey shouted to all of them: 'Get your cases and follow me.'

Harry tried to slip past her. In the excitement, he had forgotten to say goodbye to Friedrich. But Mr Grey grabbed him by the collar. 'This is a slippy one, Claire, how do you keep track of him?'

'I don't, Alf.' She took Harry by the hand and led him back to the others and their waiting cases. 'You stay with me, Harry. Won't be long before we have to go ashore.'

165

The ship docked against the wharf, gave three toots on its whistle and, as if by magic, the gang-planks began to slide out from the ship to nestle against the harbour buildings.

'We're home,' said Miss Anstey.

Chapter Thirty

June 20, 2017
Eyam, Derbyshire, England

'After your last visit, I got to thinking.' Vera's brother slurped loudly from his cup of tea. 'I went through all of Mother's stuff. Dad put it in a couple of boxes before she died. I don't think he could bear looking at it.'

They were back in the cramped living room, surrounded by books, papers, clothes and all the other detritus of a man who never threw anything away. Jayne had picked up Vera and her father from Buxton before driving over to Eyam. This time, they had all declined the offer of tea. Once bitten, twice shy.

'Anyway, to cut a long story short, I found her old Bible. The one she carried with her. Wouldn't let it out of her sight.'

He produced the old, well-thumbed book. On the cover, the gold paint of the words had nearly vanished and the spine was beginning to crack. 'Anyway, I looked through it.' He opened the first page. Pasted on the right-hand side was an ornate frontispiece.

Presented to
Miss Freda Atkins
On 4th May 1933
To Commemorate her first Holy Communion

'She loved her Bible, she did,' said Vera sadly, remembering her mother before church on a Sunday, grasping the Bible in her white-gloved hand. 'Nobody else was allowed to touch it. Only her.'

Charlie took another slurp of tea. 'Are you sure you wouldn't like a cuppa?'

They all shook their heads.

'Anyway,' he began again, 'I held up the pages and shook it.'

'You thought there might be money inside, didn't you?'

Her brother's face went bright red. 'How could you say such a thing, Vera? I was only checking for you.'

'I know you too well, Charlie.'

'Well, if that's your attitude, you can—'

Jayne held up her hands. 'Can you two fight later?' Her voice softened, becoming emollient. 'What did you find, Mr Duckworth?'

'Two letters. They were hidden behind the cover. I thought they were just padding. You know how Bibles have that spongy feel to the covers...'

'But it wasn't,' said Jayne, interrupting him before he launched into a lengthy explanation of the different textures of Bible covers. 'Do you have them?'

He handed over the letters to her.

'Can you read them out?' It was the first time Jayne's father had spoken since they had arrived at Charlie's house. He seemed pale and tired. Perhaps all the travelling was getting to him, she thought.

Jayne opened the first letter of the two. 'It's from the Mother Superior of St Michael's Home in Oldham. It's dated May tenth, 1952, and is addressed to a Miss Duckworth.'

'But Mum was married then. Why didn't she use her married name?'

'Perhaps the home knew her as Miss Duckworth. After all, it was her name when she left Harry in their care.' This was Charlie speaking, before he slurped his tea loudly yet again.

Jayne coughed once and began to read the letter:

'Dear Miss Duckworth,

'Thank you for your letter dated May 5, 1952.

'I am sorry I was not available to see you when you visited St Michael's on Monday, May 2, but I'm sure you'll appreciate that running an orphanage with forty children is a time-consuming and difficult business, and we do not have time to speak with every parent who simply turns up at the door.

'Regarding Harold, I am very happy to inform you he has been adopted by a good Catholic family and taken into their loving arms. We are sure they will be able to provide the material, educational and spiritual guidance to create a better life. Before he left us to be with his new family, Harold expressed a desire to become a priest. We are sure, if he has a vocation, and with God's grace, this family will be able to help him secure his desire.

'Yours sincerely,

'Sister Mary

'Mother Superior.'

'I don't understand,' said Vera, shaking her head. 'David Beggs was sure Harry had gone to Australia. His parents told him Harry was a child migrant.'

'And I found a Harry Britton on the passenger list of the SS Otranto. The dates matched and the record said he was from St Michael's. But this letter says he was adopted. Both can't be right.'

'Read the other letter.' Charlie was pouring himself another cup of the brown, tar-like liquid he called tea.

Jayne frowned and unfolded the second letter. 'This one is dated June fourth, 1952, and it's addressed to your father, Vera.' She began reading:

'Dear Mr Atkins,

'Thank you for you letter of May 25, 1952.

'You may not be aware of all the relevant facts of the decision to put Harold up for adoption.

'He was placed in our home on March 28, 1945. Subsequently, he was fostered to the Beggs family in 1947, as it was felt he would benefit from being in a caring family environment. In September 1951, the Beggses returned him to us. From that date until his adoption in May 1952, we note that your wife only visited him once according to our visitor's book and we have no record of any visit after New Year. We had no letter from Miss Duckworth in that time explaining her absences, nor was any money forwarded to maintain Harold's upkeep.

'This was an act of deliberate desertion and it was evident that someone had to assume parental rights and act on the child's behalf. Rather than be upset, your wife should consider herself fortunate. Harold has been adopted by a loving, Catholic family and will enjoy a far healthier and brighter future than she could possibly give him.

'I enclose a copy of the document your wife signed when she gave the young Harold over to us. As you can see, it makes it explicit that his future wellbeing is in our, and God's, care.

'I would warn you against making any attempt to retrieve him. He has settled into a new life and is very happy. Any attempt to remove him would be detrimental to his health and wellbeing.

'Yours sincerely,

'Sister Mary

'Mother Superior.'

'The bastards, how dare they accuse my mother of neglect? What were the words she used?' Vera took the letter. '"Deliberate desertion". Mum was making money to give Harry a better life, to get him back one day.'

Jayne shook her head. 'I don't understand. I was certain the person I found this morning was Harry. Everything matched up. It had to be him.'

Jayne looked at the second sheet, attached to the letter with a rusted staple. It was a carbon copy in light blue of a document dated March 28, 1945. 'This looks like the paper they made Freda sign when she placed Harry in the home.'

Regarding Harold Britton, born August 25, 1944.

I am presently unmarried and was unmarried at the time of the conception and birth of said child. Because of the circumstances of birth and having in mind the best interests of said child, I hereby agree to permanently surrender care, custody and parental authority over said child to the Sisters of Mercy.

It is agreed that the Sisters of Mercy shall have the sole and exclusive guardianship of said child and the right to place him/her in a foster home and to consent in court to his/her adop-

tion. It is further agreed that the undersigned will not induce him/her to leave the institution or family with whom he/she might be placed.

I will contribute ten shillings and sixpence (10/6) each week to the said child's upkeep and maintenance whilst he/she remains in the care and the management of the Sisters of Mercy.

I agree and pledge not to interfere with the custody, control, care or management of said child in any way or encourage or allow anyone else to do so.

Signed by Freda Duckworth.
Witnessed by Sister Mary, Mother Superior, St Michael's Home for Orphans, Oldham, Lancashire.

Jayne sighed. 'It looks like she had no rights. This allows the nuns carte blanche to do what they want with Harry.'

'She never told me she used to pay them money every week. No wonder we were always broke,' said Vera.

'It was a lot of money back then, was ten and six, love. I think I was only earning three quid a week back then and I had a skill.'

Vera was silent for a long time, biting her bottom lip, before she said, 'Perhaps that's why my mum and dad gave up. The nuns didn't want their money any more as he was already placed in a good home.'

'What do we do next, Jayne?' asked her father.

She thought for a moment. 'Two things. First, if he was adopted then we can file for the adoption papers to find out where he was sent and which family adopted him.'

'What's the second thing to do, Jayne?'

'What we should have done in the first place. Contact the Catholic Church and find out exactly what documents they have on Harry.'

'Perhaps they have nothing?' said her father.

'It's a chance we have to take, Dad. But we have to work this out. We have to find out what happened to Harry.'

Chapter Thirty-One

May 28, 1952
Fremantle, Western Australia

They all trooped down the gangplank in twos – the Astley sisters in the lead, followed by Little Tom and Harry, then came Ernie and Ginger and, in the rear, Miss Anstey with Fred and Georgie.

Harry glanced back at the ship. Friedrich was standing at the gang rail in his oily overalls, a wry smile on his face. Harry waved goodbye. Friedrich turned towards the funnels and pointed upwards. The whistle gave three long toots and a cloud of white smoke billowed from the ship.

Harry laughed as Friedrich gave him the thumbs-up sign.

'Come along, children.' Miss Anstey chivvied them along. Harry noticed her eyes were red, as if she had been crying. Where was Mr Grey? He was there on the promenade deck surrounded by the Fairbridge children, still on the ship.

Harry felt an arm on his shoulder.

'Move along, hurry up.' It was Miss Anstey pushing them into a large high-ceilinged warehouse. Queues of passengers formed in front of desks with uniformed men sitting behind them. The families who had been on-board were lined up, presenting their passports and documents.

Miss Anstey led the children to one side. 'This way, children.'

They were faced with a stern-looking man in a blue uniform, with sideburns stretching to touch the side of his mouth.

'You lot the Catholics?'

'We are,' Miss Anstey answered.

'How many?' he said, looking down at his clipboard.

'Eight.'

'Small group today. Still, the bishop has turned out to greet you,' he sniffed.

'Can you take us to him?'

'Will do. But first you need them to line up in front of Terry at the desk.'

She hurried them forward. Harry and Little Tom were first now.

'Hold out your right hand.'

'Why?' asked Harry, worried this man was going to punish them, like the sisters, with a ruler across the knuckles.

'You got to be fingerprinted.' His accent was strange, like he had a bunch of marbles in his mouth and everything was a question.

'Why?'

'It's the law. Hold out your hand?'

Harry did as he was told, followed by Little Tom. The officer grabbed his hand, dabbed all four fingers in an ink-soaked blue pad and rolled them across a form. Then he took Harry's thumb and repeated the procedure.

'You're done. Wait over there?' He pointed to a place past the table next to a noticeboard.

They stood there whilst the other children had their fingerprints taken.

'I thought they only did it to thieves and robbers,' said Little Tom.

Harry shrugged his shoulders. 'Dunno, maybe it's what they do in Australia.' He tried to wipe the blue ink off his fingers by rubbing them against his trousers.

'But none of them are having their fingerprints taken.'

The other families who had been on-board the ship were having their documents stamped and being ushered into separate lines marked 'Onward Travel' and 'Perth'.

'Is it because we're Catholics?'

'Don't think so.'

The boys from Fairbridge had also disembarked and were now having their fingerprints taken at the table next to theirs. Miss Anstey had taken the opportunity to chat with Mr Grey. Her eyes were red again.

They were gradually joined by the other children from the home, all trying to get rid of the blue ink. Finally, Miss Anstey gathered them together. Harry noticed she didn't have any blue ink on her fingers.

'Now, children, we are going to meet a very important man. You must be on your best behaviour.' She went around the group, tidying them up. 'Straighten up your jacket, Ginger. Don't forget to put on your cap, Harry.' All the time, wiping her red eyes with her handkerchief.

She led them down a corridor into a vast open area. Beneath a sign marked 'Bindoon' and another marked 'Castledare', a white-haired man in a black skirt, purple sash and purple skull-cap stood, his hands clasped in front of him as if in prayer. Behind him were two nuns and three brothers dressed in black cassocks. Behind them was a crowd of people, some with cameras in their hands, others with note-books.

Harry felt his hand being grabbed by Little Tom. 'I'm scared, Harry.'

'Don't worry, Tom, it'll soon be over.'

The white-haired man stepped forward towards Miss Anstey, his hand outstretched, palm downwards. 'Welcome to Australia.'

She nodded and made a little curtsey with her legs, bending forward to kiss the large, red ring on the man's index finger but saying nothing.

'Archbishop, can we get a picture of you with the orphans?'

'Of course you can, of course, but I'd just like to say a few words to welcome the poor children to our wonderful country first.' He held up his hands for quiet. The reporters raised their notebooks to make sure they reported his words correctly. 'Don't worry about getting it all down. Brother Michael here has it all typed out for you. And afterwards, there will be a few sandwiches and bottles of beer. I know reporting is a very hungry, and thirsty, profession.'

The men in front of him laughed in unison.

Harry and the rest of the children stood holding their cases. Miss Anstey had her head down, looking at the ground.

The Archbishop brought his hands together as if in prayer. Harry noticed the skin on his face was smooth and shiny, with a slight red glow to the cheeks.

When the Archbishop began speaking, the words came out full and loud. 'We are gathered to welcome some orphans from the towns and cities of England.'

I'm not an orphan, Harry thought, but decided to say nothing.

The Archbishop continued. 'At a time when empty cradles are contributing woefully to empty spaces, it is necessary to look for external sources of supply. And if we don't supply from our own stock, we are leaving ourselves all the more exposed to the menace of the teeming millions of our neighbouring Asiatic races. In no part of Australia is settlement more vital than for Western Australia, which, while it contributes only one twelfth of the total population, occupies one third of our whole Commonwealth...'

He paused for a moment to brush a fly away, which had been buzzing around his face. One of the sisters stepped forward to help him. Finally he continued. 'The policy at present adopted of bringing out young boys and girls and training them from the beginning in agricultural and domestic methods, has the additional advantage of acclimatising them from the outset to Australian conditions and imbuing them with Australian sentiments and Australian ideals – the essential marks of true citizenship.'

The fly returned with added ferocity. The sister stepped forward and swatted it with her sheaf of notes.

'So, it is with great pleasure that I welcome these young men and women to Australia. I am certain that, in the future, under the considered guardianship of the good Christian brothers and the Sisters of Mercy, they will become good Catholics, good Australians and good members of our society. Thank you all, and may God bless you.'

'Archbishop, could we have a picture of you with the orphans?'

'Of course, where would you like me to stand?'

'Where you are is perfect for the shot. We'll just gather all the orphans around you, with the liner in the background.'

Harry felt Miss Anstey's arm on his shoulder. He put his case on the ground and walked over to where the bishop was standing. He was soon joined by the others as they formed a circle around the man.

Harry could smell the strong odour of cologne as he stood near the Archbishop, the purple sash shining next to his head.

'Smile, kids,' shouted one of the photographers.

As the flashbulbs went off, Harry blinked. The light was too bright. Somehow, the image of the photographers, the reporters, the brothers and sisters, and the white-haired man in his purple sash, was imprinted on the inside of his eyelids. He only had to close his eyes and he could see it again, a frozen moment in time.

'Can you be part of the group too?' one of the photographers shouted at Miss Anstey. She walked over to stand behind Harry, resting her hands on his shoulders.

The lightbulbs went off again and again. When they had finished, the photographer who had shouted took her aside. 'Can we do one with you and a child? Human interest, you know.'

She stood close to Harry once more, hands on his shoulders as the lightbulbs flashed, taking shots of just her and him.

'Thanks, miss. Your name is…?'

'Claire Anstey from Perth.'

He wrote in his notebook. 'And the kid?'

'My name's Harry from Oldham.'

'Okay, Harry from Oldham. Welcome to God's Own.'

When they had finished all the photographs, and Miss Anstey had received her blessing from the Archbishop, the man departed into a large black car parked next to the quay.

As soon as he had gone, the reporters and photographers hurried away to find their sandwiches and beer, leaving the children with Miss Anstey, the three brothers and the two sisters.

One of the brothers started shouting out names. 'June and Doris Astley.'

The two sisters raised their hands.

'Go with Sister Anastasia to St Joseph's.'

'Can't we stay with the boys?' said June.

'Of course not. There are boys' homes and girls' homes. We don't believe the mixing of sexes to be beneficial to the young mind.' He glanced down at his clipboard. 'Keith Jones, Fred Whatmough, George Rice.' These three boys put their hands up more slowly this time. 'You must go with Brother Michael to Castledare.'

'I don't wanna go with 'em. I wanna stay with Ernie and Harry.'

'You are going to Castledare. They are going to Bindoon, to the Boys Town,' he said forcefully.

'I wanna go to the Boys Town, too.'

'Can't they all go together?' Miss Anstey said. 'They've become such good friends on the ship and they all come from the same home.'

'I'm afraid not. We don't have room for everybody to remain together. I'm sure you understand, Miss Anstey, that space is at a premium.' He placed his hand on Ginger's shoulder. 'The two places are not far apart. You'll be able to see each other on Sundays. And maybe we'll be able to move you later.'

'It's time for me to go now, children,' said Miss Anstey brightly, changing the subject.

She gave each of them a hug, saving a special long embrace for Harry. 'I'm going to miss you,' she whispered in his ear.

'Me too,' he replied, holding up Trevor for her to kiss.

One of the brothers stepped in. 'If we don't leave now, Miss Anstey, we'll be late for dinner at Bindoon.'

She stepped back. 'Of course, Brother.'

Harry felt his hand being taken and he was led to an old bus with Ernie and Little Tom.

As the bus drove away, he watched Miss Anstey waving to him, mouthing the words 'Goodbye, I'll miss you'. He didn't see Ginger, Fred, Georgie, or the Astley sisters. They had already vanished.

Chapter Thirty-Two

June 23, 2017
Salford, Manchester, England

It didn't take long for Jayne to find out where to go. Oldham was part of the Roman Catholic diocese of Salford and all records were available by contacting the Caritas Centre in the Cathedral Close.

When she rang, the phone was immediately answered by a confident, professional voice. 'Caritas, how can I help?'

Jayne explained the situation; her client's half-brother may have been adopted from St Michael's or he may have been sent out as a child migrant.

'Well, you are able to access the records but obviously we would have to check your identity and that of the relative first.'

'Why's that?'

'We are committed to confidentiality. These persons may still be alive, and it would be wrong for us to simply give out their past records to anybody. We have a duty of care to them and to their records.'

Jayne thought about it for a moment. 'Yes, of course.'

'Plus they may have put a veto on the records.'

'A veto?'

'Some adoptees do not what to be contacted. They may not be ready to meet their birth mother or relatives, or have simply moved on, leaving the past behind. Either way, if there is a veto in place, I'm afraid we can't release the records.'

'I understand.'

'Now, when can you come in for an appointment?'

'Do we have to come in?'

'No, the process can be completed by mail, but we always advise all those seeking adoption records to sit down with us. Sometimes the process can be unsettling, and even traumatic. We provide services to support both parties through this time.'

'I think that may be for the future. At the moment, we just want to find out the records the church holds on my client's relative.'

'Nonetheless, we would have to check your identity and that of your client. A simple photo ID would be sufficient, preferably a passport. Now when can I pencil you in? I have a spot free tomorrow at three o'clock.'

The following day, Jayne picked up Vera and drove to Salford. Her father wasn't feeling well and wanted to say in Buxton to rest.

'Shall I get a doctor to see you, Dad?'

'No, no, not at all.' Her father, like many people of his generation, had a morbid fear of 'troubling' doctors with minor ailments, preferring to suffer in silence. 'I'll be okay, just under the weather a little, that's all. You two go off and I'll rest here.'

'Are you sure, Dad?'

'Positive. I know when I'm tired.' He ran his fingers through his thinning hair. 'Anyway, I don't really want to go back there. Brings back too many memories.'

'What do you mean, Dad? I don't understand.'

Robert let out a long sigh. 'You know my dad was born in the area?'

'Salford?'

'Just off Chapel Street, not far from the cathedral. Right rough it were in the twenties. Tenements, back-to-back houses, a pub on every corner. You should read "Love on the Dole" if you want to know how it was. Policemen used to walk around in threes. It wasn't much '

'I'm sure it's different now – that was a long time ago, Robert. Times change, you know,' said Vera.

Times may have changed, but as Jayne saw very quickly, the area had not.

The Catholic cathedral still stood; solid and imposing, a rock of solidity in the world. But the surrounding area was going through the process euphemistically known as 'urban renewal', which involved knocking down the existing houses and widening all the roads so commuters could stream past to their homes in the suburbs without seeing the dereliction of the inner city.

All that was left were the shells of derelict pubs and shops, acres of waste-ground strewn with rubbish, and pothole-pitted side roads. A situation guaranteed to remain until a developer recognised the area was due for gentrification, and decided it was time to build some new apartments.

The whole place had the feeling that an urban war had been taking place. A war on communities and the human spirit.

Luckily, the welcome they both received from the woman at the Caritas Centre was warm and typically northern; honest, down-to-earth and friendly. Jayne liked her immediately. After checking their identification, Jayne produced Harry's birth certificate, which had arrived in the post that morning. 'This is the man we are looking for. He was placed in St Michael's as a young child.'

There was some difficulty explaining the discrepancies in the name of the birth mother with that of Vera, but Jayne showed the woman the letters and the birth certificates. After taking photocopies, she was happy to proceed.

'We do have some records from St Michael's during this period – I have worked on one other case there. But the records are spotty, so I would like to manage your expectations. The nuns at the time were overworked and sometimes they were not as diligent in their record-keeping as they should have been. However, if he was adopted as the letter suggests, then we should have some records to show where he was placed. If he was part of the child migration scheme, there is a central registry in London of all child migrants sent abroad by Catholic agencies during this period.'

'How long will it take?' asked Vera.

'We'll be as quick as we can, but I should remind you if there is a veto on the documents, we will not be able to release them.'

'That means the person has decided he doesn't want to meet any relatives, is that right?' asked Vera.

The woman nodded.

'What do we do then?'

'I'm afraid it means that Caritas cannot release any documents unless the adoptee removes the veto.'

Jayne stood up and held out her hand. 'Thank you for your time. You've been very helpful.'

'Please contact us if you require anything else. I'll let you know if I am sending any documents to you. In the meantime, here are a few brochures explaining the process and also some advice on the support services we provide for families.'

Vera took the documents. 'What do we do now, Jayne?' she asked as they were leaving the building.

'We wait, Vera, it's all we can do.'

Vera sighed. 'It's been over sixty years, I guess I can wait a few more weeks.'

Chapter Thirty-Three

May 28, 1952

St Joseph's Farm and Trade School, Bindoon, Western Australia

The bus had been driving across the same parched, dry landscape for nearly three hours before they came in sight of Bindoon Boys Town. The driver had stopped on top of the ridge overlooking it to let them view their new home.

Below them, a group of beige stone buildings nestled in the valley, one topped with a small dome. Others still had scaffolding surrounding and supporting them. Harry could see children climbing like zealous ants across the half-completed buildings. What were they doing?

Around the buildings, there were the beginnings of an orchard and a vineyard. Off to the right, along the ridge, a statue of Christ the Redeemer glared down on the buildings and the people below.

The driver turned round in his seat and faced them. 'My name's Brother Dawe, and that—' he pointed down to the buildings below, 'that's going to be your home for the next few years, my lovelies. Here, we're going to make men of you.'

Brother Dawe put the bus in gear and raced down the drive, through the gates and up to the main building with its distinctive dome.

A tall, thick-set man with a mop of white hair and a sharp aquiline nose was waiting for them, warming his hands in front of a brazier. He was wearing a khaki outfit that was almost soldier-like, with high boots laced up till just below his knee.

'That's Brother Keaney, he's the head of the home,' said Brother Dawe. 'A word in your English ears. I wouldn't cross him if I were you. He knows how to deal with miscreant boys.'

As the bus screeched to a halt beside Brother Keaney, Harry noticed the long, thick stick resting against the metal of the brazier.

They all picked up their suitcases and piled off the bus.

Brother Keaney scanned them up and down. 'A sorry shower of shit, Brother. Couldn't you do any better?' The accent was Irish, like a cow chewing its cud and speaking at the same time.

'Sorry, Father, there were only eight Catholics bound for Fremantle on the ship, and three of the boys were already down for Castledare.'

Brother Keaney sniffed. He reached out and squeezed Ernie's bicep. 'This one looks like he could do a spot of work. Have you done any of the building, boy?'

Ernie shook his head.

'Well, I'm sure you're going to find out how.'

'What time is dinner?' Ernie asked.

Brother Keaney laughed. 'Oh, you've missed dinner. But you still have time to help the lads over there before you say your rosary and we switch off the lights.'

He pointed to a half-constructed building on the left. A group of boys were laying the roof, while others carried hods laden with tiles up to them, all supervised by one of the monks sitting on a barrel below.

188

'Now, leave your cases here and change into these.' He handed each of them a dirty khaki shirt and a pair of shorts.

'Where's the changing room?' asked Little Tom.

'Sure, you're standing in it.' Brother Keaney pointed to the ground with his stick.

'Here?'

'As good as anywhere. Hurry along now, my Biddies, you don't want to catch your death of the cold.'

Ernie began to undo his jacket and shirt, folding them neatly and laying them on his case. He was followed by Harry and Little Tom.

'Hurry along there, you heard Brother Keaney,' chivvied Brother Dawe.

Eventually, all three were stood in their vest and shorts in front of their neatly folded piles of clothes from Afflecks in Manchester. Ernie began to pull the dirty khaki shirt over his head.

'No, no – not like that, my Biddies. We don't believe in skivvies in Bindoon. Our lads are tough not namby-pambys.'

'You mean, take off my vest and underpants too?' asked Harry.

'We have a bright one here, Brother Dawe, even if he looks a wee bit young. He's going to go far in Bindoon. That's exactly what I meant, young lad.'

It was Ernie who went first again, pulling off his vest and putting on the dirty old shirt. Then slowly, reluctantly, he let his underpants drop to the ground and pulled on the shorts, all the time watched by Brother Dawe.

The others followed him.

'And the boots too. We don't want to be wearing our good boots on the building, do we?'

They all took off their shoes and socks, laying them next to the suitcases.

'Good, looks like you're ready for a bit of graft. Brother Dawe, show them where the work is.'

Harry reached down, took his soldier out of his case and stuffed it into the pocket of his shorts.

'What do we have here?' Brother Keaney used the metal tip of his stick to prod the guardsmen sticking out of Harry's pocket.

'It's my soldier. Mum gave him to me for my birthday.'

'Let me look at it.'

Harry hesitated for a moment. Brother Keaney held out his hand.

'You heard the brother,' said Dawe.

The stick began to raise threateningly.

Harry reached into his pocket and passed Trevor across to Brother Keaney. The man peered at it down his long, straight nose. 'We don't abide with such baubles in Bindoon. You're here to become a man, not to play with toys.' He tossed the soldier on to the brazier, where it lay still on the coals for a few moments before being engulfed by flames.

'You—!' Harry lunged forward, only to met by the point of the stick driving into his chest.

'You have work to do before you say your prayers. Show them where it is, Brother Dawe.'

'This way, you lot.'

All three of them were hustled across the yard to where the boys were laying the roof. Harry took one last look at Brother Keaney warming his hands in front of the glowing embers of his soldier, the orange light dancing across his face.

The man looked happy.

Chapter Thirty-Four

May 28, 1952
St Joseph's Farm and Trade School, Bindoon, Western Australia

That evening, Harry lay in his bed, his stomach empty. Brother Keaney had been as good as his word; there had been nothing to eat. They had worked in Brother Thomas's gang, helping to put the final touches to the roof of a new kitchen block. Harry and Little Tom were told to stack the roof tiles on the hods ready for the older boys, who were aged around 12, to carry them up the ladder to the even older boys, aged 14, who were laying them on the roof, guided by the oldest boy, a strapping lad called Peter, who was 15.

'No, no, do it like the other boys.' Brother Thomas waved his hand in front of his face, warding off a particularly aggressive fly. 'Show them how it's done, Henderson.'

A tall boy, taller than Harry, detached himself from the group waiting to ascend the solitary ladder. Carefully, he placed the hod he was carrying down on the ground, making sure he didn't break any of the precious tiles. After trotting over to see them, he knelt on the red dust and began moving the tiles from the pile beneath the tarpaulin on to an empty hod. 'See, lay the first one in the corner, and then stack the rest

191

on alternate sides until you reach the top. We'll come over every time we've taken the tiles up to the roof and give you the empty hods. Got it?'

Both Harry and Little Tom nodded.

'It's pretty easy once you get the hang of it, but don't let old Thomas see you slacking. He's pretty quick with the strap. My name's Slimo, by the way.' He put out his hand and smiled, his bright white teeth standing out against the tanned face and freckled nose.

Harry shook the proffered hand. 'Been here long?'

'A couple of years. You'll get used to it. We all do.'

Harry stared at Slimo's feet, caked in dust and dirt, the soles covered in thick black skin like the hide of the elephants in Ceylon. 'Don't we ever wear shoes?'

'Not for the building. Unless we have visitors, of course. Then we have to put them on. I prefer—'

'Don't dawdle, boy,' shouted Brother Thomas from his place on the barrel beneath the tree.

Instantly, Slimo picked up the hod he had stacked and raced over to join the back of the queue of boys waiting to go up the ladder.

They carried on working until the sun had nearly set, then they were shown the dormitory where they were going to sleep.

'When you've finished, say your rosary, at least one complete round.'

One by one the boys knelt down by the side of their beds and began mumbling to themselves, their fingers working the beads.

Brother Thomas strolled up and down the central aisle between the beds, hands clasped behind his back, his sandals making a strange swishing noise as they scraped along the wooden floor.

'No talking during prayers.' There was the sound of a strap flying through the air, followed by the slap as it landed across a boy's shoulders.

Harry and Little Tom had been given places side by side at the end of the dormitory. They knelt down beside their beds, imitating the others, but neither had a set of rosary beads.

'You'll be given the rosary beads tomorrow after Mass, as long as you are good,' a voice whispered in his ear. It was Brother Thomas.

Harry could feel the man's breath on his temple; a warm puff of air with a slightly sour smell, like milk that had just curdled. He didn't turn his head as he heard the swish of the sandals on the wooden floor.

Before they had finished saying their prayers, the lights went out. The place was in complete darkness. A voice, that of Brother Thomas, rang out in the blackness.

'No talking. No getting out of your beds. And no bed-wetting. You know what happens to boys who wet the bed.'

The door closed and the room remained quiet, just the occasional squeak of the bed springs as a boy turned over in his sleep.

Even in the darkest of nights at St Michael's, Harry had never felt so alone.

He curled up into a ball, holding his hands together under his chin. He missed the warmth of Trevor, it was the one thing that held him close and protected him during the long hours of the night. The image of the red coat of his soldier burning brightly in the brazier as the brother held his hands over it, warming them, came back to him. Why did he have to burn Trevor?

Harry curled himself even tighter, trying to bury himself into the cold embrace of the thin mattress.

He was small.

He was alone.

He was scared.

A great wave of fear rose in his gullet and he felt himself choking down a sob that was trying to escape from his mouth.

He mustn't cry.

He mustn't cry.

From the neighbouring bed, he heard the muffled sounds of sobbing. It was Little Tom.

A whisper from across the gangway. 'Don't cry. Don't let them hear you cry.'

It was Slimo, whispering to Little Tom.

The door opened and a shaft of yellow light shone into the dormitory. It stayed there for a moment before becoming gradually smaller as the door was closed.

'You mustn't cry,' Slimo whispered again.

'I want to go home,' Little Tom answered.

'We all do, but you mustn't cry. It's not allowed.'

Little Tom was quieter from then on. Or perhaps he found a way to stifle his tears beneath the thin army blanket. Harry heard nothing more, except the occasional opening and closing of the door, and once, the swishing of Brother Thomas's sandals against the floor.

For a minute, they stopped at the end of his bed, before moving away.

Chapter Thirty-Five

May 29, 1952
St Joseph's Farm and Trade School, Bindoon, Western Australia

The following morning, they were awoken by Slimo just as light began to stain the sky.

'Up, get up, he'll be here in a minute.'

Harry followed the others slowly waking up, getting out of bed and folding their thin, rough blankets. One boy stayed asleep, his face bright red.

Slimo raced over to shake him awake. 'Bert, get up, he'll be here in a minute.'

The sleeping boy's mouth flapped uselessly for a few moments before he finally croaked. 'Can't, Slimo... crook... hot.'

The door opened and Brother Thomas slowly entered.

Slimo raced back to the side of his own bed.

The brother stood there in his brown habit, the rosary and strap swaying at his waist where they hung off his belt. His hair was a bright orange and tousled, like it hadn't been combed for a thousand years.

A slow, smug smile spread across his face, his hands rested on his hips and he stood in the entrance, savouring every moment.

All the boys stared straight ahead, not daring to catch his eye.

He walked slowly down the central aisle to the end of the dormitory, his sandals making that swishing sound that ended with a sharp slap. At the end, he turned and stood there, looking back at all the boys still standing at the end of their beds, before walking slowly down the aisle back to the door.

Swish... slap.

Swish... slap.

Swish... slap.

At the front of the dormitory, the hands went to his hips again and he nodded his head sagely. 'It looks like we have a lazy one this morning.'

The boys didn't say a word.

'But first let's deal with the bed-wetters, shall we?'

At each bunk, he stared at the boy standing at the end of it, and then leant over, placing his broad, meaty palm down on the frayed sheet.

If it was dry, he simply shook his head and moved on to the next bed. If it was wet, he said quietly, 'You know what to do, boy.'

The boy would then take off his nightshirt and drape the soiled wet sheet around his shoulders and body, returning to the end of his bed. After finding three boys in this way, he reached Harry.

'A new boy from England.'

'From Oldham, sir.'

'I don't care. What number were you given yesterday?'

'Number?'

His eyes rolled up into his head. 'By Brother Keaney. It's on your shorts.'

'Forty-seven, sir.'

'Well, forty-seven, are you a bed-wetter?'

'No, sir, never. I'm eight.'

Brother Thomas nodded his head, leant forward, placed all his weight on his palms and leant into the thin mattress, staring all the time at Harry. The bed squeaked and groaned as if feeling its age as well as the weight.

The man checked his palm, touching it with the fingers of the same hand before wiping it on the side of his brown habit.

Without saying a word, he moved on to Little Tom's bed next door.

Harry could see Little Tom was shaking; his foot tapping continuously on the wooden floor and his hands trembling against the coarse fabric of the nightgown. His eyes were red and wet, his hair damp with sweat.

'Another fresh arrival from England. What's your name, boy?'

'Tom... T-Thomas Livesey, sir,' he finally blurted out.

'And your number?'

Little Tom turned towards him.

'Look straight ahead, boy.'

'I dunno.'

'You dunno,' mimicked Brother Thomas.

Before Harry could move, the strap came up and lashed across Little Tom's shoulders, knocking him to the floor.

'You should know your number. Learn it by to-morrow. Or face twelve from me. Get up, you're dirtying the floor.'

Little Tom struggled to his feet.

'Are you a bed-wetter, Livesey?'

Little Tom's lips began to work against each other. He swallowed twice and tried to answer, but nothing came out.

Another smile crossed Brother Thomas's face. He touched the sheet gently with his right palm and said softly, 'It seems you are. You know what to do.'

Little Tom's whole body seemed to shake and tremble as he lifted the nightshirt over his head. Brother Thomas tore the wet sheet from the bed and threw it over the young boy's head.

'Come with me.'

He strode off, followed by the boys in two neat lines.

Harry stood next to Slimo.

'Don't say anything, it only makes it worse,' Slimo whispered out of the corner of his mouth.

They marched down the stairs and across to the bath house.

'The bed-wetters first,' ordered the brother.

The three others knew what to do. They stood in front of the shower heads, still with the sheets draped over their shoulders.

'You too.' He signalled to Little Tom.

Still shaking and trembling, the small boy stood in front of a shower head.

'Next time, you won't be so keen to wet the bed.'

He turned on the cold taps to full force. The shower head erupted with water, forcing Little Tom to step back. The sheet was drenched and his body froze under the stream of icy water. Pretty soon all of them had hands and lips beginning to turn blue. Little Tom's skin took on the quality of the paper the sisters used to write their notes. Across his chest, translucent blue veins stood out against the bones of his ribs.

Brother Thomas finally turned off the taps. 'Now it's time for the rest of you.' He adjusted the water so it was slightly warmer.

All the boys began removing their nightshirts as Brother Thomas looked on.

'Come on, forty-seven, time for your shower.' A flick of a damp towel hurried Harry along, catching him on the calf.

Harry quickly took off his nightshirt and joined the rest of them in the shower. Twenty-two boys all washing together.

'Enough, time for breakfast. I don't know about you boys but I'm famished. Get dressed and I will see you in the dining room.' He strode off, out of the bath house, whistling 'Danny Boy' as the sun was rising over the surrounding hills.

Harry rushed over to Little Tom. 'You okay?'

The young boy nodded.

'I'll get the bastard. Don't you worry, one day I'll get him.'

Chapter Thirty-Six

May 31, 1952
St Joseph's Farm and Trade School, Bindoon, Western Australia

Breakfast was the stodgy porridge Harry was used to back in St Michael's and, somehow, had grown to like. It had the texture and consistency of wallpaper paste but at least it was warm and filled him up.

Little Tom had grown soft on the voyage, missing his orange juice and toast in bed brought by Arthur, the jovial waiter from Goa. He threw his spoon against the metal plate, making a loud clatter.

All the other boys stopped mid-spoonful, their mouths open wide.

A voice from the monks' table echoed through the refectory. 'Pick up your spoon and finish your porridge.'

Tom stood up. 'Please, sir, I can't.'

The sound of a chair being scraped back.

The ominous slap of leather sandals on wooden floorboards.

The silence of the boys as they kept their heads down and stared into the brown-grey swamp lying on their plates.

A brown habit arrived at the table. 'Brother Paul has cooked this porridge for you. It is a gift from God. Eat it.'

'Please, sir, I can't,' Tom repeated.

A large hand gripped the back of Little Tom's head, forcing it down towards the metal plate.

Tom's hands went out to grip the sides of the table, but the Brother was too strong. His head was forced closer and closer to the porridge. And then Tom's strength gave in and his head landed in the lumpy mass.

Harry expected Tom to get up. His face would be covered in porridge. They would all laugh and that would be the end of it.

But Tom didn't get up.

His head was being pressed down into the plate by the thick, white hand.

Tom's arms went out to the sides, trying to push himself away. But still the hand pressed his head down.

Porridge oozed up the side of his face, covering the bottom of his ears. His legs kicked out straight and then began to struggle.

Still the hand pressed his head down into the claggy wet glue.

Harry looked up. Ernie had picked up a spoon lying on the table and drove the edge down hard into the back of the hand. The brother screamed, letting go of Little Tom's head.

The boy's head rose up, his mouth gasping for breath like a drowned man brought back to life, lumps of porridge stuck to his cheeks and nose.

The monk glared at Ernie and then at the bloody gash left by the edge of the spoon. He raised his hand and smashed Ernie across the face with all the force he could muster.

Ernie went flying across the polished floor, slamming into a wall and lying there, unmoving.

The monk removed the strap from around his waist where it sat next to the rosary. He advanced, slowly, deliberately, to where Ernie's prone body lay. 'It's your time, Wattie,' he snarled.

Only later did Harry realise, after he had tasted its bite a few times, that 'Wattie' was the name this monk gave to his strap. A pet name for the thing he loved most.

The habit of the monk loomed over Ernie's prone body. The leather strap rose into the air, paused for a moment as if looking for the perfect place to strike, then snapped down like a snake into Ernie's bare arm.

Up and down it went. The swishing sound it made was almost musical in its rhythm, across Ernie's arms, back and legs.

And then the kicking started.

Ernie curled up into a ball but the brother's sandals kicked his back again and again, a sickening thud resounding through the dining room each time the sandals struck home.

Finally, a voice from the podium. 'Enough, Brother Dominic, we will punish him properly in front of all the boys this evening.'

Brother Dominic brought the strap down on to Ernie's body one last time. Sweat dripped from his head, blood dripped from his hand. There was a madness in his eyes Harry had never seen before and never wanted to see again.

Brother Dominic stared at Harry.

For a short while, he stared back, before eventually looking down at a small stained space on the floor between his bare feet.

The monk then glared at each boy on the table in turn, forcing them to look away, one after the other.

Ernie went into hospital that afternoon after complaining of chest pains when carrying the tiles up to the roof.

He came back two weeks later but he was never the same again. The brothers had kicked whatever spirit remained out of Ernie's body.

He was transferred to another home at the end of November.

Out of sight. Out of mind. Out of luck.

Chapter Thirty-Seven

July 15, 2017
Buxton Residential Home, Derbyshire, England

The nondescript brown envelope was delivered by the postman at ten o'clock. Jayne signed for it and knew instantly what it was. Vera had been waiting none too patiently for the last three weeks.

Despite being in the middle of a new case – investigating the family background of a very well-known and very blonde TV presenter who had just done a DNA test only to find that one of her recent ancestors came from Africa – Jayne drove straight out to Buxton without opening the package.

She arrived to find the Matron waiting in the lobby.

'Nice to see you again, Jayne,' she said, in her broad Glaswegian accent. 'Vera's waiting for you in the garden. She's been on edge, what with Robert and all.'

'How is Dad?'

'About the same, no improvement really. We're still waiting for the test results. But I'll leave him to tell you himself.'

Jayne wandered through the living room on her way to the garden. As usual, the 'Golden Girls', as her dad called them, were sat together watching Cash in the Attic on TV.

'It's not worth nowt, should throw it away.'

'How do you know, Maisie Grimes? It might be worth a fortune.'

'No Toby jug is worth money, Ethel, they made millions of them.'

'Ooooh, look at that…'

Jayne hurried through before finding out what Ethel liked. Vera and her dad were waiting in their usual place in the garden. This time her father was looking very pale and, despite it being the height of summer, wore a jacket and had a blanket over his knees.

Vera looked up as soon as Jayne walked through the patio doors.

'It's arrived, hasn't it?'

Jayne nodded, handing the envelope over to her.

Even her father seemed to find some extra energy, leaning forward in his chair.

Vera's hands hovered over the top of the envelope. 'I don't think I can open it.' She held out her hand and Jayne could see it was shaking. 'I haven't been this nervous since I said "I do" to your dad.'

Her father touched the back of Vera's hand. 'Open it, love. You have to find out the truth.'

His voice wasn't strong and he seemed to have something stuck in his throat.

'Will you sit back and rest, Robert Cartwright,' Vera chided him, tucking the blanket beneath his legs. 'This envelope can wait, your health is more important.'

Robert pushed her hands away. 'I don't think my health can survive you not opening the envelope, Vera.'

She stopped fussing and picked it up. 'Okay, okay, here goes.'

She ripped the side open, carefully avoiding tearing any of the pages inside. There was a small packet of photocopies plus a typed letter within.

Vera scanned the letter quickly. 'It's from Caritas. Here are all the documents they have regarding Harry.' She carried on reading quickly. 'They caution us against contacting Harry directly without talking with them first. The initial contacts should be handled carefully to avoid emotional trauma for both parties.' She held the packet in her hands and looked at Jayne and Robert. 'It means he's alive, doesn't it?'

'We won't know unless you open it, will we, love?' Robert ended the sentence with a fit of coughing.

Jayne moved to sit by his side, putting her arm around him. 'Take it easy, Dad.'

'I'll take it easy when Vera opens the bloody packet.'

'Okay, okay.' Vera tore the packet open. 'There's a contents list; Caritas does seem organised.' She began reading. 'There's the original document Mum signed when she placed him with the home, but we've seen that already.' She laid the photocopy aside. 'The next is a letter from Mum, dated May fifth, 1952. It's in her handwriting.' Vera coughed twice and began reading:

'Dear Sister Mary,

'I visited St Michael's on May 2nd to see both yourself and my son, Harry. I waited for over two hours but I was told by Sister Tomasina that you weren't available and Harold was no longer in the home.

'I made it clear when I placed my son with St Michael's that as soon as my circumstances would allow, I would return to take him home. That's why I only allowed him to be fostered with the Beggses rather then adopted by them.

206

'My husband and I are now ready to provide a stable and loving home for Harry. We are moving back to Oldham in the near future and have already found a house to live in. It's not much, but it's a start. My husband is aware of Harry's background and the circumstances of his birth and is willing to accept him as his own son.

'Please let me know a date and a time when we can pick up Harry from St Michael's and bring him home.

'I have waited and longed for this day for seven years. I am so happy it is finally here.

'Yours in Christ,

'Freda Atkins (formerly Duckworth).'

For a moment there was silence around the small table.

Off in the distance, Jayne could hear a blackbird calling, establishing its territory against a rival. Above her head, the wind rustled through the old branches of the oak tree sheltering this spot from the sun. Next to her, she could hear her father's breathing, a clear rasp on the end of every breath.

'She wanted him back,' said Vera quietly. 'This must have been the letter she wrote in 1952.' She opened the next letter. 'And here is the Mother Superior's reply she kept in her Bible.' Vera's voice cracked. 'No wonder it broke her heart.'

Robert took hold of his wife's hand. 'There, there, love, it's alright.'

'I can't read any more. Jayne, can you do it, please?'

Jayne took the remaining letters and opened the one on top. 'This is the letter your father wrote, Vera. He's angry at the Mother Superior.'

Jayne began reading:

'Dear Mother Superior,

'I am shocked and outraged after reading your letter. How could you slander a kind and loving woman like my wife in such an awful manner?

'We have been unable to visit Harry for the last six months due to my work taking me to Manchester. It was only by chance that we found he was no longer being fostered by the Beggses but had been reclaimed by the home because "there was now space".

'To find out he has now been adopted without permission from my wife is a travesty. How could you do such a thing? My wife fully admits she has made errors in the past, but we have talked about this and are now ready to accept Harry into our home. I will adopt him as my own son and provide a loving home for him and our own children.

'Your attitude and callous disregard for my wife's feelings have made me doubt the church's integrity in this matter. I ask that you get Harry back from the family so we can look after him properly and give him the warmth and love only his mother can provide.

'Yours sincerely,
Norman Atkins.'

'That sounds just like Dad. He was slow to anger, but woe betide anybody who got in his way when he was.'

Jayne opened the next piece of paper. 'It's the Mother Superior's reply. The one your mother kept in her Bible.'

'Why didn't they carry on trying? Why did they stop looking for Harry?'

Robert patted the back of his wife's hand.

'Times were different, love. Remember the Mother Superior said Harold had been adopted by a Catholic family, one that could give him a good life. Maybe they thought he would be better off where he was. From what you told me, your mum and dad didn't have much when they went back to Oldham.'

'When I came along, they were living in a dingy back-to-back.'

'So, I wonder if they thought it was best for him. And remember, people were more devout than they are now. Your mum believed everything the church told her.'

'And I guess I came along, followed by my brother...'

'You're not to blame, love, it's a decision your parents made. They thought it was for the best.'

'But it troubled Mum, that's why she told me everything. She must have thought about Harry every day, wondering how he was, what he had become.'

'There's one more photocopy,' said Jayne, holding up a sheet of paper.

'Perhaps it's the name of the family who adopted him?' said Vera.

Jayne scanned the document. 'It's a movement order. He was sent to Australia.'

'I... I... I don't understand. The Mother Superior said he was adopted...'

'The document is quite clear.' Jayne started reading the details aloud. 'It's a movement order for "Harold Britton, on April thirteenth, for the SS Otranto, passage to Australia via Gibraltar, Port Suez, Aden and Ceylon, destination Fremantle, Western Australia".

He was being sent out as part of a group from St Michael's by the Catholic Child Welfare Council. The document – it's a ticket really – is signed by a Father Stinson.'

'What's going on, Jayne?' her father asked. 'Was he adopted or was he sent to Australia?'

'If I'm right, Dad, he was sent to Australia. I found him on the passenger list of the SS Otranto in April 1952.'

Vera's face was ashen, her mouth slightly open.

Jayne peered at the bottom of the document. 'And there's a signed release clause from a parent or guardian. The signature is scrawled but it looks like Freda Duckworth.'

Vera snatched the paper out of Jayne's hands and peered at it. 'That's not my mum's signature.'

Chapter Thirty-Eight

June 12, 1952

St Joseph's Farm and Trade School, Bindoon, Western Australia

The first two weeks at Bindoon were tough for Harry. The constant back-breaking work and lack of food made him feel tired all the time. The evenings after the rosary was said and the lights had gone out were his only time of peace.

Little Tom had been moved out on to the veranda with the rest of the bed-wetters. There, the smell of piss was so strong that Harry gagged every time he visited his friend. The younger boy didn't seem to notice it any more.

'At least I don't have to take a cold shower in the morning. None of the monks bother with me any more.'

Harry had become used to the rickety bed, the lack of a pillow and the roughness of the bed clothes, but he still slept fitfully, awoken by the slightest sound; the opening of the dormitory door, a boy shouting in his sleep, the sound of Brother Dawe's sandals as he visited the room at night.

He didn't think he could have survived without Slimo. The young boy had been there two years and knew the ropes; which of the brothers to avoid, which to butter up and which ones would help you if you asked.

Not all of them were as quick with the strap as Brother Thomas, Brother Dominic or Brother Keaney. The one who took them for their lessons after the morning's building work had been completed, Brother Sylvian, was one of those. He treated them well, trying to teach them a love of reading and writing. But Harry was often so tired in the classroom, his head resting on his arms.

One day he was woken with a gentle tap of the shoulder.

'Sure, you won't learn much like that, Harold.'

Harry blinked his eyes open. Everyone was looking at him.

'What did I just say?'

'I dunno, Brother Sylvian.'

The brother shook his head. 'Lessons are for learning, not sleeping.'

'I'm tired,' said Harry.

The monk returned to the head of the class, forty pairs of eyes following him. 'Pray to God you sleep better at night. Do you pray to Him, Harold?'

Harry was puzzled. 'I say my rosary like everyone else.'

'But do you pray to Him?'

'What do you mean?'

'Do you celebrate His grace? Do you dedicate yourself and your body to His glory? Do you ask Him to give you succour in your hour of need?'

'I... I don't think so.'

'Then maybe you should, Harold. He will listen to you. God listens to children and helps grant their wishes. But you have to believe in your prayers.' Brother Sylvian's kindly eyes scanned the whole class. 'Do you believe in your prayers, children?'

'Yes, Brother,' they chorused in unison.

'If you do, your prayers will be answered.' He clapped his hands. 'Now we will return to the parable of the five loaves and two fishes. I'm going to tell you this story from the Bible and, after I finish, I want you to write what you remember in your best handwriting.'

Harry tried to write the story. The words were there in his mind, but somehow they never appeared on the white paper in front of him. Or, if they did, they were a mass of crossings out and backward words.

It was the same with the letters he wrote home; each page ended in a mess. But he still wrote them anyway, telling his mum what he had done and giving them to the brothers to post for him.

At the end of the week, Brother Sylvian read out a list of names, asking them to stay behind. Harry's was one of them, along with Little Tom and twenty others.

'Now, boys, we have been assessing your progress over the last few weeks. It has been decided you all are better suited to a more vocational style of training – spending more time in the kitchens, the dairy and the piggery, in constructing the new buildings or in the orchards.'

Little Tom put his hand up. 'Does that mean we won't come to school any more?'

'Of course not, you will all still have to attend lessons – there will just be fewer of them and we will concentrate on learning your letters and your catechism.'

'Catechism?' one of the other boys asked.

'Stories from the Bible that will help you become good Catholics. We must feed your soul as well as your body.'

'As long as it's not porridge, I don't care,' said Little Tom.

Brother Sylvian smiled. With the other monks, such a cheekiness would have been the occasion for a beating, but with him there was just a gentle rebuke. 'We should be grateful for what we receive, Thomas. Gratitude is a positive emotion which will always stay with us, even in the darkest hours.'

He checked his watch. 'I see it is time for lunch. Run along now. Report to Brother Dawe afterwards. He has urgent repair work for you all. Remember, we all serve God in our own way and it is to Him we owe immense gratitude. After all, didn't He give us His only begotten son, Jesus Christ, to help us atone for our sins?'

Chapter Thirty-Nine

July 15, 2017
Buxton Residential Home, Derbyshire, England

Jayne picked up her mobile phone and called Caritas, switching on the loudspeaker so Vera could hear.

She was put through straight away to Mrs Traynor, the same person who interviewed them three weeks ago.

'I've been expecting your call, Mrs Sinclair. It's normal when the enquirers receive a packet of documents.'

'We have a few questions.'

'Ask away and I'll answer as best I can. We're here to help.'

'There seems to be a discrepancy in the documents. In some letters, the Mother Superior, a Sister Mary, writes that Harold Britton was adopted. But in another, a movement order, he is being sent to Australia as one of the child migrants.'

There was a long silence at the end of the phone before Mrs Traynor answered. 'I'm afraid the movement order is probably the correct document. If the child had been adopted there would be other supporting documents. Names and addresses of the adopting parents, follow-up visits, even reports from the priest of the adopting family's parish.'

'But none of those documents exist.'

'None that we can find.'

'So you believe he was sent to Australia.'

'In the absence of any adoption papers, I think that is the case.'

Jayne had to ask the question. 'Why did Sister Mary lie?'

There was another long silence at the end of the phone, followed by a long, sad sigh. 'It is something the church regrets immensely. Nobody can look into the hearts of people back in the fifties. Why lies were told. Why the truth wasn't made obvious to people. All we can do today is try to make up for the wrongs committed then as best we can. To help relatives and friends come to terms with what happened. I'm so sorry, Mrs Sinclair, I don't know why the lies were told.'

Vera had tears in her eyes. Her voice broke as she spoke. 'There's one other thing bothering me, Mrs Traynor. The signature at the bottom of the form is not my mother's. She never knew Harry was sent to Australia.'

'Is that Mrs Thompson?'

'It is.'

'I'm afraid I don't know about the signatures. The church required a signature from a parent or guardian before any child could be sent abroad.'

'But my mother wanted Harry back. She didn't want to send him to Australia...'

'I can hear you are upset, Mrs Thompson, and I understand why. I did some research on Sister Mary to see if I could ask her, but unfortunately she passed away in 1967.'

Vera couldn't speak any more; tears were streaming down her face. Robert was leaning over, his arm round her shoulders, trying to comfort her.

'Is there anything more we can do, Mrs Traynor?' he asked.

'We have given you everything we have in England on Harold Britton. The next step would be to contact Australia for the records they have of his time there. I see he was sent to Western Australia. There are two ways to find out more. You could contact the Child Migrants Trust in Nottingham, I think they have an office in Perth. Or there is a place called the Tuart Centre in Fremantle. I could send you the contact details if you like?'

'Thank you, Mrs Traynor, for all your help,' said Jayne

'I'm sorry I couldn't be of more use.' There was a pause before she spoke again. 'We recognise how traumatic these events can be for relatives. We do offer counselling to people to help them during this difficult time.'

'Thank you for your offer, Mrs Traynor,' said Vera, wiping away her tears. 'If I need anything, I will contact you.'

'The offer is there, Mrs Thompson.'

'Thank you for your help.' Jayne switched the phone off. 'What do you want to do, Vera?'

Vera's mascara was running and a tear had traced a single line through her carefully applied make-up. 'We must find Harry. Or at least find out what became of him. We owe it to my mum.'

Chapter Forty

September 26, 1952

St Joseph's Farm and Trade School, Bindoon, Western Australia

Harry understood Brother Sylvian's words about gratitude when he was told what he had to do that afternoon.

'Brother Keaney has decided we are to build the stations of the cross on the road leading to the school. It will be an example of our love for Jesus. The Archbishop will be visiting in two months so we must have it ready for his Eminence,' Brother Dawe announced.

The Italians, who supervised all the building, laid out the positions of each individual station by placing stones marked with white paint along the road leading from the main gate to the church. The boys had to drag a cart laden with stone from the quarry along the length of the road, depositing each load beside the white stone.

Supervised by Brother Keaney, they selected rough rocks for the foundation before moulding the quarried stone and mortaring it into place to build a pedestal.

If a cart became stuck in the soft earth, or the boys stopped to wipe the sweat from their brow, Brother Keaney's voice was heard shouting, 'Hurry along there, you bastards. I want Gethsemane finished today.'

This voice was followed soon after by the sound of his stick being whacked across the bottom of an errant boy or two.

Harry was working with Slimo, Little Tom, a Maltese boy called Ronnie and an Irish lad. They had been assigned the third station to build, the one where Jesus falls for the first time. Unfortunately, this was one of the furthest stations from the quarry. They were already exhausted by the time they had hauled the cart to the white-painted rock.

Little Tom looked around before flopping to the floor.

'Don't, Tom, he'll see.' Harry had become constantly aware of where each brother was at any given moment.

'I... don't... care.'

'Come on, get up. Hold this rock, pretend you're creating a pile.' Harry helped him to his feet, giving him a light stone to carry whilst the others emptied the cart.

The stone dropped at Little Tom's bare feet.

Harry glanced over his shoulder. 'Pick it up! Don't let him see.'

Little Tom just stared at him.

Harry was about to help him when he heard the voice.

'You heathens, what do you think you're doing?' Brother Keaney appeared alongside them as if out of thin air, the stick already in his hand, cheeks burning red beneath his horn-rimmed glasses. 'You, boy – move those rocks.'

Little Tom stared at Brother Keaney, swaying slightly beneath the hot sun.

219

The arm was raised, the stick extending up towards the sky. 'Did you not hear me?' The accent thicker now, like molten earth.

Little Tom blinked twice and slowly reached down to pick up the rock at his feet.

The stick dropped beneath shoulder height.

A shout from the next station along. 'Brother, can you come here?' It was one of the Italian supervisors.

'Get a bloody move on,' snarled Brother Keaney, before moving off along the road, his boots kicking up whispers of hot dust.

Little Tom aimed to throw the rock at the departing brother, but his arm was grabbed by Slimo. 'I wouldn't do that, mate.'

For a second both of them stood facing each other until, finally, Little Tom's shoulders relaxed and he said, 'I don't think I can stomach it any more.'

'Just keep your head down, mate, like the rest of us. Keep your head down.' He let go of Little Tom's arm and continued unloading the rocks from the cart.

Their little gang spent the next week making the third station. The Italians had created a mould in the shape of a cross. Once they had built the foundation and tamped down the quarried stones, they were instructed how to make the lime mortar.

Harry poured three buckets of sand into an old wheelbarrow, making a well in the centre. This was followed by pouring a bucket of lime into the well. Each time he poured the lime, the powder rose up in a thick dense cloud, causing him to cough until his chest ached. The Italian mason saw him and placed an old snot-caked handkerchief around his mouth.

The lime also stung like a swarm of wasps if it landed in any open cut or graze. None of them were immune from this pain; their feet, legs and arms were covered in cuts and bruises from the sharp stones.

After mixing the sand and lime together, Slimo came to pour water into the mix, adding a little at a time and turning it over constantly with a shovel. Little Tom and the Maltese boy, Ronnie, helped him too, using small trowels to mix the mortar, making sure it was an even colour and texture. They would cover the mixture with a tarp for the night. Next morning, they would begin pouring it into the cross-shape mould that had been fashioned by the Italians.

By the time they had finished, the concrete cross was more than six feet tall. For the next week, Harry and Little Tom had the job of keeping all fourteen stations damp to allow the mortar to set. This involved splashing water over the mould and letting it seep into the mortar.

Finally, the Italians removed the mould, leaving an off-grey cross standing proudly on its plinth, the sharp lines a stark contrast to the soft, undulating grasslands and scrub of its surrounds.

The Italians than produced hand-painted ceramic tiles for the stations and fixed them beneath the cross piece. The paintings were simple, just telling the story of Jesus and his actions on the days before his death on the cross.

Harry and Tom were given a tray of paints and told to touch up any damage that had occurred whilst the tiles had been transported from Perth.

Harry loved this work. Applying the fine paints with a small brush, ensuring the colours matched and were evenly distributed. He particularly liked applying the bright red paint on the body of Jesus in the thirteenth station, as he was taken down from the cross by the disciples and Mary Magdalene before being placed in the tomb.

The red blood was fresh and bright, not like their own blood, which was soured with dust and dirt.

When they had finished, Brother Keaney stood facing the row of crosses along the road. All fourteen stations were whitewashed, with a small wooden cross, fashioned by the boys in the woodshed, nailed above every picture of Jesus's life.

'You've done a fine job, lads. It's a fitting testament for the Archbishop.'

As he strode away, rosary jangling at his waist, Harry stared up at the final station. The picture was of Jesus resting in his tomb before the resurrection.

His face looks so peaceful, he thought, like a man who has sacrificed himself for others.

Chapter Forty-One

December 23, 1952
St Joseph's Farm and Trade School, Bindoon, Western Australia

It was just before Christmas when Little Tom came to him. One night, well after lights out, Harry felt a tap on his shoulder and awoke to find Little Tom kneeling beside his bed.

'I can't take no more.'

'Is it Brother Thomas?'

In the moonlight streaming in through the window, Harry could see the area around Tom's eyes was red and bruised.

'What have you done to your eyes?'

Little Tom rubbed them again roughly with the heel of his hand.

Harry reached out, grabbing hold of his arm. 'What are you doing?'

'It's my eyes. He says they are so lovely and blue.'

Harry heard Little Tom's voice catch and his chest grab for air as he stifled a sob. 'He came for you again?'

The silent nod of the head.

Little Tom had been moved back in from the bedwetters' veranda three months ago. He still wet the bed, but it didn't seem to matter any more. One night, Harry heard the door open and the familiar sound of sandals flapping on the floorboards. The sound had stopped at the end of his bed and he had lain there praying for it not to be him. For the brother, whichever one it was, to move on and take somebody else.

Harry had held his breath and buried himself deeper beneath the coarse blanket. 'Please let it be someone else. Please not me.'

The sandals made a sound again, moving away from his bed to the one next door. He heard a few whispered words and then the sound of Tom's bare feet accompanying the sandals out of the room.

Harry lay in the dark, listening to the wind through the trees and the creaking of the roof joists, settling after a day being heated by the hot sun. In the distance, the screech of a bird or some other animal, hunting or being hunted, in the shadows of the night.

He was thankful he hadn't been taken.

Not tonight.

Tom eventually came back and climbed into his own bed.

Next morning he said nothing, but Harry knew what had happened. All the boys knew but nobody ever talked about it. How could they?

Now Tom was kneeling beside his bed in the middle of the night, shaking with fear.

'What are you going to do?'

'Run away.'

'Where?'

'I dunno, Anywhere away from here.'

'Not much of a plan.'

'Will you come too, Harry?'

He thought for a moment. He could hear the sadness in Tom's voice, the slight catch in the throat, as if waiting and steeling himself for rejection.

'I will. When are we off?'

'I thought about Christmas Day. The brothers will take the day off after Mass, we could slip away then and nobody would know we were missing until the following day.'

'I need to write my letter to mum. I always write one at the end of the month.'

'You had any replies?'

Harry shook his head.

'Why d'you keep writing? It takes you ages.'

Harry shrugged his shoulders. 'I dunno.' Then he thought a bit more. 'It keeps her alive for me. One day she'll come and take me away.'

'But… you still want to escape with me?'

'Yeah, perhaps we can find a ship in Perth, like the one we came on. Take it back home. They have to go back, don't they, Tom?'

'I suppose so…so you're on for Christmas Day?'

Harry nodded again, before adding, 'What happens if we get caught?'

Harry sensed a shrug of the shoulders in the dark. 'Dunno and don't care. I'm not staying here no more.'

Chapter Forty-Two

December 25, 1952

St Joseph's Farm and Trade School, Bindoon, Western Australia

Christmas Day arrived. Out of the goodness of his heart, Father Keaney had given everybody the day off to celebrate the birthday of our Lord. The breakfast was still the same, though: grey-brown porridge. But everyone was given an orange as 'a special treat'.

There were no presents, other than an extra-long Mass said by a priest from Perth who was visiting. God, the man liked the sound of his own voice as he read the sermon. Afterwards, the monks retired to their rooms and the boys to the dormitory.

All except Tom and Harry, who hid in the outdoor shower block waiting for everything to become quiet.

From out of his pocket, Tom produced a piece of paper cut from a magazine.

'See, I reckon if we climb the hill, head southwest, cross over the road and keep heading in the same direction for a couple of hours, I'm sure we'll eventually reach the Great Northern Highway. There we can hitchhike to Perth or any other place the lift is going.'

'That's the plan?'

'That's the plan.'

'What are we going to eat?'

Tom produced two stale crusts of bread from his other pocket. 'Nicked 'em from the pigs. They'll keep us going until we reach Perth.'

Harry eyed the stale crusts. He could see spots of green mould growing on the edges. 'Water?' he asked.

Tom glanced around him. 'We're in the showers, let's drink our fill.' He then ran to one of the lockers where the monks kept the cleaning gear, reached behind it and produced an old bottle of HP sauce. 'It's all I could nick yesterday from the kitchen. Brother Paul was watching me all the time.'

They cleaned out the bottle, filling it with water.

'We're not taking anything else?'

'We don't have anything else. Come on.'

They ran around the back of the showers and up the hill overlooking Boys Town, making sure to keep low in a gully and out of sight. At the top, Tom paused for a moment, looking up at the sky, shielding his eyes from the sun.

'Which way now?' said Harry.

'We have to cross the road and head south-west.' Tom pointed to the road leading past Boys Town.

'How'd you know the way to go?'

'The sun. It's about nine thirty now, so the sun is over there.' He pointed into the sky. 'That's south and over there must be south-west.'

'How do you know all this?'

'There's always magazines hanging round the kitchens. The brothers leave them. When Brother Paul's not watching, I have a read.' He strode off towards the south-west. 'Come on.'

They crossed the road to Boys Town carefully, after checking that no traffic was coming. Luckily, it was quiet – just a long, thin strip of tarmac stretching off into the distance, surrounded by orange soil, rolling hills and yellow, parched grass.

They still walked barefoot, their feet hardened by six months of working on the buildings, but even they had to tread carefully on the baking tar, hopping like scalded cats on ashes. They were thankful to get back into the bush, where the bare earth or tussock grass was their friend.

After an hour of walking under the hot sun, they hit a dirt road. 'Right or left?' asked Harry.

Tom checked the map and pointed towards the right. 'The highway is over there.' He strode off down the road, its soft dirt scored with tyre tracks.

Harry ran to catch him up. 'You know, it's Christmas Day, there won't be many people on the road.'

'There'll be some. We'll get a lift.'

'And then what?'

He shrugged his shoulders like he always did. 'I don't know, Harry. We'll see.'

They walked on in silence until they hit the highway: a wider, busier road.

'Now we just stand here and wait,' said Tom.

The first two cars went sailing past them. 'An Austin and a Holden Forty-Eight. Old people, they won't stop. We need a truck.'

Five minutes later a truck came and Tom was right, it stopped forty yards past them, screeching to a halt in a cloud of orange dust. They ran after it. The driver, unshaven, with a thick black moustache and wearing a sweat-stained bush hat, leant out of the window. 'Where you going, young 'uns?'

Tom spoke first. 'Perth. Can you give us a lift?'

The man rubbed his stubbled chin. He spoke slowly, with a heavy drawl, as if he were chewing the words before spitting them out. 'Well, mates, I'm only going to Muchea, but at least you'll be on the highway.'

'That'll do.'

They ran around to the opposite side of the cab and climbed in, Little Tom in the middle and Harry near to the open window.

The driver put the truck in gear and slowly pulled away.

'Where ye from, mates? Ye sound like Poms,' he shouted above the engine noise.

'We are. Or at least, our family is. We live on a farm back there. Off to Perth to see our auntie.'

'Your dad's English?'

'Came out five years ago.'

Harry listened to Tom's lies. There was a confidence in his voice Harry hadn't heard before.

The driver peered straight down the road, staring at the black ribbon of tar stretching in front of them. 'Where did you say the farm was, mates?'

Tom laughed. 'I didn't, but it's at Mindara.'

'You've come a ways.'

'Got a lift this morning. One of the brothers, going to Bindoon Boys Town.'

'Aye, I heard about the place, them's doin' good work.'

Tom and Harry stayed silent as the driver changed down a gear to climb a small hill, the truck's engine noise increasing in pitch.

After a few minutes, they passed through Bindoon town itself. Harry had been through there often with the pig truck, taking the slops from Bindoon to a farmer.

They both stiffened as they drove down the main street, and Tom gripped Harry's hand. But there were few people around; most were at home, enjoying the delights of a Christmas lunch.

The driver just kept on going, looking neither left nor right. After they had passed through the town and were back into the open countryside, Tom spoke again. 'Why are you working on Christmas Day?'

The man seemed to think for a while. 'I work every day, Christmas or not. Had a load for Glenvar, not far from you boys.'

'Is it?'

'You don't know?'

Luckily, the man spoke so slowly Tom had time to recover. 'Course we do, Mr Elgin's over in Glenvar, isn't he?'

'Is he? Don't know no Elgin.'

'My dad works with him,' Tom said confidently.

After that, the conversation went quiet again. Obviously, the driver didn't speak much and when he did, it was like waiting for heaven to arrive as the words slithered out between his lips.

Harry was glad for the quiet. The more Tom said, the more the man would find out about them.

Outside the windows, the Australian bush swept by. Still the same orange soil. Still the same spare bushes. Still the same bleached grass.

But there were no kangaroos.

And there were no fruit trees.

The priest at St Michael's had lied to them.

They reached a crossroads and turned left towards a road signposted 'Muchea'.

'You can drop us here, mate. The road to Perth is straight ahea,' Tom said.

'I'll take youse just a bit farther. You can pick up the road again in Muchea.'

They drove for another 500 yards, the driver gripping the wheel tight. Then he pulled to the right and slid to a stop next to a sign with the words 'Police' in white against a blue background.

A young constable came out from the house. 'What we got here then, Mick?'

'A couple of runaways from the Boy's Town, Albert. I was goin' to take 'em back meself, but me dinner is on and the wife'd kill me if I'm late. You on your own today?'

'Nah, the missus is with me. She can look after the fort while I'm gone.' He opened the passenger side door. 'Out you get you two. Come on, get a move on,' he ordered.

Harry hesitated for a moment before a big, meaty hand reached in and pulled him out. Tom followed him and the driver immediately drove off in a cloud of dust without saying another word.

'You can come inside and wait while I get my keys.'

He led them into the dark interior. A young woman, hair swept back off her head and tied in a ponytail, was sitting behind a desk.

'We got a couple of runaways from Bindoon. I'll take 'em back. Won't be long.'

She nodded, but didn't say anything.

The constable left, but not before telling them, 'Don't do anything stupid. This here's my wife. If you do anything to upset her, you'll taste this.' He held up a thick fist in front of Harry's face. Harry could see the hair growing in profusion on the back of the knuckles.

The constable's voice changed as he spoke to his wife. 'Back in a minute, dear, I'll just get the car.'

The boys stood there. Harry stared straight ahead, not allowing himself to show any emotion. Tom glanced down at the white tiled floor, his bare feet dirty and stained with orange soil.

'Would you like some lemonade?'

Neither boy said anything.

The woman took that as a yes, pouring a cloudy light-yellow liquid into two glasses. 'Drink some, you look like you need it.'

Her voice was warm and friendly, and she had a little smile in her eyes.

Tom reached for the glass and drank it down in one. Harry did the same.

'You're both thirsty, aren't you? Never mind, I've made plenty.' She poured two more glasses from the jug and pointed to the seats. 'Why don't you sit down? Albert won't be long.'

Tom began to cry, softly at first, looking down at his feet. Then the sobs became louder, tears running through the dirt on his face, creating clear rivulets.

The woman got up from around the desk, and gently pushed Tom and Harry to sit down on the chairs. 'It's okay, Albert will take you back soon.'

Tom cried louder. 'We don't want to go back.'

She put her arms around both of them. Harry could smell her perfume; sweet and rich, the scent of flowers. It reminded him of his mother. He leant into her shoulder, resting his head against the spot next to her neck.

'It's okay. When you go back, the brothers will look after you.'

Harry pulled away from her. 'When we go back, they'll beat us.' He stuck out his leg and pulled up his shorts, showing the dark blue and brown bruise on his thigh, the legacy of a beating from Brother Keaney three days ago.

The woman pushed Tom away, looking at Harry and frowning. 'The brothers don't beat anybody. Why do you tell such horrible lies?' She stood up and smoothed down her dress.

'They do worse,' said Tom, without looking at her.

232

She turned away from them. 'I don't know what you mean. They don't do things like that.'

Then came the sound of an engine pulling up outside and a handbrake being applied.

Tom jumped up from the seat and grabbed the woman around the waist, holding on to her voluminous skirt. 'Please don't send us back.'

She pushed him away.

He clung on, crying even louder.

'Don't do that. Let me go.'

Her husband, the police constable, appeared in the doorway. 'Let go of her.'

Tom stopped crying and released his grip on the skirt, staring down at the ground.

'Maggie, I've told you before, you have to watch these lads.'

'I just gave them some lemonade.'

He jerked his thumb over his shoulder. 'You two, in the car.'

Harry got up and gave the woman his empty glass. 'Thank you for the lemonade,' he said.

They didn't speak to each other or to the constable during the journey back to Boys Town. Harry stared out the window, seeing the bush race past. The bush where they had walked free just two hours ago. Tom stared down at his feet, his chest occasionally heaving as a sob was strangled in his throat.

The car turned through the wrought-iron gates and drove past the fourteen stages of the cross they had spent so long building. From Jesus in the garden at Gethsemane, to his body lying in the shroud before his resurrection.

The police constable drove slowly, crossing himself as they passed each station, mumbling words under his breath.

Brother Keaney was waiting to greet them, standing on the steps as he had done when they arrived six months earlier.

'Hello, Albert, I see you've found our little spalpeens. Maggie called to let me know you were coming. Sorry to bother you on Christmas Day.'

'It's not a problem, Brother Keaney. Mick Tanner picked them up.'

The door opened and the boys slunk out.

'You two go to the dormitory. No dinner for you tonight.'

Harry and Tom sloped off to the dormitory without looking back at the constable.

'Don't you thank Albert for bringing you back?'

Harry turned and said thank you. Tom just walked on.

'Ah, don't be too hard on them, Brother. It's Christmas and I think they were just missing home.'

'They're orphans, Albert, this is their home. Maggie said they've been telling lies again about how we beat them. We do give them the strap, but only when they need it.'

'I know, Brother, I remember them walloping me and my cousin at school.'

'And you were none the worse for it, Albert.'

The constable laughed. 'You're right, I was a little terror, but the brothers soon knocked the devilment out of me.'

Brother Keaney bent down to lift a box at his feet. 'Now, I've put a bit of fruit together for you and Maggie. Picked by the boys, it was. They'll be happy for you to have it.'

'I couldn't, Brother.'

'Ah, it's Christmas, Albert. It's nothing but a bit of fruit. The boys would love you to take it.'

The constable placed the box on the front seat. 'Thank you, Brother.'

'Anything to help the police. And if you see Commissioner Kelly, please send him my regards and ask him to come and see me again.'

'I will, Brother, but he doesn't come to our neck of the woods often.'

'No matter, I'll put in a good word for you when I see him.'

'Thank you, Brother.' The constable put the car in gear and drove away.

That evening, even though it was Christmas Day, Brother Keaney had Harry and Little Tom up in front of the whole school during dinner. He pulled down their shorts and gave them twelve strokes from his cane across their bare bottoms. Tom received an extra three for not thanking the constable.

They spent the next two days in bed, unable to move.

Chapter Forty-Three

July 18, 2017
Buxton Residential Home, Derbyshire, England

Three days later, Jayne was back in Buxton. She had been mulling over what to do to continue the investigation into Vera's vanished brother. The answer finally came to her, and it was so obvious, she wondered why she hadn't thought of it before.

'I have a friend in Australia, he may be able to help us. He's a genealogist too, working on family history in Perth. It'll be much quicker than us trying to do it remotely from Manchester.'

Jayne remembered four years ago in London at one of the massive genealogical exhibitions. She had just started her own business and was actively trying to network with other genealogists. The first person she ran into was Duncan Morgan, who looked – and felt – as lost as she did. For the next two days, they attended every seminar together, walked the halls, picked up countless leaflets and, thanks to Duncan's natural gregariousness, had met more people than Jayne would ever have done on her own.

During one of their lunches, he had told her his life history; adopted as a young boy by a family in Sydney, he had been a bit of tearaway before finally going into the Australian Navy and becoming a submariner.

'When you're stuck with fifty other blokes in a long metal tube for days at an end under the sea, you better be able to get on with people, otherwise you're stuffed.'

He came out of the Navy after twelve years and then became a copper working in Western Australia's maritime police. Perhaps that was why they had got on so well. A shared love of two things; the police and family history.

Unlike her, he had stayed with the police until they kicked him out with a 'goodbye, mate' and a very generous retirement package.

He had searched around for something to do, wanting to avoid the usual awful security jobs for coppers, and lucked into genealogy.

'There's over twenty million Aussies out there, all with a bright future and no past. I help the Irish, Italians, Greeks, Poles, Yugoslavs, Germans, Lebanese, and English discover where they came from and enjoy a few schooners doing it. Who could ask for more?'

He was a lovely man. They had stayed in touch over the years, helping each other out when they were stuck and had hit the inevitable brick wall.

'Shall I give him a call? Though we may have to pay him, Vera, this is his job.'

'Money's no object, Jayne, not any more.'

Jayne checked the clock. Perth was eight hours ahead of Manchester so it would be nine o'clock at night there. Was it too late? She decided to risk it.

'Hello?' A sleepy-sounding voice answered the phone.

'Hi, Duncan, it's Jayne.'

'Jayne who?'

Jayne frowned at her dad. 'Jayne Sinclair, we met at the Genealogy Exhibition in Olympia?'

237

Silence at the other end of the phone. 'Which Jayne is that? There were so many Jaynes at the conference, I felt like Tarzan.'

Jayne laughed. 'Stop teasing me, Duncan, you know who it is.'

He joined in with her. 'Of course I do. But I love pullin' your leg, Jayne, you Poms are too serious. G'day.'

'And a good day to you too, Duncan. It's not too late to call?'

'It's never too late to hear from you. And I'm just sitting here watching Behave Yourself, which is about as funny as a Great White with a toothache.'

'How's Margery?'

'She's sitting next to me, scaring the Great White.'

A voice in the distance said, 'Hi, Jayne.'

'Hi, Margery. And how's business, Duncan?'

'Now, Jayne, you didn't ring me up on a Tuesday night at nine o'clock to ask how business is. But since you have asked, it's a bit quiet at the moment. The winter lull...'

'That's great news.'

He laughed. 'Not for me it ain't.'

'I meant, if you're not busy, you can do a bit of work for me in Australia.'

Duncan's voice changed and he suddenly became more businesslike. 'Tell me what it is, Jayne.'

'I'm going to put you on speakerphone. Listening in is my step mother, Vera, and my dad, Robert.'

'Hi, Duncan, it's Vera. Are you really in Perth in Australia?'

A muffled voice was heard down the line. 'I've just asked the wife and she tells me we are. I'm never sure myself. Nice accent you have there.'

'It's Lancashire, I'm from from Oldham.'

'Hold 'em? Funny name for a place.'

238

'No, Oldham.'

Jayne touched her step mother's arm. 'He's just teasing you, Vera.'

'How can I help?'

Jayne told him the story of Harry, Vera's mother and St Michael's. She heard an audible sigh at the end of the phone.

'Over seven thousand of these kids were sent to Australia at the end of the war. How they were treated was a disgrace.'

'I've read some of the stories,' said Jayne.

'You know, their redress money was cut in half by the government, even though it was their lack of oversight causing all the problems in the first place. Cheap bastards…'

A muffled voice at the end of the line.

'That was Margery telling me not to swear, but it gets me so angry…' There was another pause and more muffled words before Duncan came back on the line. 'Sorry, Jayne, go on – how can I help?'

'We need to find out what happened when he went to Australia. He was only eight when he was sent there.'

'Eight, you say? They sent them young. It might not be good news, Jayne. Many of them suffered emotional problems. The places they were sent to – well, let's put it this way, I would treat a dingo better. Never mind the emotional damage of being separated from your family at such an early age.'

Jayne stared at Vera. 'We know. We'd still like to find out, though.'

'You said he was Catholic and sent to Western Australia?'

'That's correct.'

'Well, there's only four places he would have been sent, all homes run by the Christian Brothers: Tardun,

Castledare, St Joseph's Farm in Bindoon, and Clontarf. From what I remember, the Christian Brothers set up a database for all the Child Migrants sent to Western Australia back in 1999. Only they can access it directly, though. Relatives have to go through Tuart Place or the Child Migrants Trust.'

'Tuart Place?'

'A charity run for the child migrants in Fremantle. Funnily enough, it's not far from the dock where most of them landed.'

'Great. When can you start, Duncan?'

'Right away if you want. I'll give the Tuart Place people a call tomorrow. You'll have to send me everything you have plus a letter from Vera appointing me as her representative. Nobody is going to let me have anything unless I have the right credentials.'

'I'll email you everything we have, Duncan.'

'Make sure you send his birth certificate. It will speed up the whole process immensely. And one more thing...'

'What's that?'

'You know you could do this more cheaply by going to the Child Migrants Trust or Tuart Place yourself?'

'We know. But we've decided we can't wait any longer. Harry is going to be seventy-three years old soon, we can't let this drag on.'

'I understand.'

A muffled voice at the other end of the line again, followed by Duncan's voice as he answered. in a whisper.

Then he was back on the line again. 'I don't know if you heard that, but Margery said I should do it for nothing – as a favour, Jayne – and I always agree with the missus. She holds the purse strings.'

Frantic signals from Vera, saying 'no, no, we pay'.

Jayne thought for a moment. 'How about this, Duncan. We'll donate the fee in your name to one of the child migrant charities?'

'Agreed. I'll get working as soon as I receive the documents.'

'They'll be in your email when you wake up to-morrow.'

Chapter Forty-Four

May 28, 1953
St Joseph's Farm and Trade School, Bindoon, Western Australia

After the attempt to run away, Harry didn't see Little Tom very often. He was moved to another dormitory closer to Brother Thomas's room and became his constant companion. There were a group of them who hung around Brother Thomas. The 'Pets', they were called by the other boys, and they were given special treats; the easiest jobs, little tea parties in his room, and they worked less, spending more time in the classroom.

Harry was told to work on the farm. At first, he was given the jobs in the dairy but he didn't mind. He liked getting up early at 4.30 to milk the cows. The first time he tried to pull those udders he failed miserably, nothing came out.

Slimo showed him how to do it.

'Look, you grab hold of the teat, give it a firm tug and a little twist with your wrist.'

A long stream of slightly milky liquid squirted into the bucket.

Harry stared at the large animal standing in front of him. The big, brown, baleful eye surrounded by long lashes stared back at him. It was the first time he had been this close to anything so big and it was as if the animal sensed his fear. 'Never seen a cow this close before. We don't get many back in Oldham. Will she kick me?'

Slimo stood up and slapped the hindquarters of the cow, and her tail swished from side to side. 'Don't worry about old Molly here. She likes being milked, don't you, old girl?'

Slimo hugged the face of the cow. Snot dribbled from two large nostrils. A long, almost prehensile tongue slipped out to try to lick his face. The eyes, with their long lashes, seemed to be staring directly at Harry.

'Are you sure?'

'Of course, she's a big softy is Old Molly.' He sat down again on the stool. 'See, just grab the teats with your hands, tug down and twist.' This time two streams of milky liquid squirted into the bucket. Followed by two more. 'It's important to get into a rhythm. One-two. One-two. One-two.'

Slimo was working the teats, his arms going up and down with all the energy of the pistons on the Otranto's engines.

Harry thought of his time on the ship with Friedrich and all the other stokers down in the engine room. It seemed so long ago now. A lifetime and half an age away..

'Pretty soon you'll have a bucket full, then you move on to Dolly.'

'How do you know when to stop?'

'When there's no more milk. Old Molly will let you know. She usually gives a little kick with her hind leg when she's had enough. There's one little perk for getting up so early and working the dairy, though.'

Slimo leant forward and placed his head beneath the teat, squirting the milk directly into his open mouth.

'Mmm, warm milk, fresh from the cow. Can't beat it. When the bucket is full, pour it into the pail over there.'

'Where does it go?'

'The milk?'

Harry nodded.

'The brothers drink most of it for their breakfast and with their tea. Some of it goes into the porridge, and the rest I haven't a clue. Don't care, either, as long as I get my share. Anyway, it's your turn. Have a go.'

Harry stared at Molly and the cow stared back at him, still chewing on the hay Slimo had placed in the rack in front of her.

'Are you sure she won't kick me?'

'Molly wouldn't hurt a flea.'

Harry sat down on the three-legged stool, and gingerly reached for the nearest teat hanging from the distended udder. Molly's hind leg gave a little kick as he touched the teat. He dropped it quickly and jerked away from the cow's body. 'Why'd she do that?'

'It helps if you rub your hands together first. How would you like somebody grabbing you with cold hands?'

Harry rubbed his hands and put them under his armpits for a few seconds to warm up. Once more he reached for the teat, tentatively touching it at first, before holding it more firmly in his fist as Slimo had done.

Above him, Molly carried on chewing her hay, paying him no attention.

'That's great, now give it a firm tug.'

Harry pulled downwards on the teat.

Nothing happened.

'Tug harder, and don't forget the flick of the wrist at the end.'

Harry tugged down as hard as he could, twisting his wrist when the teat couldn't be pulled further.

Still nothing.

Molly's head swung round to stare at him, as if saying, 'Get a bloody move on.'

'Do it more smoothly. Caress it like you would caress a woman.'

Harry had never caressed a woman. He vaguely remembered the hugs from his mum and Mrs Beggs. Was that what Slimo meant?

He tugged down on the teat again. This time a few drops of clear liquid missed the bucket, landing in the red dust of the milking shed's floor.

'That's it. Harder now, and smoother. And don't forget the little twist of the wrist at the end.'

Harry pulled down, angling his wrist so the teat pointed diagonally at the bucket. A stream of milk squirted out from the end and landed in the bucket.

'You've got it.' Slimo gave a little dance around the milking shed, his arms pumping up and down as if he were milking a giant cow.

Harry kept on milking Molly, streams of liquid landing in the bucket as it slowly filled up. He even tried using his left hand too, but he wasn't so successful with that. It didn't take long for him to get the hang of it, though. All he had to remember was to make his hands move like the pistons of the Otranto's engines.

Up and down.

Up and down.

Up and down.

This was Harry's life for now, and he didn't mind it too much. Slimo was a good friend and they only saw the brothers occasionally. The mess and smell in the cowsheds and the piggery was too much for them.

He soon got used to the cows and the pigs and the chooks. Talking to them seemed to help, making them less skittish and more friendly. Perhaps they got used to him too. The way he moved. The way he smelt. The way he treated them.

Slimo was always on hand to help him if things went wrong. Like one day, when the piglets escaped from their pens and they had to chase them round the yard, their mouths squealing and their little legs scampering away from Harry's outstretched hands.

Luckily, Slimo managed to catch them all before the brothers found out otherwise they would have been up for a beating with the strap.

Working in the farm had other advantages too. They were able to look for scraps in the pig feed; mouldy bread, a half-eaten tomato, even a bit of an apple. If Harry and Slimo checked the bucket before they fed the pigs, there was always something to eat.

The food in the dining room was still as bad as ever; maggots in the porridge, kangaroo tails floating in hot water as a soup, a mash of stale bread soaked in watered milk for dinner. Hunger seemed to be the one constant companion for the whole time Harry was at Bindoon.

He was hungry when he woke up in the morning.

Hungry after lunch.

Hungry after dinner.

Hungry when he went to bed.

An aching, grinding hunger that never left him.

In his dreams, when he had any, he often imagined a feast laid out in front of him, where he could choose any of the foods, gorging himself until he could eat no more.

Heaven.

He often wondered what happened to all the eggs, pork, milk, apricots, grapes, chickens, butter and bread they grew on the farm. He was stupid enough to ask one of the brothers once. Brother Dominic, it was.

The answer was a backhand across his head, followed by a punch with a closed fist. 'Don't be asking stupid questions. What d'ye think pays for all this?'

He knew who paid for all this.

He did.

Chapter Forty-Five

March 26, 1954

St Joseph's Farm and Trade School, Bindoon, Western Australia

All the boys were standing there in the hot sun, a warm breeze coming off the hills and blowing little eddies of red dust in front of the main building.

The speaker, one of the local dignitaries, was droning on.

Harry stood with his hands behind his back, a broad smile on his face. He was wearing a fresh white shirt and clean khaki shorts. On his feet, new sandals were chafing his heels, biting into the hard flesh that was so unused to footwear. Next to him, Slimo was whispering out of the corner of his mouth.

'I wish the fat arse would hurry up. He'd send a drongo to sleep.'

'I take this moment to welcome up on stage the Right Reverend Charles McClure.'

The audience sitting in front of the windswept stage politely clapped. A long stare from Brother Thomas encouraged the boys to join in.

There was a loud squeal, like an escaped piglet, from the microphone as the Right Reverend climbed on the stage.

'Well, that's a lovely welcome.'

Another squeal from the microphone.

'We are gathered here today, ladies and gentlemen... and boys,' he said as an afterthought, 'to celebrate the life of Brother Francis Paul Keaney, who died suddenly last month in Subiaco.'

'And won't be missed by a single one of us here,' whispered Slimo.

'His bloody stick won't be, anyway.'

The Right Reverend continued speaking. 'Brother Paul, as he was known, was born in Roscommon, Ireland, coming to Australia in 1912 to work as a policeman. And, looking at some of the boys in front of me, I'm sure his police training came in very useful.'

There was laughter from the audience seated in their chairs. Some people were from the local area, but many had driven out from Perth and Fremantle to Bindoon. In amongst them was a large contingent of clergy.

In front of them was a black casket with a closed lid.

'That's so the bastard can't escape,' said Slimo when he saw it.

'Brother Keaney joined the Christian Brothers in 1915 and dedicated his life to working to improve the life of the children in his care.'

Slimo snorted.

The speaker stopped for a moment to look out over the assembled crowd. Brother Thomas stared once more at Slimo, reaching down to the strap that was not hanging at his waist today. His hand fumbled for a moment, looking for the missing strap, before forming into a fist.

'He taught at Clontarf, Tardun and the Christian Brothers' colleges in Western Australia, coming to St Joseph's Farm and Trade School for the first time in 1942. He returned in 1948.' The Right Reverend pointed to the buildings surrounding them. 'It is not for

249

nothing he was known as "Keaney the Builder". It is through his efforts and hard work that these buildings stand tall and strong in this rugged country. All of them are a manifestation of his will. They were created by him.'

'By him?' whispered Slimo. 'I thought we built them? He sat on his fat arse and pointed his stick.'

'Shush.'

The loud noise from Brother Thomas stopped the Right Reverend from speaking for a second, but he soon returned to his notes, looking down to find his place.

'St Joseph's became known to everybody as "Bindoon Boys Town". And it is fair to say that Brother Keaney embodied all the caring, humility and generosity of spirit so wonderfully portrayed by Spencer Tracy as Father Flanagan in that beautiful film.'

Slimo snorted again, covering it up this time by coughing loudly and placing his hand over his mouth and nose. He received another long, penetrating stare from Brother Thomas.

'It is not for nothing that he was known as "The Orphan's Friend". We are gathered here today with many of the orphans he looked after with such loving care.'

The Right Reverend made an expansive gesture with his hand, taking in all the boys arrayed in front of him. 'We are gathered to lay this remarkable man, this remarkable Christian Brother, to rest in a grave close to the buildings and the school he made in his image.'

Harry shifted his weight from one foot to the other. He wished it would be all over soon and he could get out of these sandals and this new shirt, which chafed his neck.

At least they would eat well tonight. The presence of so many visitors always ensured the food was better than normal.

'Please join me in saying the Lord's Prayer.'

The Right Reverend bowed his head and began intoning the words in his deep voice. Slimo, Harry and the rest of the boys followed him, the words etched into every inch of their souls.

'Our father, who art in Heaven, hallowed be Thy name. Thy Kingdom come, Thy will be done, in earth as it is in heaven. Give us this day our daily bread and forgive us our debts as we forgive our debtors...'

As the Right Reverend said the words, Harry raised his head to stare across at Little Tom standing opposite him. The boy's eyes were wet with tears. Brother Thomas put his arm around his shoulders to comfort him.

'...And lead us not into temptation, but deliver us from evil. For Thine is the Kingdom and the power and the glory forever. Amen.'

Chapter Forty-Six

October 4, 1955

St Joseph's Farm and Trade School, Bindoon, Western Australia

Harry and Slimo laid back in one of the rows of the vineyard, hidden from sight by the new growth of leaves on the vines. They had skived off from finishing the concrete on the balustrades of the new classrooms when Brother Thomas wasn't looking. And now they dozed fitfully in the late evening sun, just doing nothing.

It had been one of those days that didn't happen often at the Boys Town. A beautiful day when all had gone well and the world was about as good as it was ever going to be.

That morning, the spring sun had risen, bringing out the best of Bindoon before the baking heat of summer. The sky was a robin's-egg blue. The birds were singing in the orchard. A gentle breeze blew over the red soil but wasn't strong enough to disturb it. Even the flies had signed a pledge not to disturb the peace.

Harry and Slimo had gone about their usual duties around the farm; milking the cows, feeding the pigs and knocking the chooks off the eggs in the hen house. In the pigs' feed, they came acrosss a whole uneaten apple hidden beneath a mound of slops.

'Must have been thrown in by mistake,' said Slimo, running it under a cold tap.

They sat down in the hen house and shared it, each one taking a bite in turn, the juice running down their faces.

Two of the Spanish nuns found them in the chook house when they came for the eggs for the brothers' breakfast. The younger of the two, a sprightly fifty-seven-year-old, found it funny that the two boys were sitting on the shelves where the chooks laid their eggs. She said something in Spanish and the elder one laughed.

'What's so funny?' asked Slimo.

'I was thinking, if you had laid an apple,' she answered in halting English.

Harry and Slimo glanced at each other and laughed.

'That's pretty funny. Laid an apple...'

She took the basket of eggs and stopped at the door of the chook house, returning with two small eggs in her wrinkled hands.

Slimo grabbed them off her. 'Thanks, Sister.' He placed one carefully on a nest of hay in the pocket of his shorts and gave the other to Harry.

'What are we going to do with them?'

'I'll show you later.'

In the middle of the morning, Slimo skimmed the top of the milk to remove the cream and poured it into an old cracked bowl they found on the tip. He cracked the two eggs into the middle of the cream and whisked it together with his finger, breaking the yolks.

'Drink it, it's good for you.'

Harry eyed the yellow mixture, with the strands of egg white floating on top. 'You sure?'

'Down it in one.'

Harry raised the cracked bowl to his lips and drank half the mixture. The cream was still warm and the eggs had cooked slightly, turning the egg white into a slimy mess. He swallowed it anyway, feeling it slip down his throat after sticking to his teeth. 'Ugh, that's awful, that is.'

Slimo took the bowl and finished off what was left in three enormous swallows, his Adam's apple bobbing up and down as he swallowed. He wiped his face with the back of his hand and said, 'Tastes horrible but does you good. My gran swears by it, and she lived to be seventy-five.'

They'd finished all their assigned work around the farm before lunchtime, which was unusual. It was as if the egg-and-cream drink had given them a whole new bout of energy.

Even lunch was better than normal on this day of days – lamb stew, which actually had bits of lamb, carrot and potato in it. Harry saw the reason for the quality of the food; a man in a suit and tie was with Brother Quilligan, going round each table in the dining room and peering into the plates and bowls. Tea cups and saucers had been laid, with a choice of orange juice, tea or milk. Even better, each boy had a large orange from the orchard given to him at the end of the meal.

Harry saw the visitor watching as he wolfed down his lamb stew. When he'd finished he took his plate and walked up to Brother Murphy, who was doling out the food.

'Please, sir, can I have more?'

Brother Murphy glanced across at the visitor and ladled a dollop of lamb stew on to Harry's empty plate.

Harry decided to push his luck. 'Could I have that piece of lamb too?'

A large chunk of lamb lay in the middle of the brown stew. Brother Murphy stared at him. For a moment, Harry thought he had pushed it too far. But slowly, and with reluctance, the ladle scooped up the chunk of lamb and placed it in the centre of the plate.

'That's enough now, Britton, we must save some for the others,' Brother Murphy said through gritted teeth.

On hearing these words, the others on Harry's table, led by Slimo, strode up to the brother and held out their plates.

For the first time in a long time, they left the dining room feeling full and happy.

The afternoon was spent with Brother Thomas, helping to finish the concreting of the balustrades on the new classrooms. When he went for his afternoon tea, they finished the job quickly and found the spot in the vineyard where they could hide.

Harry lay back in the soft earth and stared up through the leaves into the blue sky. 'Slimo,' he said, 'how'd you get your name?'

'Frogs,' said Slimo.

'Frogs?'

'When I was a nipper, me and my gran went to a lake, dunno where. Anyway, I found some frog's eggs in the water and started eating them. Must have been about three years old, I reckon. She called me Slimo and it stuck. I've been Slimo Henderson ever since.'

'What did they taste like?'

'Can't remember. Slimy, I suppose. Like the sago we sometimes get.'

Harry sat up and pulled out a blade of grass growing close to one of the vines, putting it between his teeth to suck out the juice. 'Why you here?'

'What d'ye mean?'

255

'Well, you're an Aussie, you don't have to be here. Not like me and the others.'

'There's other Aussies here.'

'Yeah, but not so many, most of us are Poms. So why are you here?'

'Dunno really. Me mum brought me here when I was ten. I'd lived with my gran since I was an ankle biter, but she passed away. Found her in bed one Spring morning. Tried to wake her but she didn't get up.' He waved a fly away from his eyes. 'Just lay there, grey and cold.'

'Was she dead?'

'That's what they said. Buried her soon after. Spent a week or two with me mam and her new feller. Ran away twice.'

'Where'd you go?'

'Nowhere. Just on the streets, wandering around all over the place.'

'What happened?'

'After the second time, they brought me here. Said it would make a man of me. What about you?'

Harry dragged his toes through the red soil, making a furrow leading away from the trunk of the vine. 'Dunno. Always thought one day I'd go back to live with me mum, but she sent me here. I guess she doesn't want me any more.'

'You still write to her, though.'

Harry shrugged his shoulders. 'I just want to tell her what I'm doing, in case she ever wants me back. But it's been three years now...'

'It's like the brothers say. Nobody wants us, that's why we're here.'

'Hey, you two, what you doing in there? Come out now.'

Brother Thomas knelt at the end of the row of vines, peering down beneath the leaves.

Slimo and Harry sat up straight, looking for somewhere to run.

'I can see you, Henderson and Britton, come out now.'

They crawled out of their hiding place on their hands and knees. As they stood up, Brother Thomas twisted their ears, giving each one a violent shank.

Harry felt the skin tear where the top of his ear met his head. The pain shot through his eyes and blood began to pour down his neck. He jammed his hand against the ear, feeling the end flop between his fingers.

Brother Thomas gave them both a kick up the backside with his boot. 'See me after dinner this evening, before you say your rosary.'

He lashed out again as Harry and Slimo dodged the kicks.

'Now get back to work, you lazy bastards.'

Chapter Forty-Seven

July 25, 2017
Buxton Residential Home, Derbyshire, England

Jayne's case with the blonde TV presenter was winding down to a satisfactory conclusion. After a lot of digging, she had discovered the celebrity's great-grandfather had been a former slave who had come to England as the servant of a plantation owner, escaping his servitude and claiming the right to be a free man. In a famous court case in 1780, his claim had been supported and he had lived out his days as the landlord of an inn in Essex.

The celebrity was delighted with the research, proclaiming her new identity in a series of television interviews, and even mentioning Jayne by name. As a result, she had been inundated with emails over the last few days but had decided to ignore them all for now.

Work could wait, her family was more important than anything else. Her father's test results had come back and there was a worrying drop in his red cell count.

More tests had been ordered and they were waiting to hear. Hopefully they would receive them soon. The wait was making both her father and Vera extremely despondent.

'How you feeling, Dad?'

They were both sitting in the day room, as they had done for the last week. Her father seemed to be feeling the cold even though it was a bright and sunny summer's day outside.

'Same old, same old. Still feeling tired, Jayne. Wish those bloody test results would come back.'

Vera put her hand on his arm. 'He's not eating, either. No appetite, he says.'

'You try eating the food here. Wouldn't feed it to the pigs…'

'Shush, Robert, that's not nice to say.'

'You used to love the food here, Dad, it was one of the reasons why you chose the place. Remember the jam roly-poly?'

Her father smiled for the first time. 'My favourite. I like a good thick custard with it, though.'

'I'll have a chat with Matron and see if they can do one soon. Might help you rediscover your appetite.' Jayne sat down next to him, moving aside a half-finished Guardian crossword. She checked the clock on the wall. Two p.m. 'Time to make the call.'

She had arranged to ring Duncan so he could tell them of his progress. 'Ready, Vera?'

'As ready as I'll ever be.'

She put her mobile on speakerphone and rang Duncan's number. The phone was answered in two rings.

'Hello, Duncan Morgan speaking.'

'Hi there, it's Jayne. I've got you on speaker with Vera and Dad listening in.'

'Good evening all.'

'It's afternoon here,' said her father grumpily.

'So it is, g'day. Now I've got good news and bad news for you.'

'Go on, Duncan.'

'I went to Tuart Place earlier this week. The people there were lovely, only too happy to help. There was a bit of problem with the difference in names between your half-brother and you, Vera, but once I showed them the birth certificate and the family tree, they were happy to proceed.'

'What does "proceed" mean, Duncan?' asked Vera.

'It means they will put a request into PHIND – it's the database for all Catholic Child Migrants into Western Australia in the fifties. Harry's documents should be stored there if he was at Bindoon. We should have an answer in a couple of weeks with a bit of luck.'

'And if his documents aren't there?'

'Well, we're buggered, to use the technical term. I'll have to work out a different way of tackling this, but we'll cross that kettle of fish when we come to it, if you know what I mean.'

'Let's hope they can find the documents,' said Jayne. 'What's the bad news?'

There was a long sigh at the end of the phone. 'I thought I would short-circuit the process by checking up on any Harry or Harold Brittons in the White Pages...'

'And?'

'Nobody with that name in Western Australia. In the other states, there's one Harry Britton in Sydney but he's three years old so I don't think he's our man.'

'Not good is it, Duncan?'

'No, it's not. But let's not jump ahead of ourselves. We should wait until we see the documents before we do anything else.'

'Why isn't it good, Jayne?' asked Vera.

'Well, it means he may have left Australia and moved to another country. Or it could mean he's not registered as part of a household. Even worse, it could mean he has already passed away.'

Vera bit down on her bottom lip again. 'Please. I hope not.'

'Listen, as I said, we can't jump ahead of ourselves.'

'You're right, Duncan, let's wait for the documents before worrying what to do next.'

'I'll email you when I receive them. Keep your heads up, folks, all genealogical research is a journey of discovery, we'll get there in the end.'

'Thanks for everything. Bye!' Jayne switched off the phone.

Vera's face was crestfallen. 'I wish he hadn't told me about the White Pages.'

'Duncan is the best researcher I know. If anybody can find Harry, it will be him.'

'Aye, don't start worrying now, love. It's just the beginning of the search in Australia.'

Vera frowned. 'I wish it were the end. I hope we can find him. He's been lost for so long. I don't know why, but I keep feeling we haven't much time.'

Chapter Forty-Eight

August 3, 1956
St Joseph's Farm and Trade School, Bindoon, Western Australia

Slimo was putting his things in his army kitbag. He didn't have much; an old second-hand pair of boots given to him by some visitor, a faded jumper with patches on the elbows, a couple of shirts, two pairs of socks and a singlet with holes in it.

He held up a pair of grundies that appeared brand new. 'Never worn these, don't suppose I ever will.' He folded them up neatly, slipping them into the side pocket of the kitbag.

There just remained his best bib and tucker; a white shirt, tie, grey shorts and brown shoes the monks had given him yesterday. 'For when you go to Mass,' they told him. He folded these as best he could, placing them on top of the other clothes, then pulling the string tight and knotting it.

'That's me done.'

'When you going?' asked Harry.

They were in the empty dormitory. All the other boys were in classes, in the woodwork room, finishing the chores on the farm, or adding the last touches to the new classroom block. Since the death of Brother Keaney, the mania for building had slowed down. Even the planned cathedral, with its elevated walkway to the main building, had been abandoned. For the moment, the boys just did basic maintenance on the buildings rather than constructing anything new.

Slimo played with the string closing the kitbag. 'When the pig truck is ready. Brother Mitchell said I could hop on the back and get a lift to the town.'

'Your mum coming?'

Slimo shook his head. 'She's too busy. Got another sprog with her new feller.' He sat down on the bed to put on the sandals the brothers had given him. They used to be Brother Dominic's, but he had a new pair now.

'Where you going?'

'Up north. Got a job on a farm near Murchison. They're going to pay me three pounds and ten shillings a week, plus me room and board. I'll come back and visit if you want,' Slimo said tentatively.

Harry just nodded.

They heard a loud beep from outside.

'Sounds like Brother Mitchell, he's always in a rush.' Slimo stepped towards Harry with his hand out. 'Look after yourself, Harry, don't let the bastards grind you down.'

Harry stared at the hand. He wanted to rush forward and hug Slimo. Tell him how much he would miss him. Explain he would never have survived Bindoon without his help. Thank him for all he had done.

But he didn't.

Instead, he shook his friend's hand and said, 'Bye, Slimo. Look after yourself, mate, and don't let the bed bugs bite.'

'I'll come back to see you when I've made a bit of money and can get some time off.' Slimo picked up his kitbag and walked to the door, turning back just before he left. 'Keep your head down, Harry. Keep your head down.'

And then he was gone.

Harry stood there in the empty dormitory. Outside, he heard Brother Mitchell's voice. 'Get a bloody move on, Henderson. We don't have all day.'

He rushed out on to the balcony.

Slimo was climbing into the back of the truck with the barrels of pig slops. He edged forward to grab hold of the bar above the cab and stared straight ahead as Brother Mitchell put the truck into gear and accelerated away in a cloud of red dust.

He didn't look back as Harry raised his hand to wave goodbye.

Harry was still waving as the truck vanished out of sight around the bend, heading towards the main gate.

He was alone now.

All alone.

Chapter Forty-Nine

October 8, 1957
St Joseph's Farm and Trade School, Bindoon, Western Australia

Slimo never came back to Bindoon, of course. Not that Harry expected him to. Not many of the boys returned once they left.

For the first couple of months, Harry missed him. But then he settled into the steady monotony of Boys Town. Up early to work with the cattle. A quick lunch. Catechism classes on Tuesdays and Thursdays. Metalwork or carpentry on the other days. Afternoons spent in the orchard or keeping the buildings maintained and clean.

He still had difficulty with reading and writing. If he concentrated and went slowly, he could read his catechism, but writing was always a problem. The letter home he wrote each month took him a week to get right.

Harry remembered the help Miss Anstey had given him on the voyage to Australia. Correcting his letters and making them look right on the page. He still had the diary somewhere, but he didn't look at it any more. It seemed like another person had written it a long time ago.

Nowadays, when he wrote something the words and the letters just jumbled up on the page. They

265

were in his head but once he wrote them down on paper, they looked all wrong.

The brothers and the other kids picked on him.

'You'll never amount to much, Britton.'

'Still can't write properly at your age, you should be ashamed.'

'Read the first line of the next page. Quicker, boy, it won't bite you.'

'He's dumb, he is, Harry Britton.'

He did better with his sums. At least then the numbers came out clearly when he wrote them, but the brothers didn't teach much about that stuff to him. Some of the boys received lessons, the favourites. Little Tom was one of those.

They met once on the steps in front of the new classrooms. Harry was just coming out to go and feed the chooks and Little Tom was going in for his afternoon lessons.

His friend from St Michael's was still fairly small, but there was a sharpness, a cleverness in the eyes which Harry had never noticed before.

'Wotcha, Harry.'

'Hi, Tom.'

They stood in front of each other, wondering what to say. Harry noticed the boy's clothing was clean and fairly new. His own was shabby, with tears in the shorts and stains on his shirt. He tried to keep it clean but there was no point any more. It would just be dirty again tomorrow.

'You still working in the dairy?'

Harry nodded. 'Haven't seen you on the farm for a while.'

'They've got me cleaning the brothers' rooms.'

'Cushy number.'

Little Tom seemed to think for a moment. 'Listen, Harry, you still writing to England?'

Harry nodded. 'Every month. No reply, though. Mum's forgotten me.'

Tom peered down at his bare feet, as if examining whether he still had five toes. Then he looked back up. 'Don't bother, the brothers don't like it.'

A frown creased Harry's forehead. 'What do you mean?'

'They just don't like it. They don't like any of the boys writing home.'

Harry shook his head. 'But I always write home. Takes me ages, it does, and I know it don't look good, but—'

'Don't bother, Harry.'

Little Tom turned to walk up the stairs, but Harry grabbed his arm. 'What do you mean?'

Tom thought for a moment. 'Meet me later at five, outside the tower staircase.' He shrugged off Harry's arm and trotted up the stairs.

For the rest of the afternoon, Harry wondered what Tom meant. At the appointed time, he walked to the base of the staircase leading up to the brothers' private rooms.

He waited for fifteen minutes and was just about to leave and go back to his dorm when Tom appeared by his side, as if out of nowhere.

'Shush, quiet, we don't want them to hear.'

Little Tom began to climb the steps to the upper floors.

'We're not supposed to be here.'

'You want to know or not?'

'Want to know what?'

Little Tom rounded on him, the whites of his eyes shining in the shadows of the dark tower. 'You're a bloody fool, Harry. Want to know why? I'm going to show you.'

'I don't understand.'

Tom let out a sigh and then spoke slowly, as if lecturing a four-year-old. 'Just… follow… me.'

Harry climbed the stairs behind Tom, keeping to the outside and looking upwards constantly to make sure none of the brothers were coming down. When they reached the third floor, where the brothers had their rooms, they crept along a tiled corridor past a row of doors.

'Shhh… Some of them may be asleep.' Little Tom stopped in front of a door near the end. He pulled out a silver key from his top pocket and showed it to Harry. 'They don't know I have this.' He inserted it into the lock and turned.

There was a loud click and Harry jumped, glancing over his shoulder to check no brothers had come out of their room to investigate the strange noise.

Little Tom pushed open the door and ushered Harry inside, closing it behind him. The room was totally black, with only a faint grey light peering in through a small window in the corner of the far wall.

Gradually, Harry's eyes adjusted to the dim light. He could see it was a small storeroom with wooden shelves lining the walls. Each shelf held a row of brown files, aligned with each other like books in a library. At one end was a stack of cardboard boxes reaching up to the window and blocking out most of the light.

'What is it?'

'Look around you.'

'It's a storeroom.'

'But what does it store, Harry? That is the question.'

Little Tom reached up and took one of the box files off the shelf. 'I found it one day, after cleaning the brothers' rooms. I was looking for some soap and I found these.'

268

He opened the box file. Inside was a stack of letters, each in their original envelopes, the addresses written in different handwriting.

Harry shuffled through them. The addresses were for a variety of places in England, Ireland, Scotland, Wales or Australia. And then he picked up one of them from the pile. The address was for Oldham and he recognised the handwriting, each letter painfully and slowly inscribed on the cover of the envelope. But it was the name on the front that took his breath away: Mrs Freda Duckworth.

'It's my letter. I wrote it when I came here.'

'Your letters and everybody else's. Don't you see, Harry? You never get a reply because they never send them. The brothers don't like us to write home.'

And then Little Tom began laughing.

Harry grabbed the letter and rushed out of the storeroom, running down the stairs past Brother Mitchell and across to the main building.

He shoved open the door to Brother Quilligan's room. The new head of Bindoon, who had replaced Brother Keaney, was sitting behind his desk, writing in the ledger in front of him. 'What do you want, Britton?'

Harry couldn't get the words out. He began to stammer. 'The l-l-l-letters… You… you n-never sent them…'

The brother took off his pince-nez glasses and placed them on top of the ledger. 'Letters from home often disturb the confidence of the boys at Bindoon, making it more difficult for them to settle in and slowing their adaptation to their new life in Australia.'

Harry held up the letter, his hand shaking. 'B-b-but I've b-b-been writing f-f-for five years…'

'And I hope you will continue to write. It will help you construct your sentences.'

'B-but... b-but you...' The words just wouldn't come out.

'But we never sent them?' Brother Quilligan finished Harry's sentence for him.

Harry nodded, shifting from one foot to another, his bare feet staining the rich red carpet.

'No, we didn't. It was the right thing to do.' Brother Quilligan's voice was calm and considered as he continued. 'But now I am angry, Britton. You have managed to gain entry into a locked room in a forbidden area. And you have stolen from that room. This is an offence in this school and in the eyes of God, for which you will be punished. Bend over the table and pull your shorts down.'

Harry just stood there, shaking. His heart was pounding and his breath was coming in short, sharp spurts.

'Did you hear me, Britton? You must submit to the punishment of God. Bend over the desk and pull your shorts down.'

Harry still stood there, unmoving.

'I will ask you one more time. If you do not obey my order, I will call Brother Thomas and Brother Dominic to hold you over the desk and you will submit to your punishment. It will then be repeated again this evening after dinner in front of the whole school.'

Harry's body went numb. The letter, written so long ago, floated free from his fingers to land on the carpet. His arms came down by his sides and his breath stilled.

He strode over to Brother Quilligan's desk and bent over, pulling his shorts down to reveal his bare buttocks.

'You must understand this pains me far more than it will hurt you, Britton.'

The bamboo cane rose slowly up into the air before it came swishing down across the flesh of Harry's behind, again and again and again.

He didn't cry out.

Not once.

When the end of the month came, and it was time for him to write home, Harry took the blank paper and burned it in the flame of a candle.

He never wrote home again.

Chapter Fifty

May 5, 1958
St Joseph's Farm and Trade School, Bindoon, Western Australia

He was alone now.

Of course, he still slept in a dormitory full of boys. He still ate with all the others. He still showered with them, the brothers watching from their place next to the hot-water geyser.

He went to the tech building most days when he had finished his work on the farm. There was a comfort in fiddling with an engine, or turning the lathe, or simply planing a plank of wood. He liked working with his hands, making something respond to his touch.

These engines, these bits of wood, these objects — they talked to him and they didn't answer back. They just did what he wanted them to do.

The other boys thought he was strange, but he didn't care. What was the use of talking with them?

He was still beaten by the brothers, of course, but not so often. He knew how to read their moods and when to avoid the bite of the weighted strap, the swipe with the back of the hand or the punch with the clenched fist.

There was another reason, too. The incident with Brother Thomas.

It happened one day in the dairy. Brother Thomas had crept up behind him and pushed his body down over the metal cage where they kept the cattle feed.

Harry had twisted around quickly, pulling out the small knife he kept to cut the ropes that bound the hay. Brother Thomas had jumped back, wary of the determination in Harry's eyes.

'No, you don't want to be doing that, Harold.'

'Leave me alone.'

The brother held up his hands in mock surrender, backing away from the knife. 'I was just joshing with you. Can't a body have a wee bit of fun these days?'

'Leave me alone,' Harry repeated, waving the knife in front of him.

Brother Thomas had backed out of the dairy, quickening his pace as he crossed the yard. Harry expected the worst that evening, at least a beating with the cane from Brother Quilligan.

But nothing happened.

When he went into the dining room, not one of the brothers looked at him, not one of them said a word. Since then, they had been wary of him, leaving him alone most days to look after the animals on the farm.

Most afternoons, when he had fed the pigs and watered the cattle, he skived off to sit beneath a Kari tree.

Somehow, this one had survived Brother Keaney and grew on its own in the middle of the bush down by the creek. He and Slimo had discovered it one day as they were looking for rabbits.

About halfway up the trunk, they had both inscribed their names and the date. Slimo and Harry. Dec 1955. Actually, Slimo had inscribed Harry's name as he could write better, even with a knife.

Harry would sit beneath the tree and try to remember his mum and Mrs Beggs and his life in England. But each time it became harder and harder, as if they were on a train pulling out of a station, their faces receding into the distance until he could see them no more.

He tried to recall his mother's voice. Or the smell of her hair. Or the touch of her lips. But he couldn't. Not any more. It was all too long ago and too far away.

After the fight with Brother Thomas, he went to the Kari tree to escape, to find peace, to remember his mother, and Mrs Beggs and Slimo.

He took the knife and cut into the bark, removing his name, leaving an ugly gash in the tree.

He was nobody.

Not any more.

That's what the brothers had told him, and it was true.

He would vanish into thin air like he had never existed.

A nobody with no name, no face, no past, no present and no future.

Nothing.

Chapter Fifty-One

September 5, 1959

St Joseph's Farm and Trade School, Bindoon, Western Australia

The end to Harry's life in Bindoon came a week after his 15th birthday.

There were fewer boys in Bindoon now; the boatloads that used to come from England had slowed to a trickle. More Maltese and some Aussie lads had arrived in the last few years, but Harry didn't really associate with them.

All the St Michael's boys who had come to Bindoon with Harry had left. Ernie, never the same after his beating, had been sent to Castledare, another orphanage. Little Tom had passed his exams earlier in the year and had been sent to one of the Christian Brothers' schools in Perth. The brothers had high hopes he would make them proud. Slimo had never come back since he had left for the farm in Murchison. The rest had vanished when they left the place, never to return,

The lack of boys meant Harry spent more and more time on the farm; driving the tractor, looking after the cows, pigs and chickens virtually alone, and making sure the vineyard was pruned and sprayed. He hardly ever went to school. As the brothers said, there was no point. He would never make much of himself.

275

Farm work was going to be his future for the rest of his life.

In the last year, his body had changed. The constant manual work had helped him develop a wiry frame; lean and strong. He was still hungry all the time, but his little perks around the farm kept him going; a squirt of milk from the cow's teat in the morning, a few eggs from the chooks, what he could steal from the pigs, and whatever stone fruit was in season in the orchard.

He lived by his wits, only socialising with the other boys when he was forced to do so by the brothers. Most of the time, he remained alone.

As he was packing his things to leave, Brother Quilligan came to him.

'We're going to miss you, Britton.'

Harry carried on packing.

'The farm won't be the same without you. None of the other boys has your way with the animals.'

Brother Quilligan adjusted his cassock over his large stomach and sat down on the bed. It creaked and groaned beneath his weight.

'Will you not stay for another year?'

'I won't, Brother Quilligan.'

'Why not, for heaven's sake? This is your home.'

Harry stopped what he was doing and stared at Brother Quilligan. This man, with his cane and his strap and his punishments, no longer frightened him. 'Can you pay me four pounds a month?'

'You know we can't, Britton. This is a school, not a business.'

'Then you have your answer.'

Brother Quilligan stood up quickly. 'Trust me, you won't amount to much, Britton. None of you boys will ever amount to anything. We give our lives to you, and what do we get in return? Nothing.' He marched over to the door, turning before he went out. 'With such an attitude, you can make your own way into town. There'll be no truck for you.'

Harry smiled. 'Mr Townsend is coming for me in ten minutes. He'll wait on the main road.'

The monk raised his finger and pointed directly at Harry, his face reddening. 'You should be grateful for all we have done for you, Britton. You were nothing when you came here, and you'll be nothing when you leave.' He marched out of the dormitory, slamming the door shut behind him.

Ten minutes later, Harry was walking down the long driveway leading to the main gate, carrying the same suitcase that was given to him in Afflecks six years earlier.

Behind him, the buildings that were built with the sweat, blood and tears of an army of young boys blended into the hills. On his left, the stations of the cross stood next to the road, each one bearing a picture of the suffering of Christ, each one a reminder of the suffering of the boys themselves.

Up ahead the farmer, Mr Townsend, was standing beside his truck beneath the arch, smoking a cigarette and waiting for Harry.

'You took your time.'

'Aye, about six years.'

The farmer threw his cigarette into the ditch beside the road. 'Is that all you've got?'

Harry slung the brown suitcase in the back. 'Yeah.'

'Not much.'

'No.'

'Anyway, you won't need anything on the farm. Not a lot there but sheep.'

'I know.'

'What did you say your name was again?'

'Harry.'

'Harry what?'

'Just Harry.'

The farmer put the truck into gear and pulled away. 'Don't say much, do ye?'

'No.'

'We're going to get on fine.'

The truck accelerated away up the hill. Harry was tempted to look back as they reached the crest. But he didn't.

Instead, he remembered the words of Brother Dawe all those years ago. 'We're going to make men of you.'

Well, the brothers had succeeded. The child had gone, and a man remained. Harry Britton was dead and another Harry had taken his place.

It was time to forget the brothers and begin again.

Chapter Fifty-Two

August 6, 2017
Buxton Residential Home, Derbyshire, England

'Are you ready, Vera?'

Jayne's step mother fanned herself with her hand. 'As ready as I'll ever be. Don't keep me in suspense any longer, my old heart can't handle it.'

'After last time, Duncan insisted on taking you through the documents one by one. He wants to explain them to you himself. He made me promise not to open them until you were listening.'

'That's good news, isn't it? It means there are some documents, at least?'

'I hope so…'

They were sitting in the Matron's office. Jayne had requested a quiet area where they could make the FaceTime call to Duncan in Australia.

Anywhere away from Victoria sponges and Argentinian Tangos.

It was a small room with a tall, incredibly green aspidistra taking up half the space. This plant was the Matron's pride and joy. She spent hours shining its leaves and encouraging it to grow even larger. Not that there was any more space for it.

'Shall I call him now?'

'Get a move on, Jayne, before Vera has a heart attack.'

Her dad's voice was stronger now. He had been diagnosed with anaemia and put on a course of iron tablets. They were still looking for the cause, but at least he was looking cheerier these days and not sleeping as much.

Jayne opened her laptop and clicked on the Face-Time graphic, selecting Duncan's number in Perth.

His face popped up on her screen within thirty seconds. 'G'day!' His teeth shone white in the video.

'Hello, Duncan, you have some news for us?'

'I do, Jayne, some good and some not so good.'

'Sounds ominous.'

'Is Vera there?'

'She is, and so is my dad.'

They both waved at the screen. Vera said, 'Is he really in Perth? Looks like he's just next door.'

'I'm definitely in Perth, Vera, and it's ten fifteen at night here. Today was a bit cold, though, it's just coming to the end of our winter. But enough of the chit-chat, I'm sure you're dying to know what I've discovered.'

'You don't know how true that is,' said Robert.

'The people at Tuart Place have come back to me with copies of the documents provided by PHIND. In Harry's file they found three documents. I'll put the first one on to split screen so you can see it.'

'I've also opened it on an iPad here.'

'Thanks, Jayne. What you're looking at is the first page of Harry's arrival record at Bindoon.'

name:	**Harold Britton**
date/place of birth:	**August 25, 1944. Oldham, Lancashire.**
parent's name(s):	**Freda Duckworth (Miss)**
age at departure :	**8**

shipping details: SS Otranto. Tilbury, Port of London. April 13, 1952.

name and location
of sending order: St Michael's Home, Oldham, Lancashire.

destination in
Western Australia: Christian Brothers

initial residence, as well as any transfers between homes and schools; and location of records on the subject, including medical, social, educational, baptismal, and immigration records – as well as sources of any records available in the United Kingdom:

Arrival: Bindoon. May 1952.
Departure :   Sept 1959.

Documents: Commonwealth of Australia Department of Immigration form for Child Migrants.

'As you can see, this shows us the details of his arrival.'

'It's pretty basic,' said Vera.

'There's not a lot of information, is there?'

'Not a lot,' answered Duncan. 'I asked for the Commonwealth of Australia form, but they said it wasn't part of the documents they were holding. They thought it may have been lost by the brothers.'

'Lost?' shouted Jayne's father. 'He wasn't a bloody lump of cargo. How could they have lost it?'

Vera patted Robert's arm. 'Don't get upset, dear, Duncan's only telling us what he found.'

'Sorry, I didn't mean to go off at you. It just makes me so bloody angry.'

'S'alright, mate. The people at Tuart can only give me what's in the records. Some of the stuff was never received by them.'

'What else do you have, Duncan?' asked Jayne.

281

'The next one is more interesting, if still very sparse. It seems to be a record of his time at Bindoon.' Duncan split the screen again and added a new document. 'The handwriting varies in legibility, I'm afraid.'

Name: Harold Britton
Birth: August 25, 1944
Arrival in Bindoon: May 28, 1952
Notes:

June 12, 1952: This child is educationally deficient. Unable to read and write with any fluency. Recommendation: Farm work and religious education. Brother Sylvian

Dec 28, 1952: Absconded from the school on Christmas Day with one other boy. Punishment administered. Keaney.

May 24, 1955: Harold seems to be well settled in the school. His care and diligence on the farm has not gone unnoticed, but he still seems to have little aptitude for learning. Sleeping in Catechism class. Brother Dominic.

Jul 2, 1958: Child punished. Brother Quilligan.

Sept 2. 1959. Britton placed with Mr Townsend, owner of Moodiarrup Estate, Great Southern, W. Australia. Quilligan.

'Is that it? After seven years in Bindoon, there are only five notes?' said Vera.

'That's all there is.'

'What about his educational achievements? What did he learn?'

'I'm sorry, Vera, there's nothing else. Just this one sheet attached to his arrival document.'

'He ran away, Vera, look – on Christmas Day. He must have been so unhappy.' Robert pointed to the screen.

'Poor Harry, what did they do to my brother?'

'There's one more attachment to the file that you should see, Vera. Please open document three, Jayne.'

Jayne brought it up on the iPad.

'This is a cutting from the Perth Mail of May 1952. The brothers must have kept it for their records, putting a copy in Harry's file.'

On the screen appeared a page from the newspaper. Beneath a headline saying 'More Child Orphans arrive in Fremantle' was a short article and two pictures. The first picture showed eight children, a woman, two nuns and three brothers surrounding an older, white-haired man in a long gown. It looked like a football team photograph, as if they were all off shortly to play some game.

Underneath was another photograph, of a young, pretty woman standing in front of a boy dressed in a school uniform, her hands resting on his shoulders. Both were smiling into camera. The caption read, 'Miss Claire Anstey of Perth with one of the orphans, Harry from Oldham. Welcome to Australia, Harry!'

'Do you think it's him? Is that our Harry?' Vera said excitedly.

'The dates are correct and the cutting is in his file, so I think it probably is.'

'And if you look at him, Vera, he's a spitting image of the boy with the soldier in your mother's photograph.'

'Oh, Harry, what a beautiful boy...He looks so happy in this photo.'

Jayne stared at the picture. 'And the woman, Claire Anstey, looks like she really cares for him. See how close both of them are.'

'I'm afraid that's all I have from PHIND,' Duncan said. 'I could go into the state records. His missing Immigration Form may be there.'

'Thanks, Duncan, this is really useful. But let me get the chronology right in my head.' Jayne scratched her forehead, while Vera and Robert continued to stare at the cutting from the Perth Mail. 'Harry arrived in Bindoon in 1952 and left in 1959 to go and work on a farm in Moodiarrup.'

'That's right. And that's where the documents end. There seems to have been no follow-up after he left the school, nor did the Brothers keep track of him. He just vanished.'

'What? What do you mean, Duncan?' said Vera.

'I checked with the current landholder of the address mentioned in the final document. He told me one of the previous owners was a Bruce Townsend, but he died in 1968. There are no records of a Harry Britton ever working at the place. In fact, there's no records of anybody working there. Apparently, Mr Townsend didn't believe in records, didn't like paying tax.'

'So what do we do next, Duncan?'

'I've checked for Harry Brittons in the old telephone directories of the time, but there are no Brittons listed.'

'He might have never owned a phone.'

'That's true, Jayne, but—'

'But what?' Vera interrupted.

'But I've researched the lives of these Child Migrants. Many of them didn't do very well after they

284

left the homes. A lot of them became drifters, moving from one farming job to the next. Others ended up on the streets or in jail. Alcoholism seems to have been very common.'

'I'm not surprised, the way they were treated,' said Vera. 'I've been reading about what happened. It was a scandal, a disgrace.'

'And that's what is even more surprising. The story of the Child Migrants broke in the 1990s. In 1994, the Christian Brothers issued an apology. There have been class actions, state inquiries, government Royal Commissions, even a badly run scheme for redress. As we speak, there is a Royal Commission investigating sexual abuse in the Residential Care Homes and Schools of Australia. I've checked all the records available...'

'And?'

'Harry is not mentioned in any of them, nor has he come forward to give evidence or claim redress.'

'Meaning?'

'Meaning when he left Bindoon in 1959, he just vanished into thin air.'

'Nobody can just vanish, not in this day and age. There must be a record for him somewhere.'

'I know, Jayne, but it looks like he did. I'll keep looking and checking the documents, but it's not going to be as easy as we thought.'

'Please keep going. I'll work at my end, perhaps I can come up with something.'

'If you have any questions, don't hesitate to get in touch. We will find him, it just takes time.'

'Thanks for all your work, Duncan, you're a star.'

'Thank you, Duncan,' chorused Vera and Robert.

'Keep your chin up, Vera, we'll find him.'

Jayne switched off the video call.

'Is that it?' asked Vera.

'I don't know. I just don't know. There must be a way of finding out what happened to Harry, but I don't know what it is yet.'

'We've come so far, Jayne – not to find him now would be terrible,' added Robert.

'I know, Dad, but as Duncan said, we've run out of leads.'

'There must be a way. Please let there be a way. Harry suffered so much, we must find out what happened to him.'

Chapter Fifty-Three

August 6, 2017
Didsbury, Manchester, England

All through the journey back to Manchester, Jayne had turned over the video call with Duncan in her mind, looking for answers.

From the bare files in PHIND, they had managed to put together a skeleton of Harry's life.

He had been at Bindoon Boys Town for seven years. He had tried to run away once but had been recaptured and punished. He was considered educationally sub-normal by the brothers, but that didn't tally with everything else they knew. Other people had described him as a bright, cheerful boy. He cared for the animals at Bindoon and seemed to be good at it. Finally, he had gone out to work on a farm when he was fifteen years old.

That was it.

The sum total of seven years of his life. There must be more hidden away somewhere.

What did he learn? How did he live? What were his thoughts and feelings? What were his ambitions? The brothers must have kept more notes about him, mustn't they?

But Duncan had re-checked with Tuart Place. These were the only records kept by the brothers in Harry's file for the seven years he wain in their care.

287

Even worse, they knew nothing about him once he had left Bindoon. It was like he had vanished off the face of the earth. Duncan had been unable to find anything either.

No records.

No telephone listing.

No contact with any of the Child Migrant organisations.

What had happened to him?

As soon as Jayne arrived home, she rushed to switch on her computer. She had to go through the documents with a fine-tooth comb. Perhaps there would be something else, anything, to give them a clue to his whereabouts.

Mr Smith was entwining himself around her legs, miaowing loudly with his tail held upright. She managed to ignore him for twenty minutes before finally giving in.

'Okay, okay, what would we like to eat?'

The cat followed her to the fridge.

'Duck with orange sauce or lamb with rosemary?' She showed him both packs of food, feeling like a crazy cat lady.

He, of course, eyed both suspiciously before licking the outside of the lamb pack.

'Lamb, it is. Sir has made a wonderful choice.' She opened the pack, spooning it into his bowl. He rushed over before she had finished and began to wolf it down. 'I only fed you this morning, you greedy beggar.'

The cat ignored her.

She returned to the computer. This case was full of the strangest complications.

Why had Harry vanished? How had he vanished? Was he dead? Or did something happen to make him go underground?

The more she read about the Christian Brothers and their treatment of the poor children who had the misfortune to be in their care, the more she worried about Harry. Where had he gone? Did he get into trouble? How were they ever going to find him?

Outside, it was another glorious summer's evening in Manchester; the peaceful end of a lazy day. Bees were buzzing around flower pots. People were watering their gardens. Off in the distance, somebody was mowing their lawn.

The classic sounds of summer in suburbia.

After three hours of poring over the documents in Harry's file, Jayne switched off her computer and went to sit on the patio steps beside Mr Smith, to enjoy the remains of the evening sun.

Perhaps they would never find him.

Perhaps he just didn't want to be found.

Thinking of Harry's story made her immensely sad. She thought back over her life. What would have happened if her mum had given up when her biological father walked out? Could she have ended up in one of those homes run by the nuns too? What would have happened then?

And what if Robert hadn't met her mum? She worried about her dad and his illness. She hoped the doctors would find out what was wrong soon. Without him, her life would be emptier than it already was.

Mr Smith gave a plaintive miaow and raced for the back fence, climbing it with all the skill of a tightrope walker. He was off to number nine again.

'Enough, Jayne, you're not going to solve this by turning it over and over again in your head. Get out of the house, go for a walk, but don't beat yourself up. The answer will come.'

She put on her walking shoes and left for Fletcher Moss Gardens. A walk around the flower beds might clear her mind. And if a pint of cider called her name from the Old Cock, well, let it sing its apple heart out.

Tonight, she was going to forget about the case for a few hours and relax.

About bloody time too.

Chapter Fifty-Four

August 6, 2017
Didsbury, Manchester, England

The answer came to her at the most unlikely time.

She had gone for her walk and stepped into the Old Cock for a glass of cider, meeting the Ridleys from number 16 in the pub.

She'd had a lovely chat with them about holidays and Manchester United and cats and the long suicide note otherwise knows as Brexit, totally forgetting about Harry and the case.

When the pub shut, she walked home. Of course, Mr Smith was still out on the prowl. She left him some water and some food in case he returned and managed to find his way in through the cat flap. Then she had gone straight to bed, the computer lying dormant on the kitchen table.

At three o'clock in the morning, she sat upright in her bed.

'That's it,' she said out loud. 'If I were in trouble, that's what I would do.'

Still in her t-shirt and knickers, she rushed down to the kitchen to switch on her computer.

Outside the patio window, Manchester was dark and sleepy. Mr Smith was still out on the prowl, canoodling with the minx at number 9, his food and water untouched in his bowls.

The computer took a while to warm up. 'Come on, come on,' she said impatiently.

The home page finally formed itself and she searched through Harry's file, looking for the image that had come to her in her dream.

Finally, she found it.

She spent a long time staring at the picture on her screen.

'Could that be it?' she said out loud.

She pulled up another document to check the names.

They matched.

It was a long shot, but she had to look into it. That's who she would turn to if she were in trouble.

It might come to nothing, but Jayne trusted her intuition – it very rarely let her down.

The clock on the wall said 3.30 a.m.

Time to ring Duncan in Perth.

Chapter Fifty-Five

August 13, 2017
Buxton Residential Home, Derbyshire, England

'You'll have to speak up, my hearing's not as good as it used to be.'

Jayne, Vera and Robert stared at the FaceTime image on the computer. The face of the woman sitting next to Duncan showed the lines of her age, but the voice was still as strong as ever. A commanding voice, used to being obeyed.

'What's that? Did they say anything in England? I'm eighty-nine years old now and I'm as fit as a fiddle but the ears have gone. Don't know where they went to, but they're no bloody use to me any more.'

Duncan had found her in one of the most expensive retirement villages in Perth. She had her own home there and was still cooking and caring for herself.

'Hang on, I'll turn the sound up,' said Duncan.

'Good afternoon, Miss Anstey, great to finally meet you.'

'You don't have to shout. I'm deaf, not stupid. Are you Harry's sister?' She pointed at the screen. 'You have the same look as him, you know. The same cheeky eyes.'

'Thank you,' muttered Vera.

'So you remember Harry?'

'Of course I remember him. A lovely boy, with a naughty smile and a bit of cheek about him. You don't forget boys like Harry.'

'You first met him on the boat?'

'No, I first met him in the orphanage in Oldham.'

'St Michael's?'

'I think that was its name, run by the nuns. I'd been living in Manchester doing training for two years at the Royal Infirmary. Surgical training. The government paid for it and I thought it was a good chance to travel abroad, see the world.'

'So you met him in the orphanage?' asked Jayne.

'That's what I already said. I do wish people would listen. I've always been a Catholic and when the diocese realised I was going back to Australia, well, they asked me whether I would look after some orphans who were going to migrate. Well, you couldn't say no when the bishop asked, so I did it. Escorted them on the SS Otranto, leaving London for Fremantle in 1952.'

'Harry was one of the migrants?'

'He was. I had to look after eight of them. None of them gave me any trouble, lovely kids they were.'

She stopped speaking for a moment. Jayne could see the woman's eyes glaze over as she was transported back to the voyage over sixty years ago.

'I met Alfred on that voyage too, but he was engaged. I never married, you know. Married to the job, I suppose, and somehow, nobody ever matched up to Alfred.'

Once again, she stopped speaking for a moment, staring into some place above Duncan's computer screen.

'Anyway, that's over and done with.' She continued speaking, the wistfulness gone from her voice. 'The voyage lasted six weeks and I looked after the children. Most of the time, though, they looked after themselves. Harry kept a diary throughout the voyage. Most of the other children made one or two entries and then forgot about it, but not Harry. He kept going right till the time we entered Fremantle harbour, even though it was difficult for him.'

'What do you mean, difficult for him?'

'I think he was dyslexic or something.'

Jayne glanced across at Vera.

'Of course, nobody knew about it then. We just thought some children were slower than others. But I knew Harry was smart, he just couldn't understand reading and writing, kept getting his "b"s and "d"s the wrong way round, and he read very slowly, as if he had to remind himself of the word every time he read it. But he was quicker than all the others put together with numbers. Loved his arithmetic, did Harry.'

'We saw a picture of both of you on Fremantle dock.'

'I remember it well. It was taken when we arrived and were met by the Archbishop.'

'You two seemed so close.'

'I suppose we were. He was a lovely boy. I remember he had a toy soldier which I had to kiss every night before he would go to sleep. He loved his toy soldier. Said his mother had given it to him.' She paused for a moment, a frown adding to the wrinkles in her forehead. 'I did wonder about those children. They were all supposed to be orphans, you see, but as far as I could make out, only one of them was. The rest had at least one parent back in England. But I suppose the church knew what was best for them.'

'Harry was taken to one of the Catholic homes?'

'He was sent to Bindoon Boys Town, I believe. He was a bit young for it, but they seemed to want him, so he went.'

'Did you ever visit him?'

'No, it was sixty miles away and I didn't have a car then, but I saw him after he left.'

'What? When was that?' Jayne asked.

'I saw him after he left Bindoon. It was about fifteen years later, in the hospital. I was Matron by then. One day, who should turn up on one of my wards but Harry. He was in a bad way, had been knocked about by a couple of thugs and he was living rough – drinking, you know.'

'When was this?'

'It must have been about 1968 or 1969.'

'Are you sure it was Harry?'

'Do I look stupid to you? Of course I'm sure. We had a long chat about life and what had happened. I don't think he had a good time at the school. And after he left he got in with a bad crowd, ending up in jail. By the time I saw him he was at the end of his rope, ready to chuck it all in.'

'What happened?'

'Well, I had to help him. In those days, the Matron of a hospital carried some clout, not like today. Harry said he wanted to go to sea, to become an engineer. So I rang up the local seaman's union. We often used to get injured men from the boats and off the docks at the hospital. Anyway, I twisted a few arms and got Harry a berth on a freighter heading for Yokohama.'

'What happened?'

'He loved life on the sea and took to it like a duck to water, even doing his leaving certificate while he was on-board. Clever lad, was Harry.'

'It sounds like you kept in touch.'

'Oh, we did.' She gestured with her hands at the four walls surrounding her. 'Who do you think pays for all this? Donald Duck?'

Chapter Fifty-Six

August 13, 2017
Buxton Residential Home, Derbyshire, England

Jayne edged closer to the computer. 'What? What did you say?'

'I said, who do you think pays for all of this? The Queen of Sheba? Well, actually, I said Donald Duck...'

'You mean Harry pays for your house in the retirement village?'

'This one's quick, isn't she, Duncan? No wonder you like working with her.'

Jayne's chin dropped to the floor. 'But... that means... You...' She stumbled over the question.

'It means Harry bought this house for me years ago, not long after I retired. And your next question will probably be, "So that means you see him?" And I will answer, yes, at least once a year and always on my birthday. He's done well for himself, has my Harry, but I always knew he would.' The old woman was obviously enjoying the whole story.

Jayne had recovered her composure now. 'But we checked for Harold Brittons in Western Australia and there were none.'

'That's because he changed his name when he left Bindoon. He told me he wanted to put the past behind him. Very mature for a fifteen-year-old. You see, for him, Harry Britton was dead. It was almost as if he had never existed, except in Bindoon.'

'If you don't mind me asking, what name did he choose?'

'Well, that's the strangest thing. Even though he wanted to forget the past, he chose a name that reminded him of it.'

'What was it?' Vera asked urgently.

'He started calling himself Harry Duckworth.'

You could cut the silence in the Matron's room with a knife. Jayne's chin dropped to the floor again, and Vera and Robert were holding on to each other, neither able to speak.

'Hello, is anybody there?' The old woman prodded the screen with a bent, wrinkled finger.

Jayne coughed. 'I'm sorry, could you say that again?'

'You going deaf too, dear? It affects us all one day. What I said was he changed his name to Harold Duckworth.' She enunciated each word slowly and clearly.

'That's what I thought you said.'

'You mean Duckworth's Tyres and Auto?' Duncan spoke for the first time.

'That's the one. Founded it when he left the sea in 1978. As he said, he stole the idea for a drive-thru tyre shop from California. Saw it on his travels, came back and made it happen.'

'What is it, Duncan?'

'Only the largest tyre and auto repair company in Western Australia. I took the bloomin' car there yesterday.'

'And one more thing.'

'What's that, Miss Anstey?'

'Well, I talked to Harry yesterday...'

'You what?' exploded Duncan.

'You may be charming, Mr Morgan, but do you honestly think I would be talking to you unless Harry had said I could?'

Again, the old lady had reduced them all to total silence.

'He gave me this number for you.' She passed a piece of paper to Duncan. 'It's his private line. He wants you to ring him.'

Chapter Fifty-Seven

August 14, 2017
Buxton Residential Home, Derbyshire, England

It was nine o'clock in the morning. Jayne, Vera and Robert were hunched over the telephone in the Matron's office.

'I'm so nervous. Look at my palms.' Vera held up her damp hands. 'I don't think I can do it.'

Robert put his arm around her. 'You've been waiting for this day for ages, love. You're finally going to speak to your brother. The brother that vanished all those years ago.'

Jayne picked up the phone. 'Shall I go ahead and dial, Vera?'

Vera nodded tentatively, her teeth biting her bottom lip.

Jayne checked the number and pressed the buttons. 'It's ringing.' She pressed the speakerphone and the sound of the dial tone filled the room.

'What if he doesn't answer? What if he doesn't want to speak with me?' said Vera.

Before Jayne could respond, a strong male voice came through the speaker. 'Harry Duckworth.'

The voice wasn't English or Australian, but a cross between the two.

Vera took a deep breath before she spoke. 'Hello, Harry, it's your sister, Vera.'

A long silence on the other end of the phone. Jayne could hear breathing; a deep, slightly breathless sound.

Eventually an answer came. 'Hello, Vera, I always knew the family would get in touch with me one day…'

And Vera began to cry.

Chapter Fifty-Eight

October 4, 2017
Manchester International Airport, England

'Now, have you got everything, Vera?'

Vera checked her carry-on bag. 'The knitting's here with the plastic needles, and my crosswords, my new book and the Sudoku Jayne gave me.'

'What about water? Are you sure you have plenty of water?'

'Don't worry, Vera's flying Business. I'm sure they'll give her water if she asks for it.'

'After I have the champagne too, of course.'

'Don't drink too much. You know what you're like when you drink champagne.'

She put her arm around Robert. 'No wonder you kept wanting me to drink the bubbly on the cruise.'

Her father blushed. 'And don't forget to leave your seat every hour to walk around. You don't want to get any of that deep-vein thrombosis on the long flight.'

Vera was finally going to see Harry for the first time. For the last two months, they had emailed, called or talked to each other every day since that first phone call back at the care home.

Harry had told her all about his life; the lost decade after he left Bindoon, working occasionally on isolated farms but spending more time drunk or in jail

302

for petty theft. How Miss Anstey had saved him all those years ago by helping him get to sea. How he had learnt all about engines from a multitude of Friedrichs. Finally, going back to Perth in 1979 and setting up his company, starting small and gradually expanding.

'I did try to find Mum, you know,' he said to her on one of their calls. 'It was 1978 and I was on a ship that had just docked in Southampton. I took a train up to London and visited the sisters at the home we stayed in before we left for Australia.'

'What happened, Harry?'

'Well, I was shown into a big parlour. All the homes had a big parlour for guests. After about an hour, the Mother Superior, a Sister Agnes, saw me. I asked to see my records. I wanted to find out if Mum was still alive. Anyway, this sister told me all the records were gone. They'd been thrown away. She was a sour-faced old cow.'

'You know, they weren't thrown away. We found them in the local diocese.'

'I don't know why they didn't give them to me or at least help me with the search.'

'You didn't go to Oldham?'

'After meeting Sister Agnes, I wanted nothing to do with the church any more. My ship was leaving a couple of days later so I went out to the movies, watched Watership Down and remembered all the rabbits I killed at Bindoon. You know, for a moment I nearly went back on the drink. But something stopped me. I was one of the lucky ones.'

'You never went back to Bindoon?'

'Nah, couldn't face the place. Oh, I read all about it; the fake apologies from the brothers, the Royal Commissions, the redress schemes and all the rest. But I wanted nothing to do with them. I was tempted when Kevin Rudd made his apology, at least I thought he meant it. But I didn't. Harry Britton was dead. They'd taken my childhood and I was never going to get it back.'

'You never married?'

'No, couldn't let anybody get close to me, especially women. Didn't really know what to do with them. I've always been a bit of a loner. Loved my job, though, and the company. I guess it was my family.'

'Well, you've got a real family now.'

'I wish I could have met Mum before she died.'

'She thought of you every day.'

Then he coughed. 'Neither of us is getting younger, Vera. Why don't you come out to see me in Australia? Maybe together we can go back to Bindoon. I can't do it on my own, but with my family, I'm sure I could face it.'

Of course, Vera had said yes. Robert wanted to go but decided to stay this time, to allow his health to get better.

Now she had checked in and they were standing outside the entry point for passenger security.

'You'd better not be late.'

'Is it time? I'd better get going.'

Robert hugged her close. 'I'll miss you.'

'Me too.'

Jayne moved away, leaving her father and her step mother to say goodbye to each other.

'Call me when you get into Perth, don't worry about the time.'

'I will.'

'And say hello to Harry for me.'

'I will.'

They gave each other one last hug. Vera's eyes were damp with tears. She gathered all her bags, waving to Jayne. 'Bye, look after your dad for me.'

Jayne waved back. 'I will. See you in three weeks.'

And Vera marched into the departure area, ready to face the obstacle course of the security and passenger checks all on her own.

Robert stood there, his arm still waving as she turned right and vanished into the belly of the beast. 'I'm going to miss her.'

'We both are.'

Chapter Fifty-Nine

October 4, 2017
The road back to Buxton, Derbyshire, England

Jayne drove slowly down the A6, careful to avoid the speed traps, roadworks and narrow lanes.

Her father sat next to her, saying very little. For once, she wasn't listening to the Manchester whine of Liam Gallagher.

'Don't worry, she'll be back soon.'

Her father smiled. 'I wasn't thinking of Vera, I know she'll be back in three weeks. I was thinking of you.'

'Me?'

'You solved the search for Vera's vanished brother pretty quickly.'

'I was lucky, Dad. I think a couple of pints of cider helped. I also remembered what you told me when I was young.'

'What was that?'

'When you have a problem, sometimes it's best to forget about it and relax, do something else, then the answer will come to you.'

'I said that?'

Jayne took her eyes off the road for a second and nodded.

'Sounds a bit too clever for me. But I'm glad you remember what I said , Jayne, even if I don't.'

'It worked for me. I went to sleep that night and the memory of that picture in the paper, of Harry standing with Claire Anstey, came back to me. I thought that if I ever had a problem I would go back to a person I trusted and loved. It was obvious the two of them were very close. Luckily, Duncan managed to find her.'

'Luck had nothing to do with it, lass, you're very good at your job.'

After the compliment, the conversation lapsed into silence. They were racing down the Buxton bypass when her father spoke again.

'You know I'm not getting any younger, Jayne. This illness, well, it's got me thinking.'

'Thinking is bad for you, Dad.'

'Listen to me. It's time you researched your own family. You must be the only genealogical investigator who doesn't know where they came from.'

'I'm not sure, Dad. I…'

'And I'm not going to be around forever. If you need any help with people, places or photographs, then we'd better do it together whilst I'm still here and can still remember.'

'Don't talk like that, Dad.'

'But it's true. Look at Vera, her mum only told her about Harry when it was too late.'

'I know, but…'

'No buts, Jayne. It's time and you know it. I've still got all your mum's stuff in a suitcase.'

'Like Charlie?'

He laughed. 'I don't throw anything away either.'

Jayne stared through the windscreen of the BMW. They were going into Dove Holes before the descent into Buxton itself.

'Let me think about it, Dad. Honestly, I don't know if I'm ready.'

'You'll never be ready, love, you just have to do it.'

'Sounds like the philosophy of your life.'

'Aye, it is. Just do it. Nike nicked that from me, you know.'

Jayne laughed. 'How do you fancy a jam roly-poly at Wetherspoon's before we go back to your place?'

'Sounds perfect, love.'

She pressed down on the accelerator as they crossed the bleak hills above Buxton. One day she would have to look into her family. Perhaps her father was right and the time was now, she had already put it off too long.

She didn't know what she would find, but that was the beauty of family history; there were always secrets waiting to be discovered.

Perhaps it was time to discover her own past.

Historical Note

Between 1869 and the end of the 1960s, around 130,000 British children, both boys and girls, and some as young as four years old, were sent to the former colonies. This is a best guess, as nobody has come up with an exact figure yet.

They were part of a child migration scheme involving children from problem families and single-parent families, illegitimate children and children whose parents had abandoned them. Despite their description at the time, very few of these child migrants were actually orphans. The majority still had at least one parent still alive in the United Kingdom.

Until 1987, the plight of these children lay buried beneath a shroud of official blindness, bureaucratic incompetence, official secrecy and downright lies. At this time, Margaret Humphreys, then working for Nottingham Council as a social worker, became aware of the children by accident when a case she was working on revealed their existence. She went on to form the Child Migrants Trust, which is still the leading charitable organisation for these children.

My own knowledge of their plight came by accident too.

I was researching in Manchester Central Library one summer's day, on June 30, 2016, when I came across an exhibition in the foyer of old inmate books, dated 1894, from a children's charity.

One of the books was open at the page for Mary Nettleship from Ardwick in Manchester. Her story was sad but unfortunately typical. Her mother had died and her father was an alcoholic. She and her sister were placed in a care home at the ages of 9 and 12. On May 9, 1895, both sisters were sent aboard the SS Vancouver, bound for Canada. There was a picture in the book taken of Mary, wearing a long black dress, with short, cropped hair and a lonely look in her eyes. On the next page were two reports from a Canadian inspector, detailing that Mary had been placed with a Canadian family in Adolphstown, Ontario to work as a domestic. She had also been separated from her younger sister.

My curiosity was aroused. How had a young girl from Manchester ended up across the Atlantic? How had her father allowed this? (In the book it stated that he couldn't be found.) Had he given permission? Why were the sisters separated? What happened to young Mary?

A week later I was in London to meet with my editors and publishers at the HarperCollins summer party, being held in the Victoria and Albert Museum. By chance, I noticed the museum had an exhibition on child migrants. I went back the following day and spent the afternoon looking at the exhibits.

The seed for the book was planted that day, and I spent the next two months researching the history and personal stories of the child migrants.

The more I researched, the more I became perturbed by their experiences of transportation to Australia.

The Australian Commission into the Child Migrants concluded that between 7,000 and 10,000 children were sent to the country in the post-war period, mostly in the 1950s. The organisations involved were the Catholic Child Welfare Society, the Fairbridge Society, Dr Barnado's, the Salvation Army and the Church of England.

In a difference from Canada, most were not sent to people's homes or adopted. Instead, they were placed in institutions to be 'trained' as farmers and domestics before entering the workforce at the age of fifteen. Again, most were boys and girls, aged between four and fourteen at the time of transportation.

My book is a novel, and all the main characters are creations. However, I have tried to remain true to the experiences of the child migrants.

Harry's early life with the Sisters of Mercy is based on contemporary memoirs and notes. The voyage out to Australia uses a wonderful book by David Hill, *The Forgotten Children*, as its main source, plus a host of archival material from government reports, Royal Commissions, oral histories and memoirs from the child migrants themselves.

The speech of welcome given to Harry and the child migrants in Perth is actually an earlier speech given in 1938 to a group of children by the Archbishop of Perth. But there are other examples in the post-war archives of the church's involvement in the White Australia policy, and a desire to increase the population of young Catholics in Australia.

Harry's experiences in Bindoon Boys Town are shocking but unfortunately confirmed by the memoirs and evidence presented at a number of Royal Commissions.

Emotional, physical and sexual abuse were all rife in the institution. The migrants were used as child labour to build the place itself; long hours of work were accompanied by severe beatings. Emotionally, they received little or no affection or love, and were treated as objects rather than children.

Sexual abuse was also commonplace in the Boys Town. Several of the former brothers were convicted of the abuse of children, but others were not charged with any offence.

As a consequence of their treatment, many of the residents have reported the inability to form relationships with other human beings as a consequence of their treatment at Bindoon. Many have also experienced problems with alcohol, drugs or an inability to settle in one place.

One of the most painful things to do is watch the children arriving in Fremantle in the newsreels of the period, seeing the smiles on their faces as they looked forward to a new life in a new country and knowing what actually awaited them.

As a Roman Catholic myself, I have no desire to excoriate the church. In truth, the abuses of children and child migrants were systemic in government homes and in other charitable institutions, both in the United Kingdom and Australia. However, the treatment of the child migrants in the four Christian Brothers institutions in Western Australia was particularly cruel, calculating and abusive.

Kevin Rudd's apology on behalf of Australia in 2009 sums up my feelings on the subject.

'We come together today to deal with an ugly chapter of our nation's history and we come together today to offer our nation's apology. To you, the Forgotten Australians, and those who were sent to our shores as children without their consent... we are sorry. Sorry that, as children, you were taken from your families and placed in institutions where you were so often abused; sorry for the physical suffering, the emotional starvation, and the cold absence of love or tenderness of care. Sorry for the tragedy, the absolute tragedy of childhoods lost, childhoods spent instead in austere and authoritarian places where names were replaced by numbers... The truth is, a great evil has been done. The truth is, this is an ugly story and its ugliness must be told without fear or favour if we are to confront fully the demons of our past.'

And what happened to Mary Nettleship, the young girl who started me on this path?

I researched her history as far as I could through the documents available in Canada. She worked as an unpaid domestic until she was eighteen, and then she married a carpenter, with whom she had four children. She settled down in Toronto to bring up her family, but unfortunately died of heart disease in 1929, aged just 42. Her husband died later in the year, leaving their children as orphans. Was her death precipitated by her early life and the domestic labour she endured from twelve years of age? We will never know.

And what of Mary's younger sister?

I have been unable to find her after the census of 1901. Did she marry? Did she die? I have not been able to find out what happened to her so far.

Perhaps, I will be able to discover the truth one day. So that she will not be forgotten like so many of the other migrant children from the cities of Great Britain.

As ever, any errors in the book are mine and mine alone. I don't believe any writer can do justice to the experience of the child migrants, but their story needs to be told.

As David Hall says in his book, 'Every childhood lasts a lifetime.'

This is true for all of us.

If you enjoyed reading this Jayne Sinclair genealogical mystery, please consider leaving a short review on Amazon. It will help other readers know how much you enjoyed the book.

Other books in the Jayne Sinclair Series

The Irish Inheritance

When an adopted American businessman dying with cancer asks her to investigate his background, it opens up a world of intrigue and forgotten secrets for Jayne Sinclair, genealogical investigator.

She only has two clues: a book and an old photograph. Can she find out the truth before he dies?

The Somme Legacy

Who is the real heir to the Lappiter millions? This is the problem facing genealogical investigator, Jayne Sinclair.

Her quest leads to a secret buried in the trenches of World War One for over 100 years. And a race against time to discover the truth of the Somme Legacy.

The American Candidate

Jayne Sinclair, genealogical investigator, is tasked to research the family history of a potential candidate for the Presidency of the United States of America. A man whose grandfather had emigrated to the country seventy years before.

When the politician who commissioned the genealogical research is shot dead in front of her, Jayne is forced to flee for her life. Why was he killed? And who is trying to stop the details of the American Candidate's family past from being revealed?

In her most dangerous case yet, Jayne Sinclair is caught in a deadly race against time to discover the truth, armed only with her own wits and ability to uncover secrets hidden in the past.

Printed in Great Britain
by Amazon